Love's
Compromise

Praise for Cass Sellars

Lightning Chasers

"This is my first book by Cass Sellars but I would absolutely read another."—*C-Spot Reviews*

Unexpected Lightning

"A mystery-thriller with lots and lots of great sex. What's there not to like?"—*reviewer@large*

Lightning Chasers

Lightning Chasers "is a rewarding read, and Sellars ensures you feel the emotions in the story. The first section of the book leads you into thinking this will be a story about relationships between a group of friends, which it is. But it is so much more. It is a murder investigation, and whilst it is not too difficult to work out who is probably responsible, the investigation and the relationships amongst the friends are what sets this apart…The romance between Syd and Parker retains the fire from the first book and our journey with them as their relationship continues to grow is one of the high points of the book."—*The Lesbian Review*

Lightning Strikes

"*Lightning Strikes* is a really lovely story of two people arriving at a point in each of their lives when they need to make a change. Parker is fresh out of a disastrous marriage with no intention of being in a relationship any time soon. Syd is a player who has never considered monogamy her thing. But you can never predict the moment when Lightening Strikes…They made a perfect couple and I felt invested in their story."—*Kitty Kat's Book Review Blog*

"*Lightning Strikes* is a butch/femme romance that is just so extraordinarily good…This is a beautifully written, scintillating, seriously hot book that is a real page turner and I will say it again, is a ROMANCE! I have no hesitation in recommending this book, go and buy it. It is one of the best books I have read this year." —*The Lesbian Review*

By the Author

Lightning Strikes

Lightning Chasers

Unexpected Lightning

Finding Sky

Love's Compromise

ISBN 13: 978-1-63555-942-2

This Trade Paperback Original Is Published By
Bold Strokes Books, Inc.
P.O. Box 249
Valley Falls, NY 12185

First Edition: October 2021

CREDITS
Editors: Victoria Villaseñor and Stacia Seaman
Production Design: Stacia Seaman
Cover Design by Tammy Seidick

Acknowledgments

Thank you to my readers and every supporter of this genre—you make it worth every word.

To everyone who has supported me through this writing journey, loved my books, and encouraged me to keep going. You are the reason I'm still writing. To my personal team of cheerleaders, including Ruth, Toni, Michelle, Linda, Inger and Kim, and so very many others, thank you for always reminding me to keep climbing.

Chapter One

Piper, damn it, could you please start drumming up business from our male members? These women are high maintenance. The last one needed champagne and a massage afterward. Seriously, how bourgeois have I become? I'm a concierge to spoiled rich woman with no life outside of coming to see you for golf lessons I don't think they even want."

"Tell me about it." Piper sighed. "Trust me, my goal is to find some underprivileged adolescent with a gift. But I'm not doing anything different, Leo. Male clients would be a nice change of pace for me too. I guess the ladies just feel more comfortable around me." She was more comfortable around them too, as a rule, but being known for her proven golf skills would be better than her rumored "social" talents.

"So comfortable they give you a house with an art studio and a BMW?" His rueful laugh suggested he was more than a little envious.

Piper brushed her hair behind her ear and returned to rewrapping the grip on her favorite driver. She sighed a little too loudly at what should have been viewed as a completely benign, platonic relationship.

"Vanessa and Frank don't *give* me anything. I'm just helping with V's game, and Frank likes someone home when he's gone, which is practically all the time. The car's certainly a nice bonus, but it's just a loan and, after all, they have *nine* cars. What can I say? Golf has been good to me."

"Yeah. And the fact Mrs. Devereaux likes to be with you more than her husband means that you're living in a tony carriage house on Beacon Terrace. Let's face it, you aren't *that* good a golfer, Piper."

"Actually, I'm good at pretty much everything, Leo." She flashed a flirty smile at him, and she wondered if his fairly accurate depiction of the real nature of her relationship with Vanessa Deveraux was simply a good guess. She had told herself a hundred times that she was merely being practical and enjoying her current setup, even though it meant that she was on call whenever V wanted her. And why the hell would she complain about that? V was stunning, wealthy, and attentive—as much as she could be.

"Including being a cocky little shit." He grabbed the appointment clipboard from the hook and glanced out the window where coaches met their students.

"It's part of my charm." She tossed the tape roll into a bin behind the counter.

"Uh-huh. Lorinda Pillson is waiting at the carts for your charms. Don't piss her off by being late."

"I won't, thank you very much. And she's five minutes early, anyway." She smoothed her palm down the fresh grip and slid the club into her bag. She longed to play a long, quiet eighteen holes with people she enjoyed being around. But that wasn't part of the day's agenda.

"Don't forget that I'm leaving at two this afternoon."

"Oh, yeah. The Holthaus art installation and cocktail party. You should sell everything if you schmooze all the Deveraux cronies as well as you do your benefactor."

"You know I hate that part the most. I'd rather drink beer with you and the guys in the clubroom." Piper cringed at the thought of mixing with the society set at the Devereaux estate. Yes, having connected clientele at every one of her receptions, thanks to V and Frank, was a bonus that made her some nice side cash, but she couldn't help but feel like someone's pet show pony at the end of the day.

"Don't worry, Stacy's making me go too." Leo was pushing her toward the door. "Go be brilliant, and I promise to rescue you tonight if it looks like it's getting too intense. Deal?"

Piper appreciated Leo's offer. He'd always supported her as an artist as well as a colleague. True friends were rare.

"Deal. Thanks. It will likely be too intense about thirty minutes after everyone gets there. I don't know what to say to these people about my art."

"They want a tortured artist story to tell their friends." Leo had a history of making bets on how long she could be present at one of her art shows without finding a corner to disappear to. She was humiliated when he had found her in the janitors' closet at her last show at the clubhouse.

"I feel it, I paint it. People like it or they don't. I don't feel the need to talk about the energy of the universe inspiring me to spill my emotions onto a canvas. It's just ridiculous." Piper knew it was a necessary evil, but she'd rather do anything but talk about the inspiration for her art.

It was personal and therapeutic and just hers. It was certainly a bonus when she sold pieces, but she didn't do it for the money. Vanessa had been insistent that soon she would start showing in galleries because people loved her work so much. It was certainly flattering to have so many people like her abstracts, but it would never feel like anything other than a personal invasion and a dull spoon carving into her very private soul.

She had often fantasized about the possible responses to "So, what were you feeling when you created this?" "Um...I was tired, a little hammered, and had some paint left over from last time." Or, her favorite, "I'd just been on a date with a woman who talked too much, and I was blasting Beth Hart and trying to block her out with cheap beer and the smell of acrylics."

She knew Vanessa would have a conniption if she were ever that honest, and the mystique surrounding Piper Holthaus, brooding artist, would be gone in seconds. But it was a nice, evil fantasy she kept to herself. It wasn't much to ask, she supposed. Maybe her life wasn't where she thought it would be at her age, but it was...

acceptable. She was successfully ignoring turning forty-five by working out harder and surrounding herself with a few friends and lots of art. She certainly wasn't planning to let anyone into the part of her heart that scared the shit out of her.

Lorinda was adjusting a blinding white cotton sweater over a mustard golf skirt when Piper approached. She threw her arms around Piper like they were long-lost friends reconnecting after a lengthy absence.

"Gorgeous Piper. I'm telling you, you and my daughter would be a match made in heaven." The delivery was half delighted squealing parent and half conspiratorial whisper.

This again, really?

She raised her hand when Piper opened her mouth to object for the hundredth time. "I know, I know. You're concentrating on your career. I hear you, but Dana thinks you're gorgeous, which you are. Even though you can't technically make babies together, they would be beautiful."

"Well, we'd certainly be set for life if I could make that happen." The joke was clichéd and hackneyed, but Piper had long since run out of original retorts to being matched up with people's daughters, sisters, or even occasionally exes.

"How about we concentrate on your follow-through on your long drives for now. You never know, we might get you on the LPGA and you'll forget my name." Piper smiled genuinely. Not because she thought Lorinda had a chance in hell of seeing the inside of any professional golf tournament—the woman was probably the worst golfer she'd ever met—but because she had mastered the game of redirecting an uncomfortable conversation without pissing anyone off. It was a control thing she relished.

Lorinda selected the pricey driver from her expensive designer bag. Piper rolled her eyes at the bag that cost nearly $2,500 and was owned by a woman who had no talent or passion for the game. Piper had overheard Carl Pillson buying it and a set of clubs as a gift, in hopes that his wife would find something else to do other than check up on him while he was away on business. Piper imagined that she checked up on him because she had once been the other woman before she was wife number four, and she knew the signs. Piper found it sad that the trade-off behind the rare wood doors of this enclave was often turning a blind eye to infidelity and making concessions about happiness to achieve contentment.

Piper used that as reason number 2,972 to never wear a ring on her left hand. She recalled her past and the faces of the women she had planned to spend a lifetime with. She skimmed quickly over the ones who made her doubt herself and ignored the images of the ones she had once believed were perfect for her. A couple still made her angry. One or two still made her sad so she didn't talk about them out loud. Ever.

"…because I don't think I'm holding my body correctly. What do you think, Piper?" Lorinda was effecting a stance at the tee box and wiggling her hips.

Piper knew the drill. She stepped behind her student, placed a firm hand on each hip, and twisted her in a direction that might aid a different player in a fruitful swing. After several enthusiastic tries, Lorinda had managed only to assault the turf repeatedly and loft one sad ball over the cart path about twenty feet away. Piper thought of the painting she could have produced or at least started in the preceding ten minutes. Instead, she was encouraging an oblivious woman who honestly had no aptitude for the game Piper loved.

The fifty-minute lesson made Piper question her own aptitude for instruction, or at least wonder why she was continuing to waste her life making the privileged better at a game most people couldn't afford to play. Oh yeah, bills. She had them. She was still paying off some legacy debt from her most recent relationship, not to mention saving for her own place and a car that she was determined to pay cash for. Driving her landlord's sports car and living practically rent-free was certainly helpful, but Piper allowed herself only momentary analysis about how much the arrangement might be costing her soul.

"Great job as usual, Lorinda." Piper draped her arm over Lorinda's shoulder and gave her a reassuring squeeze. "Keep practicing and I bet you'll see a big difference when I see you again."

"Leo said you were booked solid for two weeks, Piper. How am I supposed to get any better if some people manipulate all your time?" She pushed out her Botoxed lips in an attempt at a pout before she grinned.

Piper heard regularly about how Vanessa monopolized her just to eliminate the competition at the club. Piper shook her head and squeezed her shoulder again. "I think Cameron and Jimmy both have openings next week. It might even be good to get a fresh perspective before we meet again." Piper longed for a vacation. One where she was unreachable by anyone. She was well aware that her fantasies most often involved silence and isolation. She couldn't help it.

"It's not the same and you know it. You make me better." She glided her palm down Piper's forearm.

Piper tried not to take the honest attempt at a compliment as the insult it was, since Lorinda Pillson was a tragic golfer and, despite months of lessons, hadn't improved one iota.

"Let's get you in with Cameron next week to work on controlling your backswing technique and we can get back together on my next available date. How's that?" She turned toward the office.

"Fine. But don't expect any developments before I see you again." She slid her arm into Piper's elbow and leaned heavily against her as they walked toward the pro shop.

Piper caught Leo's amused expression as he watched them approach and rolled her eyes.

"How was the lesson, Mrs. Pillson?" He showed his very white teeth in the most artificial smile he had, which he used on everyone who came in. They seemed to adore it.

"Piper's a dream, Leo. Make sure she sticks around, okay?"

"No worries. Piper's the reason I come to work every day." He presented the lesson slip for her signature and member number that the finance department would use to bill their account.

Piper shook her head and sent her boss a steely glare over Lorinda's shoulder as she accepted a departing hug. "Be sure and call to get on Cameron's calendar next week, okay?"

"And then yours. I wouldn't miss it." Her body swayed as she threw a wave behind her and headed out in the direction of the parking lot.

"The reason you come to work every day?" Piper pulled a

black glove from her right hand and shoved it into the deep pocket of her Nike shorts as they walked into the office.

"What?" He gestured skyward and shrugged innocently. "I thought I was just joining the Piper Holthaus Fan Club. Practically everyone who's *anyone* is in it, you know." He chucked her a roll of overwrap tape followed by a box of shirts he was pulling from the storage room.

"Your jokes are…" She paused for effect before patting him on the shoulder. "Well, you keep working on them, okay?"

He pushed open the stockroom door once more and allowed Piper to pass with the armload of restock. "And, by the way, it's time for you to go. The star can't be late to her own show."

"Please come save me later, okay? Otherwise, I might piss off half of the attendees if you leave me there by myself." She dropped merchandise on a table.

"Not a chance. I won't let you bite the hand that feeds us both. Go do whatever it is that makes these people fawn over you, and I'll see you in a few hours." Leo waved in the direction of the door as Piper gathered her backpack from behind the counter and headed for the main road.

The weather was perfect, and she relished the three-block solitary walk home. She prayed that she would be able to shut the door behind her for a bit without having to engage with anyone from the main house. She inhaled the scent from the honeysuckle bushes before stopping to admire the exquisitely sculptured hedges that rose along the asphalt drive. The asphalt turned to concrete and cobblestone at the apron of the fifteen-foot gates that separated the road from the estate belonging to Vanessa and Frank. The guest cottage, just inside the circular drive, was a mirror image of the main house, only it was a tenth the size. A small arched front door sat a few yards from the driveway, but the back offered a spectacular view of the ninth green and, most importantly, afforded the cottage the kind of light an artist dreamed of. She exhaled as the door clicked shut behind her and chucked her backpack on the bench by the entry.

She stripped off her watch and ball cap as she wandered through the little bungalow to the bank of windows overlooking the ninth hole. She saw the empty easel in the studio and considered her last painting. She really would have loved more time to work with it, but Vanessa had insisted that it was going to be the star of the show, just the way it was. She had acquiesced, as usual, and now she turned her attention to the pile of blank canvases taunting her from the sunroom she used as a studio. Nothing came to her.

She hoped for some inspiration that would make her feel the way painting used to. A solo place for her unexplored emotions, a salvation of sorts that provided an outlet for the dark places in her head. She twisted a flat brush against her palm and relished the feel of the fine bristles on her skin. She placed a smaller square canvas panel on her easel and squeezed out several colors she couldn't wait to mix into the hues blending together in her mind.

She loaded the brush and stepped in to deliver the first stroke of a grayish green arching from the center. She blended and knifed the pigment into ridges and textures depicting nothing concrete but offering an aesthetic of oceans meeting endless vistas. Moments ago, she had no intention of creating anything, but now she couldn't abandon the piece that possessed an urgent energy. She traded brushes and skimmed tiny highlights over the expanse, creating distance and depth, a result that sometimes still amazed even her. Bliss. She felt that here, in front of a once empty square of cotton duck.

She couldn't move from in front of the easel, even though she knew she should be getting ready for tonight. Blues, she needed more blues. She dusted a cobalt onto the corner and pulled the new color through the edges like a hint of nightfall approaching the landscape of color. She extracted a can of beer from the mini fridge under the window. She felt for it, so her eyes could remain on her creation. Piper often thought if she looked away, she might miss something. An opportunity for the next perfect stroke or ridge of texture, perhaps. Then other times she had to walk away, abandon the project as if it had disappointed her in its pace or progress, only to return moments or sometime days later with a renewed fervor for the next touch of her brush.

The firm closing of her front door jolted her from her artist's solitude. She quickly looked at the time on her phone, which now sported a smear of white paint. She was about to have to explain why she wasn't ready to a woman who only understood art as a business and something to talk about with other people who thought the same thing.

"Why aren't you ready?" Vanessa Devereaux swept her impeccably manicured hand in the direction of the main house and the venue for the art show the Devereaux were hosting. "I swear, Piper, you act like you don't care that all this is for you."

"Sorry, V. I got lost in this piece and lost track of time. Ten minutes and I'll find something to wear and be right over." She stepped toward the slender brunette with pouty lips made impossibly shiny by copper metallic gloss. As she reached her paint-speckled hand toward her cheek, V spun away with a warning glare.

"Not a chance. New dress and I just had my makeup done. We don't need to look like we've been rolling around on a drop cloth." She pursed her lips and pointed at the stripes of color adorning Piper's thighs. "Go shower. I put new black linen slacks and a shirt on the bed. Wear those cute black oxfords I brought you from New York. They're so sexy on you."

Before Piper could respond or, God forbid, object, Vanessa was pulling open the front door. "Don't be late. Remember, this is all for you."

"My ass," Piper said through a cloud of mild resentment, and she walked quickly into the bedroom, stripping off her clothes before she stepped into the shower. She couldn't decide if she resented V for pushing these showings on her or resented herself for being the biggest sellout she'd ever met. And considering where she worked and the people she was surrounded by, that was a pretty significant statement.

She toweled off and brooded. She rarely named her paintings, though she considered numbering them sometimes, but Vanessa insisted that they have names and often chose them before Piper had a chance. Piper ruefully decided that the one she had just abandoned in her studio was going to be named *The Artist's Concession* since she was walking away from something she loved to become something she hated—Vanessa Devereaux's pet project, her good deed for the millennium and her play toy when she decided gliding along on her husband's arm bored her and she wanted the excitement that the illicit relationship with Piper brought. They had genuine affection for one another, but Piper wondered how long it would last if they were two regular people trying to make ends meet in the real world.

She pushed product through her short, loose curls and yanked the brand tag off the shirt that likely cost more than she made in a day. She scraped her fingernail over a scab of green paint that hadn't washed off in the shower and briefly considered leaving it there as part of her tortured artist costume. She knew Vanessa would blanch at a mar in her carefully created image, and it wasn't worth the fight.

Piper admired the fabric hand of her new pants. She guiltily thought how much she loved the perks of the arrangement despite the fact that she felt she was carving out a good piece of her self-respect sometimes. Quite the dichotomy. She heard the front door open and the staccato of angry heels in the marble hallway.

"Piper, this isn't the least bit cute," Vanessa called down the corridor. "Guests will be arriving any minute and you haven't even seen the placement of the paintings yet." She threw open Piper's bedroom door, clearly prepared to do battle with her for not being ready.

Piper had just sprayed cologne along her collar and casually draped a silk-cashmere scarf around her neck. She struck a dramatic pose meant to soften the tirade she likely deserved. Vanessa's face melted into a smile, and she walked over to press herself against Piper.

"I'm sorry I made you come look for me. I'm sorry I lost track of time. I know you work hard to make these shows perfect, and I do appreciate it. Really." Melting complete, Piper thought as Vanessa wrapped her arms around Piper's neck and sighed.

"It's okay, my little artistic genius. I missed you, and spending time with you makes me happy. I just hoped we would have more time before everyone arrives." Vanessa placed a delicate kiss on

Piper's mouth to avoid transferring too much lipstick. She swiped a fingertip over what had managed to cling to Piper's lips.

"We'll have all next week, right? Is Frank still flying out Monday?" When had she become the other woman? More importantly, when had she become so comfortable with it?

"Yes, I'm all yours starting Monday afternoon. Let's have a spa day, and Paul will make that Marsala you like for dinner."

Just the thought of the exquisite meals the Deverauxs' chef could whip up made her mouth water, but she wouldn't be swayed.

"You'll have to settle for an evening massage and reheated dinner, V. I still have to work, remember?" Piper gently pushed Vanessa away so they could start the walk to the front door. Despite their less than traditional arrangement, she found Vanessa to be beautiful and charming and desirable, making the curves of her body pressing against Piper's difficult to resist.

"Of course I do. You're booked for a four-hour private lesson at one o'clock on Monday, right?" She smoothed her hand over the midnight blue silk dress that stopped just above her knees as they walked toward the front door.

"How did you know that?" Piper knew the answer before she asked it.

"Who do you think made the appointment with Leo? I told him I had a friend of a friend who's too shy to come to the club, so he blocked your afternoon for me. I need to spend some time with you. Paul's going home at noon to be with his daughter after some dental procedure, and it's been too wet for the landscape crew to mow, so I rescheduled them for Wednesday." She threw a satisfied smirk over her shoulder.

"Thought of everything as usual, huh?" Piper tried not to feel manipulated since she had no vote in the matter, but that's exactly how it felt. "Guess I'll see you Monday."

Vanessa stopped and turned to face her. She drew her fingertip lightly along Piper's jaw and rolled her eyes. "I know you think I'm making decisions for you again, but I'm not. If I had to wait for you to take days off work, we'd never get any time alone."

Piper pulled her face away and walked past her. "Some of us *have* to work, you know." This was not an unfamiliar debate.

"You can have anything you want, Piper, but you're so damned stubborn, you won't ask."

"Because I don't want to be someone's charity case. I like my independence." As soon as the words left her lips, she felt stupid. How was living here in this impeccable place and driving an overpriced sports car anywhere close to independent? Regardless, she wasn't going to back down this time. "I want to make my own money, V. Why is that so hard for you to understand?"

"Piper…" The way she cooed the word cooled the ire Piper wanted to hold on to. "You're the most independent person I know. I just want you to be happy and free to work on your paintings."

"I am happy." Piper lied with practice and polish. "I appreciate everything you have done for me. Really. I just get nervous at these things." It was much easier to redirect and end the stale dispute so the evening wasn't any more of a nightmare than Piper already expected it to be. This familiar discussion had worn a rut in their odd relationship born out of the desires of a bored housewife. Two years ago Vanessa had found the new golf pro intriguing enough for repeated lessons, and before Piper knew what was happening, Vanessa had taken full-time interest in the starving artist and appointed herself as a manager Piper didn't really want. From there, she'd become Vanessa's relationship on the side who lived in their guest cottage.

"You'll be perfect as always. They love you." Vanessa rested her arms on Piper's broad shoulders and looked sweetly into her eyes. "I can't wait to be with you."

"Me too. Let's do this." Piper squeezed V's waist quickly and opened the door just in time to see a black town car drop a well-dressed couple at the bottom of the sweeping stairs to the main house.

"Tina and Blake Morrison," Vanessa whispered as she quickened her pace, waving enthusiastically. "His father owned an oil company that Blake took over right before they sold out to one of the big three a few years ago. Frank's company consulted for them and helped Blake with the acquisition. Now he's consulting for Sector Gas in Dallas."

Piper hoped she looked interested. She also hoped there wouldn't be a test. She really tried to care. Actually, she longed to find someone who was passionate about what they did for a living. Maybe it would convince her that the things she was passionate about could pay her bills one day. She silently berated herself for being such an ingrate.

She climbed the long flight of flagstone steps and felt the distance between her and Vanessa increase. It was the same every time they did this dance. Vanessa would smile and wave and gush and defer and make small talk until she hooked someone into an "exclusive meeting with the artist," who she had inevitably said was a remarkable find of hers she just had to help into the light. *Blah Blah. Groan. Kill me now. Let me hide. Pray they hate everything.*

"Piper."

Her name floated across the patio just as she was mapping her escape through the foyer.

She turned to see Vanessa flapping her hand in the air, indicating Piper should walk her way. Much to her chagrin, Vanessa was standing with the couple—*Sector something. Blake somebody.* Why was she so bad at this? They stood in front of the unfinished painting she had so hoped would be buried in a back hallway somewhere. Instead, there it sat on a display easel at the entry to the outdoor bar area overlooking the golf course. Luckily, Vanessa introduced Tina and Blake Morrison, and Piper managed to turn on the charm expected of her. They gushed about her work and dissected strokes and colors in the canvas where she could only see faults and incomplete lines.

"What do you call this, my dear?" Tina Morrison was pleasant enough.

"Uh." Piper looked at it and searched the tag for some made-up title Vanessa might have given it. She saw nothing. V raised her eyebrows as if she was hoping for brilliance but expecting failure. Piper hated to fail. "I call it *Unresolved.*"

"I see." Tina nodded as she spoke, turning her attention back to the painting before glancing back at Piper several times. "Did you feel like your life was unresolved or your art?"

Well, that would fall into the category of none of your damned business, now wouldn't it?

"I think when you pour yourself into a piece as close to my heart as this one was at the time, it's impossible to separate the two, you know? I'm sure you have a similar passion, Mrs. Morrison?" Piper watched Tina smile and blush. Piper was disgusted with herself. *I really hate being even marginally good at this.*

"Would you mind parting with it, Piper? I mean, if it means that much to you." Mr. Morrison was squinting to look at the piece more closely. Piper tried to imagine what Vanessa was going to ask for the piece, but she was never around when she talked numbers.

"Well, of course it's difficult to part with any expression of yourself, but I know that it will be appreciated, as art should be." *I'm seriously going to have to become Catholic, just so I can go to confession and cleanse myself of the bullshit that pours out of me at these things.*

"How wise, Piper." Vanessa clasped her hands to her chest. She turned back to Tina. "I can see why you want to snatch this one up. There has been quite a buzz already." She looked around the patio as if effecting a coup on the Morrisons' behalf.

Piper bit her tongue and reminded herself that some grand sum for a twenty-inch canvas would make a solid addition to her independence fund. She watched Tina Morrison nod at her husband, who removed his wallet from his jacket pocket as though this wasn't the first time his wife's nod cost him money. Vanessa steered him into the house lest the pedestrian exchange of money change the tone of the evening. Piper forced herself to entertain Mrs. Morrison until their return with a parchment tag boasting the word "Sold" in calligraphy. She offered her sincere gratitude to the couple before they were whisked away by Vanessa for a celebratory drink. She repeated her performance with Wendall Allison, Linda and Paul Gregory, and Duke Ford and his girlfriend of the moment, whose name Piper couldn't recall for all the money in the room. Four pieces sold in the first hour.

She searched several times for Leo, but admittedly the searches were quick and done from the shadows of quiet corners of less populated rooms. Vanessa caught her arm as she tried to duck into the library.

"How do you expect to make an impression if no one can find the elusive artist?" Her whisper was more of an angry hiss. She recognized it from other such evenings when she tried, with mediocre success, to escape.

"Maybe you can make me brooding and antisocial. Or tell them I felt inspired by their attendance and I may be creating a masterpiece in their honor at this very moment?" Piper was a little frightened by the look on Vanessa's face as she spoke.

"Don't make me look foolish, Piper Holthaus, or this will be the last time one of your canvases hangs in this house." She smiled, but Piper was no dummy. The smile was the lips-only kind.

"Got it. Fine. Where to?" She felt sufficiently scolded and reined in her sarcasm for the moment.

"Trent Mitchell is another one of Frank's clients. He likes *Perfect Wave*. Meeting you might seal the deal."

Piper offered an awkward nod, unsure how much trouble she was going to be in, but she had to ask. "V, um, I don't know which one that is. I never named a painting that."

Vanessa narrowed her eyes and pointed at the corner of the dining room near the meatballs and the charcuterie trays. She could manage this task. She moved quickly to the corner and the person she hoped was Trent Mitchell.

"Mr. Mitchell, I hope?" She managed a smile that usually elicited the same in return.

The pale, gray-haired man nodded without even a hint of a smile. She held out her hand, which the man took firmly in a greeting too long for her comfort. The sweaty, too-soft palm stuck to hers and his fingers squeezed a little too hard.

"I'm Piper Holthaus. Vanessa said you like some of my work and I just wanted to introduce myself and say thank you for your kind words." She gestured at the painting and tried to commit its name to memory.

"I don't remember saying I was particularly enamored by this painting." He swept his hand dismissively in the direction of the artwork. "I simply said I liked the colors. Is this your first attempt? It's not very complex, and that's being kind."

Ooh. That stung. Well, thank you, Mr. Mitchell.

"No. I've been doing this for a while. Everyone's entitled to their individual taste in art, right?" Piper backed away and hoped for a quick exit from an already excruciating conversation. "It was nice to meet you." She waved awkwardly and pushed through the first door she came to. She'd been in the main house many times but rarely paid much attention to the doors and their connection to the formal spaces. Her visits to the house consisted of formal gatherings like this one or stealthy dashes down the dark hallway to Vanessa's bed when Frank was out of town.

She found a shadowy butler's pantry and slid down the wall until her ass met her heels. She forced herself to take long, calming breaths. It was one thing to have to smile stupidly at unfounded compliments, but it was another thing entirely to have to stand by while some stranger told you that you sucked. She glanced at her watch, stunned that it had only been an hour of this torture. How much longer could she go on this way?

CHAPTER TWO

Brook angrily dusted a baking sheet with flour and arranged pastries in neat rows.

"Who do you think you are, jackass? I've been cooking for fifteen years and people love my food, you pretentious bastard." She looked down and noticed her chef's jacket was splashed with cocktail sauce and a smear of grease. She attempted to kick a bag of trash across the room but missed and stubbed her toe on the base molding instead.

"Shit, shit, shit." Brook grabbed her foot trying to fathom why she had thought branching out on her own was a good idea. At this rate and with a few more reviews like the one she'd just received, she could count on becoming a fry cook in a mediocre diner off the highway just like Meg said she would. She jerked off her stained white coat and replaced it with a clean one she drew from her hanging bag. She had learned long ago to travel with a number of replacement jackets so she always looked neat.

She pulled trays of hors d'oeuvres from the oven to cool and shoved the pastries in. She began plating fresh blocks of cheese among the tiny toast rounds she had prepared earlier in the week. Stuffed pastries and relish trays were preset for when they needed to be replenished. She refused to waste food, so she always had three trays of everything at the ready. One to lay out first, one to replace it, and one to condense the stragglers onto when they came back half full and not so artfully arranged.

She peeled the film from the relish tray and lined it up behind the tiny chocolate mousse cups she had filled while watching a documentary on Ruth Bader Ginsberg in her living room that afternoon.

She took a deep breath and tried to muster up the strength to return to the dining room, where people felt justified in publicly insulting her food. To be fair, *people* was only one questionably dressed moron, but still, who knew what everyone else thought? As soon as she pushed through the crowd, she felt her phone vibrate. She had her hands full and guests were stopping her to help themselves to the new offerings on her trays. She was desperate to grab the phone but would never be caught on a call at an event she was working. She had to let it ring and hoped no emergency would complicate her already stressful night.

Her pulse raced until she could finally make it back again to the kitchen. She grabbed her phone and her mom's voice mail said she was just checking on her and there was no need to call her back if she was busy. Whew. No crisis, no choosing between work and her personal life—she had done that too many times lately. She was relieved that she could return to obsessing about her food and rude critics. She forced her mind back to pleasing her clients and their entitled friends. "I will not let people's insults get to me. I know my food is good." She repeated the mantra under her breath as she continued working.

A noisy clatter of pans slipped from her cart. She reset the stack, restoring the kitchen's welcome silence.

❖

Piper jerked out of her self-pity when a loud metal scraping against metal noise notified her that her hideout wasn't as isolated as she had hoped. She peered around the door and saw a pissed-off woman wearing a chef's coat and a murderous expression, slamming baking sheets onto the stove grates. She heard her muttering angrily under her breath.

Piper grinned at the fact that the messy chef had a sliver of cheese stuck to the sleeve of her jacket that waved in the wind as she gestured to what she no doubt thought was an empty room. She watched her put her phone to her ear and thought she heard an audible sigh of relief.

Piper straightened and moved away from the corner that had been shielding her. She had managed a spinach puff and a soufflé bite between schmoozing sessions, and they were pretty darn good.

"I happen to love your food." She wasn't sure why she was giving up her covert corner, but perhaps she could offer reassurance to someone else having a bad night.

The chef wheeled on her in surprise. "What are you doing in here? I mean, no one is supposed to be in the kitchen." She looked around as if she realized yelling in front of some wealthy party guest was only going to add to the disaster of her day. "Sorry. I just had a moment."

"Don't apologize. I came in here to hide because my night is going about as well as yours. Some rich guy in bad plaid just told me I sucked. So, I get it." Piper leaned against the wall hosting the bank of ovens at the back of the kitchen. "The way I see it, we should pack up all the good food and go watch the wild turkeys on the twelfth green. What do you say?"

The chef blinked as if contemplating the odd suggestion by a perfect stranger. She recovered quickly.

"Ha! I wish, but I have three more hours of putting up with picky wannabe-foodies while they pretend to like some unknown artist's work with clichéd names like *Weeping Fire* and *Broken Dreams*. God, why is everyone so fucking pretentious?" She seemed to forget that she was trying to reign in her anger.

"*Weeping Fire*? Shit. That *is* awful." Piper was determined to find out which of her paintings Vanessa had labeled with such a horrible moniker.

"Isn't it? I mean, the painting is okay, but the name kicks it right in the toilet for me." She busied herself arranging a tray of crudités and prepping more puff pastries for the oven, not once looking at Piper. "I hope I didn't offend you. I mean, you may think the art is great. I'm just having a bad night. The oven is heating unevenly, my salmon guy showed up thirty minutes late, and the crostini is soggy. First-world problems, huh?"

Piper smiled and watched the remnant of sleeve cheese finally hit the floor. The chef was strangely magnetic in a haphazard way. Not classically beautiful, necessarily, but she was kind of mesmerizing in the sharp way she moved and spoke. Her blunt-cut nails were well manicured, but given they were currently covered in bits of pastry and parsley garnish, it was hard to make a proper assessment. Her brown hair was knotted into a small messy bun at the nape of her neck. As she turned to slide a tray into the oven, Piper saw her white cotton jacket said "Myers" in slanted font.

"Myers. Is that a first name or a last?" Her voice was suddenly husky and playful as her sole focus became making the unraveled woman a little more raveled, or at least willing to commit to conversation with her.

"Uh, it's a last name. Brook is my first name." She stopped to look at Piper for a second and wiped her hands on a towel. "I've been pretty rude. I'm sorry. Not the best way to drum up clients for my business."

"Oh. An entrepreneur? Nice." She held up a fist to meet Brook in the most sanitary handshake she could think of given their surroundings and Brook's tasks. Brook washed her hands after the fist-bump anyway.

"Right now, we're calling it 'pray the bills away.'" She grimaced and managed a quick smile. "I guess we'll see what happens."

"Well, if I threw expensive parties and had wealthy friends, I'd hire you. But I can probably only assemble a couple of golf pros on a pizza budget if you get desperate."

"I might take you up on that if things continue to go like this." Her rueful tone said she thought that this might be the last in a few challenging business moments.

"My name's Piper, by the way." She resumed her lean on the oven wall and watched Brook continue to work.

"Nice to meet you…Wait. Piper? As in Piper Holthaus, the artist?" Her eyes were huge, and she froze with a pan suspended in her hands.

"In all my Weeping Fiery glory." Piper couldn't help but laugh at the ludicrous title and the shocked look on Brook's face.

"God. I am a totally fucking disaster. I need to find a job working underground where I'm not allowed to talk to other humans." She brushed her sleeve over the moisture beading on her forehead. "I should just go out there and fire myself, so you don't have to."

"Why would I do that? It is a completely wretched name for a painting, and the reason I'm even in this kitchen is because I'm hiding from people who want to talk to the fractured artist with an axe to grind with the world. I could give a royal crap if you hated my work. After all, there are a good twenty or so people pretending to like it, so I'm good."

"Well, you're quite a breath of fresh air this evening. I needed that. And by the way, I think your art is great."

"If it redeems me at all, I didn't name any of my pieces. Vanessa did." Piper wanted Brook Myers to know that she was anything but pretentious. It was remarkably important for some reason.

"Wow. She is quite a mover and a shaker. I guess you're lucky to have her backing you." She tilted an empty pan onto a rack and then dried her hands on a towel looped over her shoulder.

"Considering I've been avoiding her and everyone else out there for the better part of thirty minutes, I'm guessing this might be my last hurrah." Piper shrugged and wondered if she would actually mind.

She could picture herself in a one-room lakefront cabin, alone, painting for the therapy of it. Maybe a tiny converted warehouse downtown somewhere. Then she imagined the stacks of paintings barricading her in the tiny space where they would eventually find her, wallowing in her solitude and talking to herself.

She shook her head to erase the mental image and refocused on Brook as she pulled a tray of bubbling mini-soufflés from the oven and arranged them on serving platters. She held a cocktail napkin out to Piper and picked up one of the trays, holding it in her direction. Piper assessed her ruddy complexion, which she surmised was less sun-kissed and more oven-flushed.

"You're welcome to hide in here all night if you like, but you might as well face the music at some point. Consider me your role model." Her delivery was considerably more chipper than a few moments earlier. She had adeptly arranged lettuce leaves that managed to end up looking like a symmetrical doily under the round pastries.

"How so?" Piper was intrigued. She chose what looked like a cheese puff and a stuffed mushroom, placing them on her napkin.

"I plan to walk up to the pretentious bastard who hates my food and offer him a soufflé." Brook smiled as she filled in the gaps made by Piper's selections.

"Good for you. Go show 'em how it's done." She popped the mushroom in her mouth, making an appreciative moan as she chewed.

"I think I shall." Brook took an audible breath and spun out the swinging door with her soufflés and her head held high.

Piper finished the cheese puff and immediately wished for another. They were truly fantastic. She knew she had been gone too long and peered out the small window in the door. She wondered if she had completely pissed Vanessa off. She caught Leo and Stacy passing the food display and heading for a bartender carrying tall trumpet flutes of champagne. Piper felt a little bad. The longer she was gone, the more conspicuous her absence was going to be. She would face it again. In a minute.

Brook wore a crooked, knowing smile when she pushed back into the kitchen. "You might want to think about heading back to the party. I heard Mrs. Devereaux assure someone that you had to step out to handle a family emergency but that you couldn't wait to discuss *Brink of Danger* with them."

"Seriously? *Brink of Danger*? Sounds like a series drama destined to be canceled right after the pilot airs." Piper stared at the door willing herself to walk through it.

"Here." Brook went to a cabinet and pulled out a bottle of wine, decanting a healthy few inches into a glass. "It's not fancy, but it's better than going out there stone cold sober. I mean assuming you drink, or like wine, or…stop talking, Myers."

Piper took the glass from her and drained its contents. Dry

white wine did nothing for her, but somehow, it felt like a little bit of team courage, courtesy of the new friend she would much rather stay and talk to.

"Thanks. Wish me luck." She handed back the empty glass and forced herself to reenter the melee. She instantly wished she could go back to hiding in the kitchen and talking to someone not tasked with liking her just because the Devereaux did.

Piper smiled as she approached an obviously livid Vanessa. She adeptly covered her fury as she introduced a couple whose names Piper would never remember.

She gripped Piper's sleeve and squeezed just a little too hard. "Piper, darling, please tell them about *Frozen Intuition.*"

Are you kidding me? I can't begin to make up a story for that crap title.

Vanessa stared until Piper spoke about the painting they were standing beside.

"Oh, right. I guess I was in a pretty dark place when that one came to me. I stayed up for three days until I had mixed all the right hues to adequately match my need for closure after a particularly rough patch in my life." Piper did her best to look as if she was feeling the imaginary recall all over again. In reality, she had called in sick from work due to a chest cold and painted it while lying on the couch, bracing the canvas with her knees. Several of the brush strokes happened when she fell asleep still holding the paintbrush.

"So, you really do leave a piece of yourself on each canvas, like Vanessa says." The woman wore a knot of pearls and clutched her husband's arm as she spoke.

"Vanessa knows me so well." *This is how sociopaths are born. If I keep doing this, I might forget when I'm just making shit up. The ID Channel will make a series about me:* The Artist, The Axe, The Anarchy.

"Thank you, Piper. It was so nice to meet the woman behind the work. I'll let you get back to your other guests. Best of luck." She reached for Piper's hand, and Piper thought it was the kind of pitiful gesture some college counselor might offer someone who decided to become a street mime instead of a brain surgeon.

"And thank you." She stared after the couple that Vanessa was now steering toward the negotiation station. It was actually the bar, where she offered them a drink and told them how many people would likely want the painting. If they decided to make the wise purchase, Vanessa would tell them that she thought they might be the night's celebrity.

Piper found Leo and Stacy and made small talk until they'd had their fill of hors d'oeuvres and free booze and headed home. Piper looked around at the thinning crowd and ducked back into the kitchen without giving the destination much thought.

"Need a refill?" Brook was condensing two trays of berries and chocolate onto one.

"God yes. *Frozen Intuition*, she named it *Frozen Intuition*. What the hell was she thinking?" Piper briefly considered how easily she had clicked with Brook and was shorthanding conversations after knowing her for mere minutes.

Her good-natured laugh instantly relaxed Piper. "I guess she was trying to make it sound evocative. It's a little stilted, if I'm being honest." Brook stopped as if to gauge Piper's reaction to her comment.

"You're being too kind. It's just awful." Piper suddenly felt like she was hawking cheap hotel art at a convention hall. She knew her work was nothing more than a fire sale for people who didn't know what else to do with their money. She had to stop it before she ended up hating art altogether.

Brook stepped closer, her hands still covered in berries, and nudged her shoulder against Piper's. "It could be worse. We can't choose who likes our stuff. We just have to be happy someone does." She used her wrist to slide a nearly empty platter of cheese toward Piper and nodded for her to help herself.

Piper watched her return to arranging the fruit, noticing the spray of faint freckles along her slim nose. "So, when are you done with this shindig?" She wanted to stop thinking about art and schmoozing and focus on finding out more about someone who didn't try to act impressed by her because Vanessa convinced them they were. Piper lamented that she wasn't around very many real people anymore. She desperately needed to change that.

"Half an hour to finish serving and an hour to clean up, why?"

"I wasn't kidding. Twelfth green, wild turkeys, and some cheap beer. I need a little break from tonight. I thought you might too." Piper fully expected her to reject the offer, but she made it anyway.

Brook looked shocked and then sad. "I wish I could. Really. It sounds peaceful, but I take care of a sick family member and I can't leave her alone for very long. Thanks anyway." She turned back to the food, which punctuated the end of the conversation.

Piper watched her for a few seconds more and wondered which part of that was a lie and why it made Brook so sad. She chucked her business card on the table near a purse she assumed belonged to Brook.

"If you ever need a break, chances are I will too. Thanks for the talk and the wine. I really enjoyed meeting you." She watched her until she looked up. "By the way, your food is awesome. You're going to do great."

"Thanks. I enjoyed meeting you too." Brook returned to her platter and Piper slid out the back door to the patio, hoping to avoid another sales job. She stood on the stone terrace as the last guest carried a painting to their car. She was terrified to know what it had been called and thought it best if she didn't ask. She heard Vanessa's unmistakable footsteps behind her.

"*Before the Rain* sold for twenty-one hundred, in case you care to know." Her voice was hurt and dismissive and she stopped several feet away.

"I don't even know which painting that was, V." Piper felt guilty that she hadn't been more appreciative of the ridiculous marketing done on her behalf. She just couldn't forget that pieces that once moved her and were once a part of her felt like mass productions in a twisted Hallmark catalog.

"It was the small blue one you finished last month. You told me it took you longer to finish that one than the giant commission piece you did for me when we first met."

"Oh, yeah. I liked that one." Piper softened her tone since Vanessa looked fairly defeated. "Who bought it?" She doubted she would know the name, but she hoped it made her seem appropriately interested.

"Trent Mitchell." Vanessa's tone was an incongruous mix of triumph and resignation.

Piper had no trouble remembering him. "He practically told me I was a novice hack. What the hell does he want it for?"

"I think he was just trying to get the price down." A hint of a smile formed on Vanessa's lips.

"You love this, don't you?" Piper shook her head and joined in the smile as she relaxed against the low stone wall surrounding the terrace.

"He told me you were rude. I told him you were brooding. He told me you were unknown, I told him you were newly discovered. He told me he couldn't decide, and I told him the piece he was talking to you about already sold for twice the offer price and he wrote the check for fifty percent over list so someone didn't outbid him." Her now melodic tone suggested she particularly enjoyed separating the arrogant fool from some of his money.

"He'll probably shove it in the back of a closet somewhere," Piper grumbled. She caught Vanessa's eye and they shared a private second, despite the public space.

"Maybe. But as I see it, brooding artist that I adore: one. Pretentious ass: zero." She glanced around to make sure no one had walked close enough to hear the exchange. She was fully aware of the pretense and façade of the world she chose to live in.

"Adore, huh? How did I get so lucky to have a beautiful woman like you say such things?" Piper stepped closer to Vanessa and spoke quietly.

"You make me look forward to waking up in your arms and forget how much work being Vanessa Devereaux is," she whispered as sadness clouded her eyes again, but this time it had nothing to do with art or Piper's refusal to be part of the game.

Piper broke eye contact and turned as Frank Devereaux

lumbered out on the patio and tucked his arm around his wife's waist. He dropped a glancing kiss on her forehead.

Piper couldn't help but think the gesture felt more like ownership than affection. She wondered if it felt like that to Vanessa too.

"Good show, Piper. My wife outdid herself tonight." He studied her intensely.

His booming voice always made Piper want to shush him, but he never seemed to notice Piper's recoil.

"I think you practically sold out." He looked at his wife and smiled.

The comment was a little too close to the bone. "V did a fabulous job, as always. Thank you for the hospitality, Frank."

"Anytime." He tilted a rocks glass full of his customary whiskey and drained it. "I like knowing Vanessa has someone here that she trusts when I'm gone. Consider it payment in trade."

Piper stared at him as he spoke. He knew the deal. He always had, but it was never spoken aloud. It was ridiculous if Piper thought about it too much. He jetted off to wherever for days or weeks at a time and did who knows what with God knows whom, while Piper satisfied the needs of his lonely trophy wife.

"Well then, I guess we both win. Thank you, just the same." Piper smiled. At least she hoped she was smiling and not grimacing like she'd smelled something bad.

"Anytime." He looked at Vanessa for a minute as if he had something profound to say. Instead, he said, "I'm hitting the bed. May have a call later, so I'll stay on my side tonight."

Piper knew that was code for the other side of the house where an office, movie room, and a bedroom suite were set up for him. A plethora of excuses like late night or early-morning calls, illness, snoring, or restlessness would regularly put him on the opposite side of the estate from his wife. Vanessa knew the excuses and had told Piper that she had stopped caring. If he wanted a divorce, it would cost him dearly.

Their prenup said if she left him, she'd clear a couple of million and the beach house. If he left her, or cheated on her? Four million and the Shadow Glass Estate house worth considerably more. Piper marveled at the commerce of their relationship as Frank ambled away and Vanessa tried to look unaffected.

"I bet you're tired." Piper winced at the platitude, but what else did you say to someone who had an open cage door but refused to fly?

"Yeah, pimping you out is a lot of work." She did her best to look lighthearted.

Piper noticed that the sentiment of her words didn't reach her eyes, and probably wasn't anywhere near her heart.

"I wish I could hold you tonight. Might make you sleep better." Piper ran her hand over Vanessa's arm, careful that no one saw. She began to walk toward the front steps.

"You know it would. I just have to hold out for Monday." Vanessa turned and followed Piper down the stairs and across the drive to the front porch of the carriage house, now lit by only the moon. Piper opened the door that there was never any reason to lock and Vanessa followed her in.

"I wish I could stay." Vanessa looked past Piper down the hall.

Piper detected the precursor to tears brewing in her eyes. "Yeah, me too, V." She actually wanted nothing more than to be alone, but Vanessa needed to hear the words that cost Piper nothing. She pulled Vanessa against her chest and whispered, "It'll be okay. I'll make it better on Monday."

Vanessa accepted the kiss that Piper pressed gently to her lips. Piper was bad at relationships, horrible at finding the right woman, but pretty phenomenal at making women feel like they were at home in her arms. The juxtaposition was profoundly fucked up, but at least someone went home feeling better. It just wasn't ever Piper.

CHAPTER THREE

Piper sipped too-hot coffee and added numbers to the club's inventory sheets she populated every morning. The outer door swung open, and she hoped to hear a coworker's voice instead of a member's. Somehow, she didn't think she could muster up any believable charm quite yet.

"Have you made enough to retire yet?" Leo's morning voice sounded like gravel and pepper, but to Piper it was soothing and comfortable in the most platonic way. Leo was her clarity in the very unreal world they both visited every day. He got to return to reality much more often than she did. She wondered why she was jealous that he got to go home to Stacy outside these gates and live among real people.

"I'm saving for a car and so I can buy my own apartment first. I figure I only have to sell *half* my soul for that, right?"

"Depends. Are you trying to buy a Maserati, or will you settle for a normal car?"

"I would settle for a used Z4 in black." She drove the one from Frank's garage and loved the feel of it. She thought it was the perfect indulgence without being over-the-top like the rest of his accumulation of stuff. She briefly considered that Vanessa felt like part of that accumulation. Piper certainly felt like *her* property on occasion.

"Well, after the other night, you should be close. I saw five different paintings being carried to the car in a few hours." He raised his eyebrows. "Impressive, I'd say."

"Thank you for showing up. I know it's a chore for a weeknight given the too-muchness of it all." She made air quotes around the phrase.

"Pipe, you're the only one that feels like it's a pain. The rest of the regular people feel like they get a peek behind the curtain."

"I suppose." She contemplated the weird class system money created. She thought about her mother, who had worked her whole life without any help. Her grandparents had disowned her mother when she chose to live her life against their wishes by refusing to marry into a wealthy family. Piper's mother would tell anyone who wanted to know that money always smelled funny and sleeping with it didn't change that.

Leo's voice snapped her out of her meandering thoughts.

"What's eating you? That you aren't some tragic bootstrap story you get to sell to the *Times* someday? That you didn't hold out until you were discovered for being some organic talent living behind a dumpster? Piper, it doesn't make you less of an artist because some wealthy woman claimed you as her discovery."

"Doesn't it? Maybe the people I want to love my art for art's sake, for the evocative nature of it, aren't invited beyond the pearly gates. And by that, I mean the guarded kind, not the afterlife kind."

"The trouble with you is you keep looking at the gift horse and wondering why you can't love them for what they're offering."

"Because it feels like pandering, Leo. Like selling out to the nth degree." Piper was finally able to put a fine point on it. "I don't believe any of those people gave a rat's plump ass who I was, what my paintings represent, or what they mean to me."

"Oh, poor Piper. So misunderstood. Do you think the artists who sell their work in some South Bay bistro get a call from the owner who just sold their painting of stylized pasta say, 'Gee, did you make sure they understood what I was feeling when I sketched that meatball?' Get the hell out of your own very special head. It's art. Good art, but art nonetheless. In the eye of the beholder and all that shit. Get out of your head and stop thinking that people want to feel anything other than simple discoveries about their own reaction to art…in all its forms. Just because you create it doesn't mean you can dictate how people should go about appreciating it."

"You, my dear Leo, are infuriatingly obnoxious and a bit accurate. The last thing I want is to be self-important or bourgeois about what I create. I just think maybe there is some happy medium somewhere." Piper hoped she would find it someday.

"You can think about that while you drag Mr. Daniels around the links. Get out of my space for a few minutes so I can get some work done." He pushed through to the back room, leaving Piper to consider how much she valued him and his regular reality checks.

She smoothed her hair back with her thumbs as she slid the ball cap back on her head. She retucked her golf shirt into her black pants and smoothed her palms down each thigh. She actually had a real client to teach.

She had heard Perry Daniels was a pretty talented golfer for whom she might have to be an *actual* golf pro. Women were great golfers, she just rarely got those. If she was honest with herself, her normal client lessons were basically therapy sessions interrupted by rudimentary pointers on swing and body mechanics for bored members who decided to spend an hour with her before they lunched overlooking the first tee.

These were not hours that required her to muster up all her skill and years of experience playing semi-pro golf; all she had to do was make people feel like the center of her world and her attention.

After all, that's how she and Vanessa met. Frank had gifted her a ten-session package of lessons with Piper, and between the coaching and the conversation, they found common ground and an unintended bond. Piper didn't anticipate them satisfying each other's most basic needs, but once it had started, she made no effort to stop it. Vanessa took an interest in her art, and it all sounded like a tawdry novel.

Piper would do anything to further her art career, but she refused to admit that part of the achievement was at the expense of her self-respect. A weird equation, given her concessions made to and for her art as it related to Vanessa Devereaux and her current living situation. She intended to be professional now. To take on this new client and earn her pay today. She looked forward to the challenge.

As it turned out, Perry Daniels didn't want counseling or coaching, for that matter. He needed his entourage, or various portions of it, standing around cheering him on as if he were a wildly popular singer in a mediocre band.

Perry was over-tanned, over-processed, and over-confident. She discovered that the reputation concerning his golf skills was exaggerated at best, complete pandering at worst. He seemed to want to talk more than he wanted to golf, though he managed a few passable swings in the general direction of the intended hole. She was completely unprepared when the gas company executive dropped his club in his bag and didn't select another.

He stepped closer to her, and Piper stepped back.

"You know, Piper, we talk about your little cottage industry out here. All of the wives on your lesson card." His smile, if one could call it that, looked somewhat like a worm sliding off a slippery rock.

Piper cringed. "We?" Who else had the time or inclination to discuss her? She glanced at the small group of men and wondered if they really weren't paying attention or were just attempting to look like they weren't.

"We wonder if you're trying to fuck *all* these women. That's the rumor. We sit around and watch which of the wives are begging to take your lessons. None of us think it's because they aim to challenge their husbands out on the course. We all think that the golf pro chick strokes their egos and then whatever else needs stroking, since their husbands are out drilling other women."

"Well, that's quite a commentary on the condition of modern marriage inside the walls of Shadow Glass Estates, isn't it?" She refused to display any physical reaction, but acid rose in her throat.

"Don't be naïve enough to think that it only exists inside these walls. And none of us think you're here because golf would be a better sport."

"None of us? I suppose I should be flattered that captains of industry are actually spending time talking about little ol' me, considering I'm no threat to any of you and my reputation is much inflated."

"No one's threatened by you, you're right." He stood rod straight now and rested a hand on his clubs.

She mused that if they had been in some lowbrow bar and she had been another over-hormoned guy, there would likely have been some chest bumping and crushing of beer cans.

"We are simply amused by the fact that someone like you thinks she can offer a woman more than we can."

Piper felt the challenge. Was it meant as one? Of course it was. Her initial reaction wanted to suggest how she could, indeed, offer more than they could. Maybe not money, but she could engage a woman sexually without costing them their self-respect. Something, she imagined, that wouldn't happen with inferior narcissists like Perry Daniels. Piper was many things, but she wasn't condescending, nor did she ever leave a woman wanting more or wishing that they were never with her. Something she was sure men like Daniels couldn't claim. Women, no matter what their class or income level, wanted to be appreciated and admired and respected. And then to be driven over the edge by someone whose goal was to make them experience ecstasy.

No, Mr. Daniels wasn't there to glean tips on a perfect swing, but this wasn't the first time she worried about her job at the club because some dick wanted to throw his weight around. She took a deep breath in order to assure that her voice and reply were even and measured. "I can assure you, Mr. Daniels, I am here to teach golf to whoever needs my help. You can tell everyone you're talking about me with that's my only intention."

"Whatever you say, Piper. Eyes are on you." He made the silly two-fingered gesture from his eyes to hers.

"Better golf means keeping your eyes on the ball, right?" She smiled and hoped that her attempt at levity would redirect the uncomfortable exchange.

"Let's face it, sweetheart, I really don't need lessons, but it can't hurt to hear what you've got since I'm here." He sauntered back to his bag and selected the wrong club.

Piper inwardly cringed at the reductive term, but she would never let it show. She watched his approach to the ball, the club hanging loosely in his grip. His pelvis was thrust forward like it was doing the playing for him. From what she had gleaned about his personality, it probably was.

"Watch this," he called back to his cronies drinking Bloody Marys near the cart path. He lofted the club behind him and swung like he was intending on pulverizing the little white ball. Instead he skimmed the top and it rolled limply to the rough just below them.

"Let's call that stroke interference and you take another shot." She walked over to pick up the first ball so that in case the burst of laughter escaped, she could perhaps mute it with some distance. Not much distance, however, thanks to Pro Golfer Daniels.

Perry checked behind him, seemingly grateful that his pals didn't appear to be watching. "This course is not what it used to be. The grounds people must be new."

"I'm sure that's it." She coughed into the crook of her elbow and masked the grin she could no longer stop from forming.

He swung again and managed a passable mid-fairway drive that she could have helped him improve on, but she wouldn't waste the energy.

The lesson was over in a scant forty-five minutes, but sixty seconds with Perry Daniels could be measured in months. She was never so happy to get his signature on the club sheet and throw up a dismissive wave.

The door to the club room hadn't fully closed when she growled in Leo's direction. "Why do I work here again? That guy was a total dick." She chucked a towel toward the laundry bag and missed.

Leo raised one eyebrow and dropped his chin to his chest. "Because thirty hours a week here gets you the equivalent of full-time pay anywhere else and again, you drive a Bimmer."

"I borrow one, and yeah, keep reminding me. It helps me not hammer a divot tool into the skulls of people like Perry Daniels. I don't think they would let me have an art show in prison." She was keenly aware that too much rumor where she was concerned could cause some difficulty at the club; however, she also knew that most people wouldn't challenge the Devereaux as long as she was Vanessa's favorite.

"You could have one, it just wouldn't be nearly so profitable." Leo pushed the schedule clipboard at her. "A new member is showing his arm candy girlfriend all the trappings of country club life in twenty minutes. Try to burn off the bitchy by then, okay?"

She glanced at the sheet and hoped this one would tip well or be marginally good at golf. She dared not hope for both.

The ensuing lesson was nothing more than a repeat of Lorinda's except this one was young enough to be Piper's daughter and the septuagenarian's granddaughter rather than his girlfriend.

Piper caught herself replaying the intriguing kitchen conversation with the enigmatic Brook Myers as she made stroke suggestions. She wondered if their common opinion of bourgeois excess made her more attractive or the fact that Brook wasn't the least bit in control made her seem like her spirit sister.

When she finally made it home Monday afternoon, she pushed into the overstuffed chaise lounge and googled "Brook Myers Catering." She checked the door several times because she knew she wouldn't be alone with her thoughts long.

The website for a catering company came up, but her picture appeared nowhere. If Piper was honest, she wanted to study her a little closer. She couldn't decide exactly why.

CHAPTER FOUR

The clatter of keys and heels echoed in her foyer as Vanessa sighed too loudly and pushed an enormous box through the large arched doorway.

"Pipe, wait till you see what came today. You are so going to love me."

Piper took a reflexive step back. She never wanted to hear the L-word from Vanessa. She would definitely never say it. It was heavy and dishonest and fraught with all the emotional weight she never wanted to be steamrolled by again.

"Look." Vanessa didn't seem to notice Piper's visceral reaction.

"What is it?" Piper could deflect better than anyone. It was her superpower.

"Only the best easel money can buy." She looked at Piper expectantly, like a parent bestowing a first bike to a five-year-old.

"I like the one I have." Piper never stopped to think how her words landed on the other person. She could be too direct, and sometimes people could be wounded by her delivery.

"You mean the duct-taped plywood A-frame piece of crap you insist on kneeling in front of?" Vanessa was defensive and wounded.

"Um, yeah. I guess." She hadn't noticed that her easel was deserving of such a disparaging description. To Piper, it felt a little like a well-fitting pair of jeans.

"Look at this one and give it a chance, please?" The last word sounded like begging.

"Of course. And thank you." Piper reminded herself that people needed a little stroking and that their feelings needed a little caretaking.

She walked to the large box and extracted the Diamante beechwood easel she could never afford. With its 550-pound capacity and pneumatic height adjustments, Piper wondered if it would enhance her art or somehow diminish it. She pictured dripping paint on something so expensive and winced. She plastered a grateful smile on her face and turned to Vanessa.

"What did I do to deserve you, V?" Piper knew the intention was good. Vanessa wanted to do something to make Piper happy, and being an ungrateful shit about it wasn't the right thing to do.

"You make me happy, and let's face it, you have a way of turning me on just a little." She walked into Piper and tucked against her.

Piper was happy to have saved the moment. "I do, huh?" Piper's voice dropped an octave as her strong fingers gripped the thick hair at Vanessa's neck. The game had begun and they both knew it. The door was locked, Frank was away, the staff had gone home, and the surreal cloak of isolation was drawn around them.

They could have gone to the main house, but Vanessa liked it in Piper's bungalow. Piper liked it because she was fairly certain there was no electronic surveillance, and she could be as loud and as in charge as she wanted when she made the lady of the estate succumb to her.

She clutched the column of hair more strongly as she drew Vanessa's head back to expose her neck. Her teeth skimmed Vanessa's skin, and she relished the mewling sounds when she increased the pressure.

"You mean because I can make you feel like you've lost control?" Piper's teasing words were the best part of the game.

"Yesss," Vanessa managed to whisper.

"Because I can make you beg for me to take you?" Piper walked her backward down the hallway a few steps, as much to start the trip to the bedroom as to assert her control.

"I need you." Vanessa delivered the words in Piper's ear.

It was guttural, visceral, and expected. Piper couldn't stop it. She didn't want to. This made her engines fire. It also fortified the barrier between her and her own true feelings. It was purely physical.

She pushed Vanessa into the bedroom and stroked her hand under her blouse until Vanessa took over, pulling it over her head and tossing it to the side.

"It seems like someone wants to be naked." The words were taunting and provocative and intended to get Vanessa to focus on her.

"I just want to feel you against me. You know what you do to me." The words were breathy and desperate. Vanessa's fingers clawed at Piper's belt.

"Of course I do." Piper was in the place that made her comfortable. The one where she was in control and delivered the expected experience but was undone by none of it. That was safe. She slid her mouth near Vanessa's ear and watched in her peripheral for the moment when she was completely under her spell. Piper skimmed her hand under her skirt and claimed her.

"There. Right there," Vanessa begged as Piper skimmed her fingers along her center. Vanessa arched against her hand and Piper stroked inside her, slowly at first, gently. The time for gentle and slow was quickly eclipsed by Vanessa's demand for more.

Piper relished the sound. Nothing felt better than Vanessa driving her nails into Piper's back while Piper disappeared into the abyss of satisfaction that being in charge brought her. She knew what Vanessa wanted. Her other superpower was knowing that, delivering it, and never being weakened by it. At least, that's what she always told herself.

Vanessa's body changed under her hand, under her mouth. Vanessa's release was potent and reminded Piper how much she loved the feeling of Vanessa's body against her even though it was, and would always be, temporary. Piper curved against Vanessa's torso and exhaled for probably the first time in her complex week of pretending to belong. It was a lot of work hiding from the world.

Piper wrapped her arms around Vanessa and felt content. It wasn't bliss or any part of happy, but contentment felt like a welcome compromise. Like lemon tart substituting for chocolate mousse. It wasn't perfect, but the taste still satisfied the craving for something sweet. Piper felt herself slipping into sleep.

❖

"Piper? I made us some tea."

Piper woke to the feel of Vanessa arranging the covers around her and the smell of herbal tea. "You let me take you to bed *and* serve me beverages?" She managed to open one eye and shoot a soulful glance in Vanessa's direction.

Vanessa reclaimed her side of the bed and rolled to rest her head on Piper's shoulder. "I know you aren't always going to work at the club." The dejection wasn't hidden under her whisper.

The post-sex conversation Piper dreaded came without much prelude this time. "Well, you're working pretty hard at this art thing for me, so I hope I'll be doing that instead." Piper knew Vanessa was fishing for reassurance and some sort of fantasy where she wasn't Frank's kept woman and Piper wasn't a side piece that Vanessa could manipulate with art shows and a new easel.

"That just means I'll be without you, and it makes me sad." She twisted the chunky diamond ring on her left hand as she spoke.

"You could always come with me." Piper didn't want a relationship or anything permanent with Vanessa any more than Vanessa did with her, but it was the game they played.

"You know I can't leave." She traced a fingertip across Piper's collarbone.

"Can't or won't?" Piper knew she was entering dicey territory, but she couldn't help herself.

"My life is here." Vanessa's reply sounded rehearsed, mostly because it was.

"No, Frank is here, and I'd hardly call him your life."

She ignored that and kept talking. "You know how you say you want your independence? Well, I had mine. I worked in an office fifty hours a week and I barely scraped by. I ate in a diner once in a while and that's what I called a social life. I don't ever want to go back to that, Piper. I don't want to depend on anybody to pay me what they think I'm worth."

"That's one hell of an exchange, V. If you don't love him, do you really want to live off of him? I mean, how is that *real*?" Despite the fact that Piper had no desire to forge some permanent structure with Vanessa, the fact that she settled so readily was unbelievable.

"Love is a fickle thing, Piper. My broker, however, is not. My ability to do what I want and travel where I want means a lot. That's real enough for me." She rolled away from Piper as she declared her independence as she saw it.

"Right, I can see why you wouldn't want to give that up for a fulfilling emotional relationship instead." The cynical side of Piper snuck out and she caught herself making a case for a relationship she didn't want.

"Are you really saying that's what we would have?" She tilted her head and looked at Piper.

"I think you know exactly what it would be." Piper intentionally left the question unanswered. Regardless, she knew that Vanessa would never live the simple life by choice, and Piper would never venture into a relationship for love's sake again, so the die was cast. Piper had never been shy about her past relationships or her lack of desire to be in a new one.

"How about we stay in bed for the rest of the day?" Vanessa was clearly happy to change the subject.

Piper thought about it for a moment and then thought how much she would love to paint. "How about you open some wine and I do a little painting? You could be my model." She nuzzled against her neck and nibbled at the spot that made Vanessa instantly weak and compliant.

"Well, since you only paint abstracts, I'm not sure what kind of model I would be or what the resulting painting might look like."

"Very true. Maybe you could have a glass of wine and read one of your magazines or shop through one of those catalogues that keep coming here."

"Well, you certainly have reduced me to the empty-headed cliché, haven't you?"

"Not at all. I enjoy your company, but I really want to get some painting done. An afternoon off is rare during the week." God, what she wouldn't do to have the time to herself to simply paint, without having to beg for it.

"So, now aren't you happy that I booked out your Monday at the club?"

"Of course I am. I'm just still deciding how I feel since you, or more accurately, Frank, is having to pay an hourly rate to the club so I can be here. It makes our arrangement take on an unsavory light."

"Oh, stop it. You're not a hooker." Her tone was exasperated.

"No, but it does feel a little like I'm a gigolo," Piper half joked and ignored the other half that said that she was exactly that.

"How about we just enjoy this afternoon and tonight and stop talking about nonsense that doesn't make any difference to anyone, and certainly not to Frank's wallet."

"I suppose," Piper said. It still felt strange that she was essentially being rented out by this woman in the big mansion while her husband was off working and doing who knew what else or who else. She reminded herself that it wouldn't be much longer. She was getting closer and closer to her goals and her work was selling more and more quickly. She wouldn't delude herself into thinking that those sales wouldn't dry up once Vanessa was no longer her de facto agent. Either way, she would make it.

Two years' worth of rent and expenses in the bank would give her the cushion she needed to leap into art full-time. She had to make it. There was no trust fund waiting for her, no rich relatives hoping to bequeath their huge estate to her. Self-sufficiency would come from hard work no matter what that looked like. She was sure, however, that she didn't want it to look like this for very much longer.

Vanessa had drifted into a quiet sleep again and Piper's thoughts skipped back to Brook. She wasn't going to pretend that she didn't find her intriguing. She wondered about her story. She hadn't felt that curiosity about anyone in a long time. Curiosity. Yeah, that was it. Platonic curiosity.

After several fruitless protests to remain in bed, Vanessa

relented when Piper headed into her studio. Vanessa finally followed and pushed herself into the corner of the chaise lounge. It wasn't long before a large catalog full of overpriced home furnishings was flopped open in her lap and a thin-stemmed wine glass dangled between her elegant fingers.

Piper stared at the white square of canvas vised into her expensive new easel, which had taken only moments to erect. She wondered if she would feel bad the first time paint dropped onto the wood. Vanessa had to know that it would get messy, but Piper still felt guilty. She found a wide, smooth brush and pressed it into the dollop of red paint and then into the white. She wasn't particularly happy with the resulting shade of pink. She wiped off the brush and painted over it. She pushed more of the red paint onto the canvas to mask its pastel predecessor.

She was rarely in a red mood, but when it happened it was deep and thick and fiery. An hour had passed. She only thought to look at the time because Vanessa was pouring her second glass.

Vanessa didn't seem to notice Piper staring at her. Vanessa was beautiful. Ink-black silky hair, perfect skin, matching manicure and pedicure. Even her lounge-around clothes looked expensive. The fleece of her joggers managed to crease perfectly, a stark contrast to Piper's preferred paint-speckled lounge pants. She would never let herself fall for anyone again, particularly someone with Vanessa's dedication to high-end everything, but she could appreciate the view and the person she could be with her.

Piper didn't respect her life choices. Vanessa had traded a free existence for an expensive one. Piper knew how insanely hypocritical that was given the fact that she'd pretty much done exactly the same. She kept telling herself that the difference was that her situation wasn't permanent. It was a temporary means to an end, not a choice. It made her feel marginally better.

She drew a chisel point brush along the red pigment forming the swollen hip of a woman. She rarely attempted figurative pieces, but she was compelled to try. This wasn't Vanessa. Vanessa was perfectly sculpted by genetics, her personal trainer, and her plastic surgeon. She likely wouldn't take kindly to the slightly exaggerated swell of the waist in her painting. But it was sensual and compelling, and the image stuck in Piper's mind. She stroked the paint along the subtle V between the figure's legs, rounding the strokes slightly.

"Are you almost done?"

Vanessa broke Piper's concentration and demanded her attention when she wasn't ready to give it. Painting was therapeutic. It was a zone, a place she could go and be with herself, her thoughts, and her art. When she was jerked from it, it was uncomfortable, and the reentry felt jolting.

"Yes, I'm almost done." She managed the words, she hoped, without sounding annoyed. "Can I have like twenty more minutes. maybe?"

Vanessa looked up from her catalog and sighed. "Yes, my temperamental artist. Please take as long as you want to create whatever the next masterpiece is."

"That almost sounded mocking. But since you work so hard at selling them, I'm going to assume it wasn't."

"Of course not, Piper. I would never mock your work. I think you're amazing. I just want a little us time before we have to go back to the real world."

"You mean the real world where Frank only acts like a husband but stays on his side of the house?" She stole a glance to gauge how the thoughtless comment had landed. Vanessa's expression remained banal.

"Doesn't that bother you? I mean that he never stays with you?" Piper fleetingly wondered why she was picking at this particular scab.

"I suppose it should. I should want a full marriage and companionship and attention from him, but honestly, I prefer to get that from you."

She sounded wistful, and Piper watched her shift and roll her shoulders as if to relieve herself of the tension of the subject.

"You mean you would prefer to get it from me despite the fact I can't give you all the trappings that Frank can, correct?" Piper imagined that some psychologist somewhere would accuse her of pointing out the flaws in others that she most disliked about herself.

"It's not just the money, Piper. Stop making me sound like a horrible person."

"I'm not. Look, we both know what the deal is. I'm in no position to have a relationship and you've already got a pretty all-encompassing one. We'll continue to enjoy each other's company the way it is. I'm not making more out of it, I just worry about you. You seem sad."

"I suppose it's sad when this place feels empty. That's why I don't like it when you talk about leaving."

This wasn't the first time they had poked this exact bear. Piper waffled between honestly caring for Vanessa's happiness and protecting herself.

"Let's not talk about it anymore, okay? It'll put a damper on our night. What were you tapping into your phone so intently?" She glanced down at her own phone and noticed that ninety minutes had passed since they left the bedroom. Time rushed by when she had a paintbrush in her hand.

"I was texting Paul to see if he could throw something together for dinner."

"We could have just had pizza, you know. Money complicates things."

"Stop that. No, it doesn't. I just wanted you to have something a little healthier. I worry about how you eat. You live like a bachelor." Vanessa needed to care about something. There was a nurturing side to her that came out every so often.

"I hardly think so. I work out and I play golf and I try not to drink too much beer. That sounds like a pretty healthy routine to me." She looked guiltily at the stock of discarded beer cans now numbering four.

"Exactly my point. Paul's primavera is wonderful, and his crepes are even better. Just trust me on this."

"Vanessa, I've been trusting you for two years. I'm not very hard to get along with, you know." The dance around each other's feelings and this dynamic was as familiar as it was futile.

"On the contrary, Piper, you are one of the most difficult people

I've ever met. That's why I can't get enough of you." She managed a smile in Piper's direction.

"I'll remind you of that when I'm grouchy and you're mad at me."

A few minutes later the bell buzzed, and Vanessa dashed for the door. Piper heard her explaining to the chef how the resident artist was too involved and engrossed in her work to eat properly and she had told her how good this dish was. She was sure all the staff had a good damned idea what was going on, but Vanessa still made a show of explaining it away each and every time. Piper didn't care much about appearances. Part of the problem of becoming a well-known artist was that appearances were a big deal, and she didn't manage that very well. But still…there would come a day when she wasn't someone's dirty little secret.

They sat in comfortable silence, save the appreciative noises after each admittedly delectable bite. Piper had to concede that the food was pretty good. And a damn sight better than pizza.

"Thank you." Piper nudged her knee against Vanessa's.

"Of course. Anything for you. You know that." She placed her knife and fork at the perfect two-o'clock position on her plate and turned to look at Piper. "Look, I know this arrangement isn't where you saw yourself five years ago or even two years ago, but I love that you're in my life and I really like our time together." Vanessa's voice faded off.

Piper took her plate and placed it on the nearby end table. "We're both where we're supposed to be." She believed it and thought it sounded placating to a woman obviously fighting with her feelings. But neither outright honesty nor a total lie felt right, either. "Nothing is ever ideal. And maybe it shouldn't be. It makes things interesting, right?"

She pulled Vanessa over to straddle her lap. She was happy to end the conversation that wasn't headed anywhere good. Just like their relationship. Piper pulled Vanessa to her and kissed her deeply. This was going to be a long night. And it wasn't going to be about sleep.

CHAPTER FIVE

Piper's only client on Friday canceled, so she opted to take a few hours off. She didn't mention her newly discovered freedom to Vanessa when she had called to say good morning, and she didn't feel the least bit guilty. She had a right to time on her own, after all.

She waited for the art store to open at nine, then she spent an hour and $157 on art supplies, a good deal thanks to a buy one, get one free sale. She wedged the canvases into the tiny sports car and hoisted two bags full of discount tubes of paint into the trunk. Then she headed toward the gourmet grocery in search of a different sort of inspiration. Cooking wasn't something she did often, but she wasn't bad when she set her mind to it. She had a craving for fresh bruschetta and pasta with some homemade mushroom Marsala. She quickly filled a basket with a variety of mushrooms and began looking through the offering of onions under a wooden-framed chalkboard proclaiming the largest organic produce selection in the city. She stepped around a woman crouched near a potato barrel and continued to search through the bins near an older lady examining green onions.

Piper spoke out loud to no one in particular. "Does anyone know if green onions and scallions are the same thing?"

A voice from the vicinity of the potato bin answered quickly. "They are, actually. Just the same. People think shallots are the same too, but they're very different." The woman who answered didn't look up from her task of selecting potatoes. She was methodically placing them into her basket.

Piper stared down at the thick mass of haphazard brown hair as the cadence of the woman's voice struck a familiar chord. She stepped around her in an attempt to achieve an angle that would allow her to see her face.

"Thanks. I'll remember that." Piper watched her finally stand and drag her dusty palms down the thighs of her jeans, still looking down at her potatoes.

"Can I ask what you're making?" Her voice had a smooth tone and an even more familiar element now.

"Mushroom Marsala." Piper felt strange talking to someone she couldn't look in the eye.

When she finally turned to face Piper, the recognition was immediate.

Brook spoke first. "Piper. Hi!" She offered a surprised laugh. "It's Brook Myers, from the party at the Devereauxs'. Remember?"

"Hello there. Of course I do." Piper smelled a hint of Brook's perfume, or perhaps a lotion with a subtle lily-of-the-valley scent. Her smile was engaging, and Piper couldn't help staring at her mouth as she spoke.

"I feel like I should apologize for my mini tantrums and emotional outburst the other night. It wasn't very professional." She shrugged self-consciously and awkwardly balanced the heavy basket of potatoes and a gallon jug of milk.

"Are you kidding? You fed me, hid me, and entertained me. Now, I think you should bill me. Besides, I did my share of kvetching to you. I believe you were completely justified, anyway."

"Likewise." Brook checked her watch, and mild panic crossed her face. "Well, it was nice running into you."

"You look stressed. Let me help." Piper took the basket of produce from her and gestured toward the checkout stands, abandoning her own basket on the floor.

"Thank you. Yeah. Kind of completely stressed." Brook managed a laugh. "A catering job this afternoon, a tasting after that,

I'm still unpacking from a move where I significantly downsized, and I can't find anything. Besides that, I probably should go home and make dinner before I leave again."

They got in the line behind a small child buying one cookie, his mother watching fondly as he managed his own transaction. The distraction seemed to make the creases in Brook's forehead relax.

"I take it you're having potatoes?" Piper nudged Brook with her shoulder and smiled.

"Nah. These are for the parmesan potato puffs I'm making for the baby shower. I gave up on sleep at four o'clock this morning to start cooking and realized I didn't have enough potatoes. Tomorrow will probably be the same routine. Luckily, I love cooking."

"I had an early morning myself, but not quite that early. I read that we get too little sleep as adults."

Piper watched as Brook's brown hair fell in front of her eye and she tossed her head to encourage its retreat. When it was her turn to pay, she handed the checker exact change and collected the potatoes in a cloth bag.

"Remember, I've proposed a stress reliever in the form of beer and some wild turkeys on the twelfth green." Piper wondered why she was shamelessly flirting.

"I do remember. That sounds like the closest I'll get to a vacation this year, so stand by in case I can take you up on it."

Piper followed Brook to a white minivan that had seen much better days and handed her the bag, which she placed on the passenger seat.

"You still have my card, right?"

Brook was rushed, she knew, but Piper didn't want to end the conversation.

Brook nodded and offered a huge smile. "Nice running into you, Piper. And remember, if you decide to cater your next art show, I'll give you a great deal."

"I look forward to next time, whatever happens." *What the hell was that?* Piper thought she likely sounded like some creepy barfly with an agenda. Why did she find this bundle of stress with a bag full of potatoes so sexy?

She waved as Brook pulled away and realized she had accomplished nothing. Making dinner now sounded less appealing than stopping for an order of nachos on the way home. She took inspiration anywhere she could find it, and Brook seemed to inspire her to return to her paints.

❖

Brook jerked the wheel to enter the far-right lane. A truck blew its horn at her and she considered flipping him off but stopped herself. *Remember, you never know what someone's going through today. Ignore the impulse.* Her grandmother's voice echoed in her head.

She wished she could call her grandmother and beg for the advice that she sorely missed since her death a few years ago.

How could she get out of this mess? How could she end something after fifteen years without destroying what they had experienced together? Those were heavy questions for another day. When had she become okay with dreading her evenings, cursing her circumstances, and succumbing to her stress? She silently vowed to straighten out the life she had signed up for but not anticipated in any way.

"Hi, Meg." She fought the impulse to fall into the routine of calling Meg honey or sweetheart or babe. They weren't there anymore, despite Meg's refusal to be realistic about the painful shards of their shattered relationship.

"You ever coming home?" The gritty sound of her delivery meant last night's liquor consumption wasn't sitting well on her recently awoken constitution.

"I had to get some potatoes from D'Angelo's. I haven't been gone more than forty-five minutes." She knew that Meg couldn't have been up for long and had no concept of the amount of time she might have been gone.

"This business is taking all your time. When do we get any time together?"

Brook tried not to raise her voice when the frustration of her life began spilling over. What was the point in spending time together? Meg was either drunk or passed out. There wasn't quality time, only caretaking and crisis management. She'd realized months ago that her life had simply become managing the next crisis or fallout from Meg's drinking, her unemployment, her family tension, and her bad behavior. Add a new business, a move, and financial strain, and Brook had ticked all the boxes of the stress that came from demands exceeding resources. She was tapped out financially, emotionally, and mentally. She just had to figure how to fix all of it in the five minutes a day she had to herself, if you could call showering at four a.m. alone time.

"Can we just talk when I get home, please? I'll see you in ten minutes." The only acknowledgment from the woman who used to bring her flowers weekly was an abrupt click as the call ended.

Brook tried to ignore the clutch of anxiety squeezing her chest as she stopped at the curb in front of their tiny house. At least she was feeling something. She headed in through the back door and started unloading produce onto the counter. She pulled fresh parmesan from the fridge and began immersing herself in menu preparations. She should have sought Meg out, but she would appear in the kitchen soon enough.

As if on cue, Meg wandered through the doorway of the kitchen and dragged out a stool from the tiny bar area. Brook started at the jarring noise of the feet scraping across the linoleum.

"Anything I can have a taste of?" Meg was sober, but after all, she had only been awake a couple of minutes. Brook was grateful for the distance from the night before, which had consisted of Meg consuming a fifth of Jack Daniel's and firing coarse, hurtful words at her. She'd learned to be grateful for the small things. But she longed for a life where discord wasn't inevitable.

"You could try one of my new mushroom pastries?" She slipped one out of the toaster oven and handed her the steaming hors d'oeuvre on a hastily torn paper towel. Meg took it and eyed it suspiciously.

"Maybe I spoke too soon, my stomach isn't feeling great." Meg swallowed loudly and blew out a shaky breath.

Hangover. It's called a hangover! Brook wanted to scream but she bit her tongue quietly, continuing to cook. "I'm sorry you aren't feeling well."

"I think it must be something I ate."

Meg was serious. Brook wasn't stunned that she attempted the hackneyed excuse or thought Brook was so dense as to believe that anything she ate fourteen or so hours ago could be responsible. But that wasn't a fight they were going to have this morning if Brook could help it.

"So what's all this for?" Meg abandoned the mushroom pastry on the counter and slid it away as if the mere smell of food was turning her stomach.

"Prep work and a little experimentation before this afternoon's baby shower, remember? Then I have to take samples to a potential client. This Devereaux party might have been the break I needed." She had met a couple at the Holthaus art show and hoped to land the catering gig at their next gathering. She desperately hoped this was the first step on the path to her business's success. She dreamed of the day this painful relationship would be behind her and she could concentrate on a job she loved. Maybe even start her own retail business one day. She artfully arranged the samples on a travel platter and snapped the lid over the ridge of the glass dish.

The morning felt lonely despite the person she had known most of her adult life sitting across from her. She felt completely on her own. She wondered if Meg felt it too. She certainly didn't acknowledge that anything was off. Sometimes Brook's anger toward Meg felt mean, but most times it felt justified. It seemed their entire universe revolved around Meg's next drink, and Brook resented it, resented her for it. The accompanying bitterness seemed to have taken over her feelings for her partner.

When Brook needed support, she handled it herself, since Meg wasn't equipped. When the good stuff happened, she no longer wanted to share it with Meg, almost as if she didn't deserve to participate. She felt bad for being so angry. After all, Meg was sick, but the difference was she refused to get better or do anything to aid in her own recovery. Hell, she refused to even admit there was a problem. If Brook was honest, any recovery was too late for their relationship anyway, but them being together was probably the only thing standing between Meg and the absolute bottom.

"I don't remember you telling me about that." Her tone said that she knew that it wasn't because Brook hadn't told her but that she hadn't been in the frame of mind to pay attention.

Brook told herself every day that she couldn't stay in this much longer. It had been too many years and there had been too much water under the proverbial bridge for her to find any of her once-passionate feelings for the brilliant Professor Morris. She had waded too far through the rubble of her shattered life to go back and try and pick up the pieces. And yet, taking that final step to end things seemed nearly impossible.

Brook ignored Meg's statement. "I'm making all my signature items, including the parmesan potato puffs you like. I could land a pretty big client if they like my food."

"What's not to like? No one ever said that you couldn't cook. They should love your food. I wish I got more of it."

The beginning of a genuine compliment was quickly tied with a ribbon of guilt. Per usual, it was a caress before a punch.

Brook glanced at Meg now holding the mushroom pastry near her nose as if testing for any intestinal revolt. She managed a tiny bite without comment.

Brook thought how much she just wanted peace. A hundred times a day it went through her head. *I just want a little peace.* She had once read an article talking about people involved in emotional and chronic substance abuse situations who had CAT scans that showed part of their brains to have died. She knew she focused more on her broken relationship than anything else, which was extremely unhealthy. Everything was in flux. She could ask for financial help from her family, but she was determined to do this on her own. As far as Meg's addiction, that was up to her. She had invested too much time and lost too much of herself because of it. Somehow, she had to figure out a way to get beyond it and start over.

Brook filled insulated carriers with food while keeping an eye on Meg, who was looking increasingly green and unstable. The half-eaten hors oeuvre was back on the napkin.

"Do you want me to help you take the food to the van? I don't want you hurting your back." A glimpse of the old supportive Meg peeked through on occasion, which used to make Brook nostalgic. Now it felt like too little, too late.

Brook studied her and thought she might pass out before she made it across the threshold, let alone all the way to the street.

"No. But thank you. Why don't you go lie down? I'll be gone for a while anyway." Brook didn't know how many times she had suggested Meg go sleep off her hangover. It was usually so she could enjoy the ensuing silence. She was almost sorry she would miss this one.

"Maybe I will. Don't forget about the barbecue at Matt and Tanya's tonight." Meg pushed off the stool and wandered down the hallway to the bedroom.

Brook changed quickly and corralled a few wild strands of hair into the bun at the nape of her neck. By the time she was ready to leave, Meg was sprawled across the center of the bed, snoring loudly. She paused a moment and tried to reconcile that image with the strong, brilliant woman who once made her pulse race. No time for that now.

The van smelled like an oven full of divine savory treats. She found a renewed passion for presenting her delicacies to her clients and tried to ignore the tiny sad cottage that had never felt like home.

CHAPTER SIX

Piper's phone rang just as she walked away from the clubhouse and her last client of the evening. It had been a long one and she could feel it in her shoulders. It was a local number she didn't recognize.

"Hello?" She moved quickly into the bushes as she answered since a Bentley was barreling down the dark residential street, unlikely to be looking out for pedestrians.

"Piper?"

The connection was scratchy, and Piper pressed the phone closer to her ear. "Yes?"

"It's Brook. Can you hear me? Am I catching you at a bad time?"

Piper's heart pounded at the sound of Brook's voice. "Not at all. How are you?" She hoped she didn't sound like a giddy teenager in high school when the cool kid talked to her.

"I just found out that I got the job. I mean...the one I was telling you about at D'Angelo's Market. Not that you needed to know that, but I thought I would tell you anyway." The ensuing laugh sounded nervous and adorable.

"Brook, that's fantastic. Congratulations. What's the next step?" She wanted to keep the conversation going any way she could.

"Well, stress some more, plan the menu, stress about that, second-guess myself, hire a helper, and try not to freak out."

"No freaking out, okay? You got the job, which means they

loved you and you're well on your way to being the go-to cater chef around here, trust me."

"That's a long leap. I think stressing for a few more months is a safer plan."

Piper heard the roar of the engine quiet to a dull rumble, perhaps stopped at a light. "Ready to take me up on the evening-on-the-green destresser? It is clinically proven to work miracles."

"Oh really? And what clinic is that?" Brook's tone was teasing.

"Well, it was really independent study and a single researcher who happens to have the same name as me, but I promise it works." Piper matched her playful tenor.

"How's tonight? I actually think I could use one of those," Brook replied.

Piper wasn't prepared for her to actually accept and stuttered for a second. "Uh, yeah, I mean sure."

"Unless you're busy," Brook said quickly.

"Not at all. That sounds great." Piper was still standing in the brush along the road and hoped no one would notice her there.

"What time is good?"

Piper could hear the rev of the van engine once more. "Does now work?" She glanced down at her work clothes and decided they sufficed.

"Actually, yeah. That's perfect. I'm about twenty minutes away and I'll bring the beer."

"I'll meet you at the gate, okay?" Piper knew it was easier than making a formal request to the guards. She tried to walk at a normal pace to the entrance, despite the sudden butterflies of excitement swarming in her gut. She felt drawn to Brook. She looked forward to a conversation not sliced into snippets in a frantic kitchen or a public market.

She had barely reached the cobblestone apron of the property when Brook made the turn into her path. She walked past the guard shack and ducked under the gate arm. She waved at the guard, indicating that Brook's van should be able to pass.

"I'm supposed to log in every vehicle, Ms. Holthaus." Chuck held the clipboard under his arm and held up his pen.

"I know, Chuck. She's just driving me back to the house. She's a friend." Logging the arrival of her personal friends at the gate always felt a little too Big Brother for Piper, not that she had many visitors. She gave no indication that she was going to give up Brook's name as she jumped into the passenger seat of her van and waved at him.

She watched Chuck shrug in resignation and hit the button to raise the orange gate arm.

"Don't I have to sign in?" Brook looked nervous as Piper pointed at the open gateway and the dusky two-lane road.

"Nope. I handled it. Just head toward the pro shop." Piper knew the club parking lot would be deserted for the balance of the evening.

Brook drove slowly through the advancing darkness and pulled into the distant parking spot Piper pointed to. She turned in her seat to face Brook.

"So how did I get so lucky?" Piper scanned Brook's face and tried to determine the mood that put her in a dark parking lot with her on a Sunday night. Her hair had sprung from her bun in wild strands and Piper resisted the urge to smooth them back to their original place.

"Actually, I probably should have gone home, but I didn't feel like hanging out at the neighbor's barbecue. I just didn't want a crowd tonight. I made a work excuse and thought I would take you up on your offer. It sounded much more peaceful."

Piper wondered about the story behind the cloudy look in Brook's eyes. "Well, I'm glad you did. I'll do my best to live up to my marketing pitch." Piper opened the passenger door and grinned over her shoulder at Brook. "Come with me."

Piper walked them to a shiny black golf cart with a plastic enclosure. If the official club cart was seen after hours, it would cause fewer raised eyebrows than one of the generic rental carts might. Many a cart had been commandeered by bored Shadow Glass kids, so residents were on alert to any such mischief.

Piper pulled away, driving close to the wood line and taking advantage of the shortcut to the twelfth green. She backed the cart onto a secluded carpet of pine needles overlooking the valley and the lights of the homes dotting the vista.

Brook exhaled loudly. "Wow, you were right. Pretty awesome view. I can see why you call it a stress reliever." She scanned the horizon, looking a little more relaxed.

"I'm not done yet. Grab the beer and come with me." Piper reached into the cargo space to produce a tarp and a few large towels. She led Brook to a higher clearing with a view that was better yet. She spread out the tarp and the towels and indicated Brook should sit first.

"How did you find this?" Brook's eyes skimmed the course and the view as she folded onto the towel.

"Lessons with a lot of bad golfers and searching for a lot of bad balls. You can't even see this place from the fairway, which means I've seen a lot of ball kicking and hole dodging. But no one has ever caught me tucked in here."

"Thanks for sharing it with me. I needed this." Brook took a long sip of her drink and plucked at the tight white T-shirt escaping from the waistband of her dark jeans. "It's nice to have a drink without having to worry about contributing to someone else's issue."

"Want to talk about it?" Piper could tell she needed to talk.

"Things don't make sense right now." She briefly shut her eyes and tilted her head back as the breeze ruffled her hair.

"Don't feel like you have to talk about it. Why don't you tell me about your new clients?" She didn't want to intrude. Piper wondered if she had crossed Brook's mind as often as Brook had crossed hers since the night they met.

Brook looked relieved at the subject change.

"It's the Warners on Pine Crest. They were at your art show and liked my food. They're hosting some company reception in two weeks and need a *lot* of food for a *lot* of people. I'm not positive that I'm not in over my head, but I took a leap anyway and told them I'd done lots of parties like this." She wedged the bottle between her thighs and leaned back on her elbows. "I totally lied. I've *worked* parties that big, but I've never done one solo."

"You can do it. Your food is awesome. I'll be on standby if you need a minion." Piper stole a full body appraisal of Brook and admired her long, full figure stretched out beside her. The distinct curve of her hips made Piper recall the half-painted figure waiting for her in her studio. Clearly, a subconscious force had directed her brush to recreate a replica of the woman laid out before her.

"You better hope I don't have to take you up on that. The event planner is providing floor staff, so all I have to worry about is having enough food and stamina. It will be a lot of prep work." She turned and smiled.

Piper couldn't look away. Brook's eyes slid to hers and held her gaze.

"What?" Piper threaded her fingers together so she wouldn't reach up and trace the line of freckles that dusted Brook's pale skin.

Brook took a few second before she replied. "I was just noticing your eyes. They're a very interesting color, kind of a shade of brandy. I like it, very unique."

She continued to study her until Piper felt goose bumps along her arms. The connection warmed her as Brook eyes burned her.

She shifted and concentrated on focusing her attention on conversation. "Um, thanks. I owe them to my dad, I guess." *Well, maybe Brook did notice me.*

"He must be a good-looking guy." Brook took another pull from her beer.

"Actually, I don't know. I've never met him. My mom had bright green eyes, so I have to assume mine look like my dad's."

"I'm sorry. That must be hard." Brook moved her bottle and turned on her side to face Piper, clearly relaxing and unintentionally replicating the pose of the faceless woman waiting on her canvas.

Piper shrugged. "I never knew any differently, so other than the occasional father-daughter event that popped up, I didn't think about it much." Piper mirrored Brook's pose and thought it was a good idea until she realized she could feel Brook's breath on her cheek when she spoke. The dark space between them was close and intimate, and Piper liked it too much. She sat up again but couldn't make herself turn away.

"What about your family?" The subject seemed safer than nonexistent fathers and Brook's appraisal of her eyes.

"My dad's a good guy. Likes to take care of everyone, works too much, so I worry about him and his health, but I leave that to my mom." Brook reclined fully onto her back and stared up at the sky.

Piper noted that she now looked relaxed. "What does he do?" She stopped herself from touching Brook's arm, which lay only millimeters from her thigh.

"He works in shipping. He and my mom own an import business."

"Is it successful?" Piper was grateful to talk about Brook's family and avoid revealing any more about herself.

"They do pretty well, and my dad's clients love him." She smiled, as if talking about her dad made her proud.

"What about your mom?"

"She worked with my dad when he first got started but then she chose to work from home so she could be there for us. We were pretty lucky." The apparently pleasant memory caused a wistful look to settle over her face.

"You were. I didn't see my mom much as a kid," Piper replied without a hint of envy. "My mom worked two jobs to support us, but I think it went a long way to making me independent."

"I'm sorry. That must have been hard," Brook said for the second time. She hoped she hadn't brought up any difficult feelings for Piper. She liked the fact that keeping her talking meant she could keep looking at her without it seeming strange. Her eyes were truly the most unusual color she had ever seen. Yes, most of the population had brown eyes but hers were pale and almost metallic with flecks of gold.

"Again, I didn't know any different, so it seemed completely normal to me." Piper shrugged.

"I assume she passed since you talk about her in the past tense?" Brook almost cringed as she asked the question. People's reactions varied on the topic of a late parent.

"Yeah. Almost ten years ago now. Cancer." Piper glanced away.

Brook reached out and stroked her fingertips lightly down

Piper's arm. She spoke quietly. "I'm so sorry." Brook had hoped that something more eloquent or creative would come out of her mouth, but a lame apology was all she could manage.

"It was a really long battle, so I was happy she got to be free of it when she went. We said everything we needed to."

Piper covered Brook's hand in what Brook took as a thank-you, but a small chill followed regardless.

"Well, I believe that saying your piece when things are over feels like the best closure. Like you can move on without too much baggage."

"Sounds like a woman trying to downsize in the baggage department." Piper leaned in as if for emphasis and then sat back again.

Brook couldn't quite sort out her sudden reaction created by the nearness, so she just answered honestly. "Truth be told, I could walk away from everything right now, but Meg isn't...um...I mean, we aren't exactly in the same place. She drinks too much." Brook shocked herself with the simple revelation.

"Ahh. People tend to stay where it's comfortable. She isn't ready for you to leave and she depends on you for everything, right?"

Brook nodded. Piper was more than intuitive. And yes, she *had* become Meg's crutch. Her enabler. She couldn't survive perpetually drunk and checked out of life if Brook didn't pick up the pieces, pay the bills, and make excuses for her. Her sister bought her the booze. At least Brook had stopped footing that bill.

"She does. More and more every day, it seems. It's my fault, though. I let it happen."

"But you have a heart and you kept hoping it would change, I'm guessing."

"Get out of my head." She smiled a little. "You sound like you have some experience with this." It was a dubious membership in a painful club.

"Three years with Michelob's biggest fan. It took me a long time to figure it out and even longer to finally cut the cord." Piper held her eyes. The look was compassionate and sympathetic.

"Sorry you went through that." Brook felt even more comfortable now. "How did you do it? Get out, I mean?"

"I took her to her mother's house and told her that she was staying there. We had a month-to-month lease, so by the time she sobered up from a four-day bender, we were out of the apartment and her belongings were delivered to her mom's garage. I kind of sound like a dick, huh?"

Brook could almost feel the freedom from that. "Not at all. Sounds like a really good plan. I'm afraid it won't be quite as easy after fifteen years." Brook felt the dread that always rode shotgun in her mind as she contemplated her way out.

"Wow. That's a long time to live with a substance problem."

"In fairness, it's only been the past five, although that sounds bad enough." She tried to remember what it felt like to be in love with Meg, but those feelings were from a different lifetime. "I never would have expected that my life could end up like this." Why was she sharing so much? New friends didn't appreciate the full unload of a bad relationship story.

"What does she do?" Piper set her half-finished drink back into the carton so it wouldn't tip over.

"Did. She was a law professor. Now she's the commander of the giant ugly recliner and the river of Jack Daniel's flowing through our living room." Bitterness felt more like a vise when she said it out loud. She didn't seem to have to soften it for Piper, though, and it felt like being heard for the first time. She unclenched her fists and spread her fingers, stroking the cool fabric of the towel, and relishing the relief that came from exhaling her story.

"What will she do when you leave? I mean, I assume that's the plan." Piper rested her chin on her knees as she spoke.

"Every day. That's my plan every damned day when I wake up to the mess she left from the night before or every time I have to make excuses to friends and former colleagues because she didn't show up or forgot a relative's birthday. I want her to go to rehab and get her life back, but that kind of public acknowledgment isn't how they do it in the Morris family. It's all about appearances and position. Her dad was a drinker, but no one ever talks about it. I guess she can go there for a while. Until her parents figure out what a handful she is." Brook caught herself. "Wow. I didn't mean to throw all that at you. I didn't even know I had all that cued up."

"It means you don't get to vent much. I've been there, so I'm the perfect audience."

Piper squeezed Brook's knee for a few seconds, forcing a wash of goose bumps to frost over Brook's thigh.

"You're responsible for getting her to a safe place, but that's where it ends. It took me a long time to get there. Don't waste your life living Meg's for her."

"Wow. All true." Brook felt the pressure return. "I know I need to pull the trigger; I just always find a reason not to." She knew she had to find her courage. Somehow Piper sitting next to her on a dark golf course made her feel some of that strength build.

"When was the last time you remember a simple, perfect moment?" Piper nudged the edge of the bottle's label with her thumb.

Brook thought for a moment. "I'm not sure what you mean?"

"The last time you took a mental snapshot that made you feel whole. The moment that every time you revisit it in your mind, it takes you back to simple, calm, and a little bit perfect. Your happy place, I guess, if you want the cliché." Piper's voice drifted off and she stared through the trees.

"I get it. Let me think."

They sat in relative silence, save the occasional night bird or lizard rustling through the brush and a few crickets chirping their contribution to the orchestra of nature, which felt like a much-needed blanket around Brook's shoulders.

"Point Reyes, at Tomales Point," Brook said finally. "I went there when Meg had a conference close by. It's a protected area where Tule elk are safeguarded from hunters and poachers. I went out one afternoon because I couldn't take another bunch of law professors patting themselves on the back all evening. Meg wanted to ditch too, but she had to make an appearance. So, I took the car and hiked to a secluded spot where you could see the ocean, and this herd of elk wandered past. I watched them for what seemed like forever. No one was around and I felt like I was given special tickets to this amazing show where wildlife wasn't in danger from people and they could just exist in this beautiful place.

"The sun began to set, and they started to move away. This red-orange sky started melting into this gold circle on the ocean when the last bull ambled across my view. He had huge horns that created a striking silhouette against the colors. He stopped in the middle and turned to look in my direction, as if he knew I was watching. He stared at me, absolutely still for probably a full minute, and I thought that no photograph could ever capture the perfect calm of that picture in my mind. I worry it will disappear one day." Brook dragged her fingertip under her eyes.

"That's exactly what I meant. I can almost see it too." Piper leaned into Brook. "Do you go there when things get crazy? I mean, you should. A little mental vacation from the pressure of being a caregiver."

"You make it sound like I'm providing for an invalid." Was it true? Had she become one?

"I've been there. It feels like that sometimes." Piper's voice was soothing, blending into the quiet of the evening rather than adding a layer to it.

"I do wonder sometimes what would have happened if Meg had been alone when she started to drink too much. I mean, if I hadn't been there to clean the house, make sure she ate, reminded her to go to work when she still had a job, or take care of every other responsibility she abdicated when she drank. I wonder if she would have stopped sooner. Would she have caught herself and stopped?" Brook pressed her hands over her face and held them there. Oh, how much she would love to be on that bluff overlooking the ocean again. She fought the threatening tears.

"Okay. Let's play that out." Piper crossed her legs into a lotus position and faced her. "What if she would have continued until she was fired much sooner? She was evicted, and her parents weren't there to help? What if she had nowhere to live or got arrested or worse? And she never had anyone there for her? She never knew what being in a loving relationship was and there was never a reason for her to stop drinking?"

"I guess you are trying to make me stop feeling sorry for myself, huh?" Brook dropped her hands to the tarp and blew out a deep breath.

"No. I'm trying to tell you what no one told me. That you aren't responsible for someone else being irresponsible. Yes, it's a disease, but when you have a condition, you seek help. You set a broken arm, sew up a cut, take medication for an issue. I know I'm simplifying it, but it's true. When she's ready to get help, she will. Nothing you do or say at this point will change the path she's choosing to be on."

"Words of wisdom from someone who's been there, huh?" Brook felt heard and understood for the first time in ages. A little glimpse of the life she once had and still craved. One she hoped to have again.

"I don't relish the place you're in right now, but you'll be so happy when you break free from it. I'd love to see your smile reach your eyes like it did when you told me about sunsets and elk."

Brook bit her lip. When was the last time she felt this content? And with someone who looked like Piper, which was most certainly a bonus. "I can't tell you how much this helped me tonight."

Piper rose on her knees and reached across for the remainder of her beer. "I'm very glad to hear it. I hope we can do it again."

Brook was in the middle of appraising the athletic body over her when her phone vibrated. She immediately felt her heart drum. Anxiety roiled at the choice between answering it and running away from this roller coaster. She squeezed the soft key on the side of the phone and knew her evening was over. The text demanding her anticipated arrival time came seconds later.

Piper sat back and locked eyes with her. "I take it you need to get back?"

"I suppose I should." She didn't want to lose the contentment she felt sitting here, in the dark, with an attractive stranger. "I'm sorry."

"Why? I get it. Better to stop the battle before it escalates. I remember it well." Piper stood and held her hand out. Brook pressed her fingers into Piper's palm and pulled up to stand next to her.

"I want you to know that this was the best hour I have spent anywhere in a long time." She pulled against Piper into a hug and thought she heard her gasp. "You okay?"

"Perfect. It's been a pretty awesome hour for me too. Glad you could make it. Let's do it again?" Piper poured out the remains from their open bottles. Neither of them had finished much of their second beer.

"Thank you. I would really like that. It was nice to have an adult conversation." Brook could have stayed another two hours and felt guilty about being attracted to someone when she was in the midst of her own turmoil.

"It's been my pleasure, Chef. Truly." Piper gathered the tarp and towels, wadding them into a ball and shoving them into the cart's storage compartment.

Brook climbed back into her seat and cursed the fact that she wasn't allowing herself to enjoy the quiet ride through the trees, thinking of nothing but the condition that Meg might be in when she arrived home. When they stopped at her van, she turned to Piper.

"Just so you know, you've made this hot mess feel pretty human tonight. Thank you." She wished she had found out a thousand things about Piper instead of letting her alcohol-bathed home life take center stage.

"Keep in touch, okay?" Piper opened her door.

"Try to stop me." Brook couldn't suppress her grin when Piper pulled her in for a really warm hug. She drove away with a singular goal. She needed to find some regular happy so evenings like this didn't come as such a surprise.

CHAPTER SEVEN

Piper woke to her alarm blaring "Everybody Dance Now" loud enough to ensure she wouldn't sleep through it. She slapped at the nightstand, cursing herself for agreeing to an eight o'clock lesson for the Youngs so they could make their annual Italian Riviera trip without changing their flight. She dragged her weary body from her warm bed. She would admit to loving her benefactor's money for two things: an awesome mattress and a bank of the best shower jets all aiming at her at once.

She gave herself a few extra minutes to wake up and review last evening, where she could have happily stayed all night. Brook was in a tough place that was certainly familiar to Piper. She could have used a friend when she was in the same spot. She could be a shoulder for Brook, despite the lingering thoughts of a few midnight fantasies where Piper woke up very naked with Brook Myers. But given what Brook was going through, and the fact that she was in a relationship, there wouldn't be anything between them other than friendship. So be it. The fantasies could still be hot. She was looking forward to the short walk she had to get to work, giving her time to refocus on golf and not the time she'd spent on the course a few hours before.

She pulled a Shadow Glass golf shirt over her head as she shuffled to the kitchen to start her coffee pot, just before she heard her front door open. She tried to decide why it bothered her more this morning that she never had any expectation of privacy where Vanessa was concerned.

"Morning Piper, darling." She sang the words before she even shut the door behind her.

"Morning." Piper prayed for the caffeine that would make her feel more human, not to mention tolerant. "Why are you up so early?"

"The Youngs told me they were meeting with you this morning, so I wanted to be sure you were up. They are among your most ardent fans, you know." Her all-business-all-the-time-voice sounded shrill and bossy, and Piper wanted none of it this morning. And she wasn't a teenager who needed a reminder to go to work. She managed it just fine every single day.

"Okay. So not here to praise me on my morning personality?" Piper pulled a frozen meal out for her lunch.

"Hardly your best quality." Vanessa eyed her nutritionless choice overtly.

"Duly noted." Piper ignored her and slipped the meal into her bag.

"How about after your lesson, we go to Marysville and rent a boat for the afternoon?"

"That would be great if I didn't have four other clients after the Youngs. Sometimes I think you forget that I have a job and not a hobby." Piper's tone was curt, and she made no effort to temper it.

"Don't be so obnoxious. Cancel them. They'll rebook." Vanessa flicked her hand as if brushing lint off her expensive slacks.

"Um, no. Because I can't on so many levels, not the least of which is, I'll be fired."

"I'll just take care of you." Vanessa had said essentially that same thing a hundred times, maybe a thousand, and Piper wanted to choke her every time.

"No. I want a life outside of squatting in your husband's carriage house, V. What would happen if I did something to piss him off? Or he found someone else he wanted to live here—or you did? I have to be able to support myself. You remember how that works, right?" The comment was unnecessary, but Piper stopped fighting to filter her annoyance at this particular exchange.

"Don't be a jackass, Piper." The saccharine smile had turned into an annoyed warning glare.

"How is reminding you how the other ninety-nine percent live being a jackass? You used to be part of the majority."

"Yeah. And I hated it." Vanessa, once again, made no excuses for her compromises. She was where she wanted to be.

"I don't love it, but I want to have something to show for my work in ten years, and I can assure you, I won't be sleeping with a man to get it." Piper knew that was a low blow and almost wished she could take it back. Almost.

Vanessa's head snapped up and she stalked closer to Piper.

"Who the hell do you think you are, Piper? You aren't better than me." Her brow creased as much as the Botox would allow.

"Never said I was. You just forget that your offer to be my patron comes with a price I'm not willing to pay." Piper couldn't really believe that she was being so brazen. She was stomping on very thin ice in big boots and she knew it.

"I don't understand why you have to be so stubborn or fucking judgmental." Vanessa stepped back from the counter. "I just wanted to spend time with you and spoil you a little bit, and this is the thanks I get."

Piper rarely heard her curse, so she knew she must have royally pissed her off, but she couldn't stop. "Stubborn? Self-respect and self-reliance aren't stubborn. I won't apologize for saying it or thinking it." Piper glanced at the clock on the stove. "And now I'm going to be late." She poured the coffee and attempted to screw on the lid of the travel mug, which infuriatingly refused to thread properly. She snatched it up after her second attempt and wrapped a napkin around the neck.

"I am not some brainless trophy wife." Vanessa wasn't finished and followed Piper to the door.

Piper spun around to face her. "And I'm not your charity case. Stop asking me to be a kept woman so that you have company in your golden cage." Piper knew she would pay for that comment dearly, but she had to go and didn't have time to analyze her next move. The look on Vanessa's face said that she had stepped way over the line.

Piper grabbed her windbreaker and stormed out. She thought how strange it was to leave her home with someone else in it. Someone who could do anything she wanted to prove a point. She reminded herself that it wasn't and would never be her home. They had been here before, but she didn't think it had ever been this raw.

She marched down the road at a rapid clip, hoping to burn off the frustration she always felt with Vanessa, but particularly intensely this morning. The point where she had reached her limit was fast approaching. The only problem was Plan B was costly and required a leap of faith that said she could live as an artist without the help of bored rich people.

A black Jaguar pulled to a stop beside her and Sandy Young waved manically out the window.

"Ride, Piper?"

"No, thank you. I need to warm up. See you shortly." She continued to walk directly next to the slow-moving car.

"Okay. See you soon!" Sandy chirped.

Nick Young didn't move or even turn his head. He wasn't engaged, and Piper wondered what that must be like, to spend all your time with someone who didn't move you, didn't stimulate you, like it appeared that his wife didn't. In Piper's ideal world, she just wanted to come through the door and stand in her studio, inspired, driven, engaged. She coveted none of Shadow Glass's dark secrets and profound compromises, all in the name of money and power. It all felt like a great big, sad, dirty concession. She thought about the mess she had left in her kitchen with Vanessa and the choreography it would take to fix it. Fucking exhausting. But wasn't she making some of those same compromises? What did that say about her?

By noon, the Youngs were on a plane to Italy, slightly more educated on the best backswing techniques; Kendra James could now tell the difference between a wood and an iron; and Taylor Manning was finally convinced that gophers would not pop up in the middle of her shot and be whacked by a ball. Mrs. Manning was a bit dim and had the personality of dry toast. Piper was sure, however, that she herself was getting dumber by the day just by spending time with these people. A few large tips and an early afternoon end to her shift helped make it all a little less painful. God, was that just as much a concession? Of course it was.

She pushed through the front door of the carriage house and immediately found the large yellow note stuck to the mirror in her foyer.

Hope you remember how to paint on the floor.

And there it was. Vanessa had taken the new easel and, as it turned out, the old one as well, to prove a point. Piper wouldn't say anything because she refused to beg for things she could live without, and if she was honest, Vanessa was one of those things.

She spread an old white painter's cloth on the floor, dropping the red woman canvas into the middle, then she shed her uniform shirt and slacks. There was something intensely freeing about painting without worrying where it might land in the posh surroundings. For forty minutes Tori Amos serenaded Piper as she pressed her brushes into the paint and forced it to comply. She slowly bent the arches of acrylic into a piece of art; a crimson, fraught, arching statement that matched her mood and, by extension, the woman occupying the center of her attention. Her meditation was unceremoniously broken when Vanessa marched through her door.

"You have no right to judge me." She didn't bother with any greeting and seemed to pick up exactly where they left off hours ago.

"I didn't," Piper lied. "You choose to feel judged when things people say don't sit well with you. It was the truth, whether you like it or not." Piper walked on her knees to the opposite side of the canvas and stroked a swath of color onto it with the heel of her hand, which held a dollop of black paint. She coaxed it further with a pallet knife.

"You're pretty ballsy to say those things to me. You've always thought I settled." She stood at the edge of the cloth with her arms crossed tightly over her chest.

Piper *did* think she'd settled, but she certainly wasn't going there again. It wasn't worth the fight that would take up the rest of the time she would rather be painting.

"I'm sorry. I was in a hurry. I appreciate everything you do. Honestly." *And if you stopped trying to rent me for your temporary entertainment, I'd really appreciate that as well.*

"I'm guessing you want your easels back." Her voice had softened a bit.

"That isn't why I apologized." She certainly wouldn't beg for some overpriced toy she never asked for. She wanted to note that she *had* bought the old one long before she met Vanessa, but she didn't bother.

"I'll ask Tom to bring them back." This was as close to apologizing as Vanessa would get. "Why are you in your underwear?"

"Because I felt like painting as soon as I got home, and I was going to be crawling around, so I just went with it. Come down here and put your hands in the paint. Smear it all around with your fingers until you get lost in the look and the feel of it." Piper looked inexplicably for common ground.

"Don't be ridiculous, Piper. You know I hate getting dirty."

This wasn't dirty. This was organic and essential. She couldn't imagine not connecting with it like that. The smell of the paint, the feel of the pigment oozing between her fingers, even an errant smear along her cheek she could feel drying.

"How about you go shower and I'll meet you in bed where you can remind me why I can't get enough of you." Vanessa was resetting the chessboard so they could start the game once more.

Piper couldn't help but feel like one of the house staff whose job it was to satisfy the lady of the estate, no matter the request or the vitriol of the preceding eight hours. Pathetic. She felt pathetic for still being there. She felt more so when she reminded herself that cheap rent and a bunch of compromises were allowing her to get to the next stage in her career. The lines weren't all drawn on the plans yet, but she was close. In a few months, closer still.

"Can you let me finish this piece? I would love it if you stayed and talked to me while I finish. You can even come up with a name for it as I go, if you'd like?" She actually hated having anyone watching her paint, but if it prevented another fight and allowed her to stay where she was, she'd concede.

"I *have* developed quite a knack for naming them, I think. Don't you?" And instantly, her ire dissipated in the face of compliments. She kicked off her shoes and tucked a leg under her on the chaise, suddenly more relaxed and, to Piper's relief, placated.

"You certainly manage to come up with things I never would have thought of." Piper hoped that the truth of the statement would eclipse the fact that she was hedging and maneuvering around the actual sentiment.

Piper abandoned the thoughts and stroked some wisps of white paint with her fingertips, creating the image of light behind the darker colors, and muted the edges of them. She was happy with the result and continued the technique on the opposite corner of the canvas. She sat back on her heels and surveyed the results of the past two hours. She noticed the brown wisps of hair framing the face of the anonymous figure staring up at her. The thought of attending to every detail of the canvas woman excited her. The thought of working on ten more pieces energized her. The thought of her first lesson in the morning made her feel like running away. People who supported themselves doing what they loved were the luckiest people alive, she thought. It would be her one day. She realized that it might well be a rockier road that didn't offer free room and board, but it would be worth the price.

Piper glanced over as Vanessa flipped through a catalog, no longer watching her. She thought about coming up with a new excuse to avoid sex. It wasn't because she didn't enjoy it. She did. But she'd always think about the seedy side of their arrangement and all the things Piper would rather experience with someone she trusted. She wondered when blanket avoidance of anything relationship had become just avoiding something with Vanessa.

"One day." Piper didn't realize she had spoken aloud until Vanessa jerked her head from the magazine.

"One day, what?" She pursed her lips and waited for an answer.

Piper panicked. There were probably a hundred plausible answers, but she couldn't think of one.

"Uh, um, I was just wondering if I would be able to finish this in one day." It was weak, but it would do since she hardly thought Vanessa could care less.

Vanessa's phone rang before Piper knew if she sufficiently bought her explanation. "But I didn't think you were going to be here for dinner." Vanessa rolled her eyes as she listened.

Piper could hear Frank's thundering baritone from ten feet away.

"That's not much notice, Frank. Do you really need me to go?" She uncrossed her legs and perched on the edge of the cushion. She unclipped and finger-combed her hair, which fell in silky strands around her shoulders.

"No, of course, it's fine. I didn't have any plans. I'll be ready."

She stood as she disconnected and looked apologetically at Piper. "He wants me at some fundraiser with Nelson Banford. Remember the lawyer for Frank's company?" She didn't wait for an answer. "There's some sort of whiskey and cigar reception and then dinner at the Parliament. I have to go."

Piper had been to the Parliament once before with Vanessa. The appetizers alone cost as much as an hour lesson at the club.

"It's okay. He wants his wife with him. It's understandable." Piper endeavored to look sad even though she was secretly thrilled that she could finish her piece in peace.

"A trained monkey could be more useful than me. I hate Nelson Banford. He is a pretentious social climber who just cares where his next leg up comes from."

Piper bit her lip because drawing the obvious parallel between Nelson Banford and Vanessa Devereaux would be dangerously stupid or stupidly dangerous. It would also force her to visit the dubious commerce of her own life.

"It's okay. I'll just be here painting. I think this should be called *Peace in Pieces*. What do you think?"

She managed a kiss to Piper's cheek from the edge of the sheet that she stepped cautiously around to leave. She called back over her shoulder, "We'll see."

Piper waited to hear the door click closed before she said, "My fucking painting. I'll name it what I want."

Piper could hear the tap of Vanessa's heels as she stalked across the cobblestones. The impatient horn of her husband's waiting vehicle followed within a few minutes.

As she painted, Piper recalled the relaxed conversation with Brook and wondered how she was. She could have called, she supposed, but she knew well that new friends showing up in a domestic crisis could only make it worse. She would wait for Brook to reach out. She considered whether friendship, all Brook needed, was what she wanted. It had been a long time since she had even considered someone worthy of more than a few calculated hours of her time. Brook was somehow different.

Brook felt the heavy weave of the sofa on her cheek and realized that she had fallen asleep in the living room. A rare day without a list of commitments felt like bliss, and the silence of the house—no television, no music, no random TikTok videos playing from Meg's laptop—felt like a gift.

Brook subconsciously enjoyed the moment until the question of why it was so quiet crept in. She arched back to confirm that Meg's tired, sagging recliner was indeed empty. She squinted past the lamp in the hall and could see no further lights. She moved the curtains on the window to the backyard and also found it empty. Taking a weary breath, Brook swung her legs off the couch and pushed herself up to go find Meg. She opened the front door to confirm that her van was still parked along the curb and then she called toward the bedroom as she walked down the hall. The tiny house was hardly a search challenge, but she always had the dreaded thought that one day she would walk in and find that Meg had passed out for the last time, that the drug she clung to for life would one day take it.

She found the rest of the house just as dark, and there was no sign of Meg. Her keys lay in the basket by the door and the house was otherwise in order. She opened the back door only to come face-to-face with a man carrying a bocce ball and a Blue Moon complete with an orange wedge jammed in the top.

His presence surprised her, and she took a startled step back.

"Hey! Meg told me to come get you. You're Brook, right? I'm Tommy. Everybody calls me T-Boy."

Brook felt her pulse race as she examined all the possibilities. Meg had fallen, passed out in the street, been picked up by police for some disorderly charge, had a heart attack. The possibilities were endless, but Brook knew she would have to fix whatever it was, and she summoned all her energy. She grabbed her purse from the floor and prepared to follow him.

"Where is she, Tommy?" She shut the door behind her and tried to prepare herself for the worst as Tommy walked casually in front of her. "How bad is it?"

He looked at her curiously, obviously trying to figure out what she meant. "Well, if you mean the game, it's real bad. In case you didn't know, it's not normal to have to fetch a bocce ball from the neighbors' yard." He laughed heartily as if he had made quite the comic declaration.

Brook was confused and exasperated. "I don't care about your game, what happened to Meg?"

"Nothing, except she has bad aim." He held the polished red ball aloft and spun it in his hand. "She made it a shot-for-points game, and she's winning even though she's had more shots than the losers. We actually had to go to the store for more Jack. That girl can drink!" He was talking over his shoulder as he steered them toward the house next door.

Brook's shoulders slumped as the relief and realization that Meg wasn't hurt settled in. The ensuing fury came at the fact that, once again, Meg's drinking was the center and subject of her day. She followed Tommy toward the increasing sounds of cheers and shouts of celebration. The loudest one she recognized as Meg's.

"Drink, asshole! You lost this round and you know it!" Meg held a half-empty half-gallon bottle of whiskey as she shakily decanted some into a shot glass, passing it to an equally unsteady female in cutoff shorts and a tank top. She managed to chug the liquor to chants of "shoot it back, shoot it down, drink it all, just don't drown." Meg didn't miss the opportunity to fill her own glass and drain it.

Charming. Brook wondered how they had lucked into neighbors like these. The driveway was stacked with rusty muscle cars and aging trucks while the backyard seemed to sport every grown-up toy available, from Jet Skis and dirt bikes to ATVs.

Meg had yet to notice her standing a few feet away.

"Hi." Brook only trusted herself with the one word in case her simmering displeasure for the scene and her partner came out too loudly.

"Hey, babe!" Meg words weren't sharp; it was the stage where she was on her way to being very drunk but hadn't realized it yet. "Everyone, this is Brooklynn, my girlfriend. She doesn't socialize very much because she works a lot." Meg drew out the words for emphasis and to complete the tired dig.

Brook offered a quick wave and tried to assess the situation. If she asked Meg to come home for her own good, she would never hear the end of it and Meg would inevitably embarrass her in front of the group of strangers. She waited for the party to resume so she could fade into the periphery. It happened fairly quickly given the prevailing degree of inebriation. Brook watched and listened to the Animal House–style conversations. She kept an eye on Meg and then gave up trying. She actually thought about the quiet evening she could have if Meg passed out early, which was a certainty at this point. She felt guilty for reveling in the potential outcome, but she had learned to claim serenity whenever she could find it.

After an hour, Meg could barely stay upright, having consumed a stunning amount of her familiar whiskey crutch. If Brook let it continue, there would be no getting her home. She considered that the average person would have suffered alcohol poisoning if they consumed what Meg did almost nightly. She cared about Meg, loved her even, but she now pitied her more and resented her even further. Her doughy, gray pallor and her dull-eyed expression were in no way reminiscent of the bright, fit, intelligent woman who used to captivate Brook, challenge her, and take care of her. Brook had long buried that woman and resigned herself to caretaking the self-destructive child Meg had become.

"Time to go, Meg," she whispered close to her ear.

"Why, because I'm having fun and you're a big wet blanket every time I'm enjoying myself?"

Oh, for heaven's sake. The script was the same, the argument identical. Brook chose to hide her exasperation.

"Yes. That's it. You know I don't sleep well when you aren't at the house with me. Besides, I'm making some food I need you to help me taste. You can have a drink and we can continue the party at home."

As if Meg needed an excuse to explain her tapping out of the raucous party, she turned to the crowd. "Hey! The warden here needs me back to the cell block, but I'll head back over if you guys are still partying later."

Jeers and calls to Brook declaring her a party pooper inspired laughs and condolences to Meg for her "whipped" status.

Brook waved and steered Meg as quickly down the drive as she could, trying to ignore the comments.

She knew the new Meg very well. They wouldn't be in the house five minutes before she'd begin to berate Brook for being boring, no fun, and a workaholic. She would tell her that she longed for the sexy woman she used to be instead of the stick-in-the-mud who forgot how to be fun. Then she would pass out for the night wherever she fell first. She wouldn't eat because it might trump the buzz she'd spent all day chasing. She wouldn't remember anything in the morning, nothing she said to Brook and nothing she did. Most of tomorrow would be spent managing the chronic hangover, and they wouldn't talk about the evening that put her in that condition.

Brook knew what was coming. All of it. The script didn't change. She realized that of all of the contemptable facets of Meg's current life, she hated herself the most for still being here. It felt like a sentence that would never be commuted, and she wondered, once again, when she might get up the nerve to make a plan.

Only thirty minutes later, Brook sat with a book and a reheated bowl of Chinese food. The only sound was the distant snore from the bedroom where Meg had sprawled across the mattress on top of the covers. She pulled a blanket from the end of the sofa and reveled in the gift of solitude.

She reviewed the conversation with Piper. She was sharp and driven and entertaining. She loved the creative side of her and wondered how on earth she managed to remain single. Women like that, especially ones who looked like Piper, rarely stayed on the market long. She knew they were just friends, and had to be since Brook would never cheat, no matter how over her relationship was. She wouldn't date anyone until it was finished completely and there was no question of some unhealthy rebound, either. The fantasy was pleasant, but her thoughts circled back to how that might happen. It was all on her. Up to her.

"This is your own damned fault. Do something." She said it out loud as if the directive would be less likely to get lost in the muddle of her thoughts if she did.

She pulled the blanket over her and curled into the sofa, grateful that she could, for just a few hours, have some peace. She fell asleep to the memory of lying beside Piper under a blanket of stars.

Chapter Eight

S aturday evening, Piper found herself without plans. Vanessa had accompanied Frank to a corporate retreat in the country for a few days and Leo was vetting locations for Stacy's parents' anniversary party in Marysville. She scanned the "To Do" section of the local independent paper and decided to drive downtown to the Wine and Art Fair. A little culture, a little wine, and a little checking out the competition. She was always interested in other artists. The crowd would make her anonymous and solitary without being alone. A perfect evening—private time with art and her thoughts.

The first booth was John Cashman's watercolors. They were lovely. The prices were crazy, and she wondered if he ever sold a forty-inch canvas for $8,500 at a street fair. Maybe people had different levels of impulse income that she couldn't fathom. His smaller pieces, the few that there were, still sported a price tag beyond her monthly salary.

She sampled wine and bought a couple of bottles of a Pinot Noir from a local vineyard. She perused a booth offering stunning handmade titanium jewelry and skimmed through at least a hundred pieces until she found a unique bracelet. She had searched for the tiniest one she thought would fit Vanessa. She held it in her hand just long enough to feel silly buying a ninety-dollar bracelet for the wife of a multimillionaire. She placed it back on the table and wandered out through the crowd.

"Can I interest you in a stuffed mushroom?"

Piper felt the voice as much as heard it and turned to follow the sound. Brook held out a napkin and a skewered hors d'oeuvre to a gentleman in a Hawaiian shirt and a straw hat who seemed to be quite fond of the offering, since he snatched her business card immediately upon swallowing. He thanked her and walked away mumbling something about a cocktail party for his wife's birthday.

"What does a girl have to do to get her own free sample?" Piper offered a sideways grin and a bit of a flirty nod at Brook, who turned around quickly.

"For you? A little of that artist charm and a please might do it." Brook arranged an assortment of treats on a napkin and handed it over. Piper noted that she looked relaxed, surrounded by her culinary creations.

"I'll do my best. I didn't know you were doing this show."

"Super last minute. A friend who owns a bake shop couldn't use his spot and gave it to me for free. I couldn't pass it up."

"Good for you. How did your baby shower go the other day? We never got around to talking about it."

"Oh yeah. I kind of dumped my drama on you instead, huh? They loved the food and I got two more leads. It's certainly picking up, but it sure is time consuming when it's just you." She spoke in a reduced tone, obviously not wanting to give away the secrets from behind the entrepreneurial curtain.

"You'll be booked solid before you know it." Piper looked over Brook like she was a painting. She caught herself trying to decide if her thin mouth made her broad cheekbones more pronounced or her cheekbones made her mouth look smaller. Then she decided that was a pretty dumb thing to be spending time on while she stood near the woman she had tried to capture on canvas since their conversation on a dark golf course. "And, just so you know, you can vent to me any time."

Brook rearranged samples on trays, and Piper thought she saw her blush. "Thank you again."

Piper refocused. "How about some coffee when you're done?"

Brook looked uncomfortable and Piper tried to soften the moment. "It's okay. We don't have to. I just enjoy talking with you."

"Oh, no. I would love to spend time with the elusive artist. We all need good friends, right? I'm just not very good when it comes to planning fun stuff. Because…well, you know."

"No planning necessary. Why don't we go after this thing closes?" Piper would trade her uncomplicated evening off for a cup of coffee and a nice conversation with Brook any time.

"Well, I have another two hours and I'm a little bit sweaty. Hardly coffee date material. Not that it's a date or anything." She put out her hands as if to ward off any misunderstandings.

"Well, I don't think there's a dress code at coffee shops, and they also don't test you for sweat."

"You don't mind hanging around? I could really use a Death by Bean from Marco's, if you don't mind waiting?" Brook seemed to give herself permission to enjoy the idea.

"Perfect. Why don't I help? If you don't make me talk to people, I can refill the samples or something?"

"Free help? I'll take it." She pushed an empty silver platter at Piper and pointed to the baking sheet of stuffed savory pastries under foil. Piper picked up tongs and started arranging them onto her platter before beginning again with a tray of sweet ones. The booth was busy, and she noted how good Brook was at dealing with people. She would deftly find a common interest, make cooking suggestions or, in two cases, book a potential cocktail reception and a rehearsal dinner.

Piper thought about how quickly time passed when she was painting. It was nothing to compare to how fast two hours had gone with Brook. By the time they had cleaned up and loaded up her cart with trays and utensils, it was ten o'clock.

Brook scraped the sleeve of her jacket across her forehead. "I am so done serving and smiling. I can't tell you what a relief it is when these things are over." She led the way, pushing the last cartload through the alley to her van.

Piper dragged the large cooler to the back of Brook's van and perched on the bumper. "I'm afraid I have bad news."

Brook turned a gave her an inquisitive look. "Hit me."

"It's already ten and Marco's is closed. Can I interest you in a sparkling water on this lovely coffee table?" She swept her hand over the pebbled plastic top of the cooler and produced a bottle of water from her bag.

"Well, it's not glamorous, but I will take you up on it." She smiled at Piper and held out her hand for the drink. She shrugged out of her white chef's coat and folded it over a cart that she had secured to the side rails inside the van with a bungie cord.

"So tell me more about you, famous artist," Brook said as she relaxed against the door.

"Please. I am not famous. I like to paint, and some people have decided they liked a piece or two. I'd rather hear about you anyway." Her Public Relations teacher in high school had drilled into them that the best way to endear yourself to people was to make the conversation about them.

Brook offered a dubious smile. "You already know pretty much everything, so it won't take long."

In fact, it took another thirty minutes. Piper hung on every word and asked her a plethora of questions. She loved that Brook was smart and ambitious. Piper craftily confirmed that nothing of her relationship status had changed.

"Why don't you tell me about you? How are you not dating anyone?" Brook took another swig of the water. She slipped her feet out of her shoes and pushed further against the door of the van, revealing tidy, unpolished toes. "Busy? Gun-shy?"

"I have someone I spend time with, but it's definitely not a relationship."

"Ah. So a friends-with-benefits kind of thing?" Brook smiled and drained all the water from her bottle.

"Sounds pretty clichéd, huh?" Piper suddenly felt embarrassed by the disclosure. It was worse than a simple friends-with-benefits thing, in a way.

"Heck no. You get to be out at ten thirty and no one is wondering where you are. Sounds pretty fabulous to me."

"Sounds like a woman with a heavy decision to make." Piper grabbed an opportunity to see into Brook's plans a bit further.

"I know it's over, so the decision's been made. The other night—hell, every night—just confirms what I already know. It's only complicated when I think of logistics." Brook squeezed the empty bottle and twisted it in her hands, the plastic making an ugly sound.

"I'm a pretty good sounding board if you want to run the plan by me."

"Thanks, but I'm okay. I just keep putting it off. There's so much to figure out after you decide you want to leave. And then I have to remind myself to stop making excuses. I no longer have a real companion waiting for me so she can hear about my day. Now I have a roommate waiting to point to what was broken in hers."

Piper nodded and remembered the similar feeling she had when a chronically drunk and disorderly Wendy danced regularly on her last nerve.

"My only advice is to do it before the house catches fire." Piper didn't mean to sound so bitter.

"Sounds like you've searched through some wreckage." Brook narrowed her eyes and leaned in slightly.

"You don't know how much of me I've watched go up in flames when relationships have ended. It's not the belongings I cared about. I think I lost actual pieces of my soul in each one." Piper didn't do emotional disclosure, so she wasn't sure where this was coming from.

"I don't know how much of me is left at this point. She can have all the material stuff. What there is, anyway."

Piper tried to remember when she had connected with someone like she did with Brook. She was sharing private, painful things for no reason and, for once, she didn't think to run for a more benign subject.

"How long have you known you wanted to leave?" Piper saw the stress in Brook's face return.

"It seems like forever but, in reality, only a couple of years. This disease sneaks up on you, you know?" She blew out a breath as if talking about it increased the weight of it. "I kept thinking that she was just going through a rough patch and she would come out of it, but instead it got incrementally worse until I didn't recognize her anymore."

"Why are you having a hard time leaving?" Piper tried not to think about her attraction to Brook as she asked her about her painful life circumstance. That wasn't fair to either of them, really.

"She doesn't take care of herself anymore. She's become ridiculously dependent and I let it happen."

"Do you own property together?" Piper could see the emotional toll this continued to take on Brook.

"Actually, I sold the house to start my business, and now we're renting a little bungalow off Naglee. I mean, it was my house, so I don't know how all that works or if she'll come after me for money. It would just be out of spite, since she can get whatever she needs from her family and I don't have much left."

"Nasty business." Piper squeezed Brook's arm and gave her a smile she hoped didn't portray pity.

Brook jumped and reached for her phone playing "Purple Rain." She silenced it but immediately stood up.

"I guess I need to go. This was unexpected and really nice. Thank you."

Piper noticed how quickly reality, or at least the reality of addiction, could change Brook's constitution. Meg was obviously on the other end of "Purple Rain."

"Let's plan on that coffee?"

"I really don't know when, Piper. But thank you." The relaxed Brook was gone, and a taut, nervous woman had taken her place. "Do you need a ride?"

"Nah, I'm only parked a few blocks away, I can walk." Piper hated Meg for the calm she stole from Brook. Since she didn't know her, it was unfair.

"Thanks for the break. It was good." Brook shoved the cooler through the back opening and slammed the door. A few long strides and she was sliding in behind the wheel.

Piper followed and held the door open. "If you change your mind, call me. If you need anything, you have my number."

"Sure. I'll be fine but thank you." Brook pulled the door closed.

The engine barely had a chance to start before she pulled away, leaving Piper alone on the dark road, feeling the lack of contact she so relished from their previous evening together.

Brook was certainly intriguing, but clearly far from available for anything other than friendship, and even that seemed tenuous. Piper wanted to be Brook's friend, and heaven knew she needed one. The fact that Brook was living in an untenable situation made Piper sad and a little concerned. It felt strange to feel protective over someone she barely knew.

❖

"Sorry, Meg. I'm leaving now. I was just talking to some potential clients and I lost track of time." She considered why she had lied. It wasn't like she was doing anything wrong.

"Maybe you should find something interesting to do at home. I can't just sit here waiting for you all the time."

Brook heard the signs of how her evening was going to end in Meg's tone. "I've never asked you to do that, Meg. I'm trying to make this business work."

"You could be an overnight success if you'd just get out of your own way."

"I'm not taking the easy way. I want to know I'm good enough to make it completely on my own."

"As long as the princess is happy. Huh, Brooklynn?" The acid in Meg's tone was unfiltered.

Brook sighed and pulled to the side of the road. When these arguments first began, she had the energy to do battle. Now, the distance between the beginning and end of her stamina to fight was almost nonexistent. "I can't just sit at home if I want to be successful."

"Oh. Like me? Nice shot, babe. Well, the waste of oxygen will be here whenever you decide you want to come home."

"I'll be there shortly." Brook could hear the exhaustion in her own voice, almost as much as she could hear the whiskey in Meg's.

She pulled back onto the road headed for the place she lived. Not home. She didn't have one of those anymore, and the resentment about that threatened to consume her.

She could no longer remember when she looked forward to pulling into her driveway in hopes of throwing her arms around esteemed law professor Megan Morris. That woman was barely a memory. Duchess Meg of the Decrepit Armchair had given in to the family legacy of substance and surrender.

The retreat had been gradual. She'd agreed to teach fewer hours each semester, solicited substitutes until she ran out of them and then canceled entire weeks of classes because of one made-up illness or another. Her grades were often late and her nights with a cocktail even later. Brook had mentioned it, massaged it into an encouraging ego stroke about how many of her students looked up to her, but nothing worked. Finally, the university asked her to step down when they likely began to suspect her of drinking at work. Brook could smell the alcohol constantly, so she doubted the fragrance had been lost on students and faculty.

Brook saw the glow of the living room light in the small rental. It sat close to the street, tucked between two much larger and now taller homes that had been renovated. The house looked like it could be swallowed up by its surroundings. Brook wondered if she had felt some kindred emotion when she had agreed to rent it.

She could see Meg watching television and sipping from the ubiquitous rocks glass in her left hand, remote in her right. She stopped along the curb and mentally inventoried what she had to bring in tonight and what could wait in the van. She loaded her cart with perishables and quickly assembled a plate of food for Meg, hoping it might absorb some of her alcohol and ire.

She thought about how she'd left things with Piper. She'd been abrupt, she knew. But she couldn't let herself feel what Piper made her feel. Maybe it wasn't just Piper, although she seemed like something special. Maybe Piper just represented what it felt like to be free.

❖

Piper wanted to call and check on Brook. She could pose as a client in case Meg got suspicious. *What the hell am I hiding for?* But she knew the game and didn't want to make things worse for Brook. She wasn't trying to insert herself, she was genuinely concerned. She could be just her friend, would be. Perhaps a guide down the road that Piper had already traveled.

When she pulled onto the drive, Frank's Tesla sat conspicuously in front of Piper's home and Piper had to carefully maneuver around it to park in her allotted niche off the driveway space. *A rather fitting metaphor, isn't it?* Piper maneuvered around the big expensive dude that took up too much space so she could claim the little piece of what he let her borrow. She shuddered at the distasteful comparison and slipped inside.

She began pulling ingredients out of the fridge. Brook's samples were long gone from her stomach. She craved a little Italian cooking, and kitchen creating might take her mind off the intriguing woman with the colossal problem. She defrosted spinach, emptied ricotta into a large bowl, and added a variety of seasonings and some fresh garlic.

Within a few minutes, Vanessa stepped into the carriage house wearing yoga pants and a trendy V-neck T-shirt tied at the hip.

"Did you go work out?" Piper wasn't feeling the game tonight.

Vanessa looked down at her outfit. "Well, earlier." She sounded indignant and perhaps a bit insulted. "I just thought these were cute and you might like me in them."

Piper accepted that her evening was going to be this way. Passive-aggressive volleys when Vanessa set her up so she could tap compliments and reassurances in her direction. Ones she didn't get from Frank.

Piper's words betrayed her true thoughts. "Of course I like you in them." She slid her arm around Vanessa's narrow waist and pulled her in for what she intended to be a brief hug. Vanessa had other ideas. She threw her arms around Piper's neck and began to sob. Piper was shocked and then resigned.

"What's wrong?" She wasn't sure she wanted to know. "Let's not be sad tonight."

Vanessa exhaled a shaky breath.

"I had a fight with Frank because he decided not to be home for my birthday."

She looked up at Piper. Her watery eyes looked desperate and miserable, and Piper was glad she wasn't responsible for putting that look there this time. Despite the awkward nuances of their dubious association, she cared for Vanessa in her own way.

"I'm sorry, V. I wish I could make it better." She'd forgotten Vanessa's birthday as well. She couldn't imagine the fallout from that.

"It doesn't matter. I don't really care. I just made plans because he said he was going to be home this time."

Piper realized that Vanessa had actual feelings for Frank—not deep, loving, abiding feelings perhaps, but feelings nonetheless— and was hurt at his dismissive treatment.

"Where is he going to be?" She managed not to ask with whom.

Vanessa rolled her eyes. "You know, where he always is. Some random business meeting that can't possibly go on without his presence." Her sarcasm was potent.

"Well, he's missing out on the opportunity to spend the day with you. He's a fool." Piper knew already what she would be expected to do. "How about you and I spend your birthday together and *I'll* take you to dinner."

It was the least Piper could do. No one should spend their birthday alone regardless of the unholy mess that was her marriage. It would make Vanessa happy and make up a little bit for the fact that Frank was a giant narcissistic asshole.

Vanessa brightened immediately and instantly began planning where she would like to go.

"I'll even take the afternoon off," Piper said.

"Can't you take the whole day off? I bet we could fly to the city for a minute and have supper at Braylow."

It was fascinating that people could consider that sort of trip for a birthday dinner even feasible; however, she wanted to pay for their outing, and she wouldn't be, couldn't be, nearly that extravagant.

Spending their day celebrating on Frank's dime wasn't in Piper's comfort zone.

"How about we go to May Garden in Rivers? They have a fabulous menu and nobody from Shadow Glass will be over there on a weeknight. And yes, I'll take the day off." It would still tax her budget significantly, but it was at least doable, and their food was divine.

"I don't care if they are." Vanessa became indignant at the mention of them being caught out together socially. "I'm allowed to go to dinner on my birthday with my friend."

Piper smiled. "Of course you are. And that's what we'll do." Piper pushed Vanessa toward the island playfully and dropped an apron around her neck.

"Since you're here, I could use a little assistance." Her spirited tone and abrupt change of subject elicited a wary look.

Piper pulled the ties around Vanessa's waist and pushed her toward the mixing bowl.

"I'm not sure I *want* to be your assistant, Piper." Vanessa's tone was finally relaxed and hinted at playful.

"Too late." Piper held out the soap and turned on the water in the sink for her to wash her hands. "Now it is time, Mrs. Devereaux," Piper said formally and grandly after Vanessa dried her hands, "to get your very manicured fingers dirty."

She plunged Vanessa's fuchsia-painted fingertips into the bowl of wilted spinach and ricotta and forced her hands to contract around the ingredients.

Vanessa squealed at the sound and feel of the cheese mixture squeezing between her fingers. "I just got a manicure, Piper. That's awful! I can't imagine that proper chefs do it this way."

"Well, if they don't, they should." Piper smiled and bumped Vanessa with her hip. She took great pleasure in pouring in a cup of fresh parmesan cheese on top of her hands.

"You did that on purpose to see me squirm."

"I like to see you squirm, V." Piper's teasing spoke of the evening where she capitulated to the unconventional nature of the relationship and surrendered to what she found fun about it.

"I'm talking about cheese, Piper."

"Yes. Me too. All you have to do is get it all mixed up so I can layer it over the noodles, and you can be done."

"Then what?"

"You'll see." Piper laid a layer of noodles in a glass dish. Within minutes, they assembled the meal. The ensuing moments served to create a distraction that Vanessa seemed to need and that Piper was grateful for.

In no time, the lasagna had cooked and formed the delightful crispy noodle edges. Piper set it on the stove to rest and pushed place mats onto the table for their midnight feast. When Vanessa appeared behind her, Piper pushed her onto the center of the surface.

"I hardly think this is sanitary, Piper." Her protest didn't sound very forceful.

Vanessa obviously relaxed as she submitted to Piper, under the command of her mouth and hands. Piper figured dinner could wait while she compelled Vanessa's complete surrender.

Ninety minutes later, Piper was amused as she watched Vanessa, sated and full, dance around the kitchen, actually cleaning dishes, with rubber gloves, of course. She finished the pedestrian task without complaint. Piper enjoyed these moments where things felt real with Vanessa, but they were too few and far between. The circumstance of their entanglement was growing heavier by the day, but Piper kept that summation quite to herself.

"Do you want any dessert?" Piper held open the freezer and pointed to a low-calorie ice milk that Vanessa had put in her fridge a few weeks ago.

"Sure. I suppose I'll just work out doubly hard tomorrow."

Piper shook her head. Vanessa was tiny, but every day was spent trying to live up to some trophy wife ideal.

"If you work out anymore, I think you might disappear."

"Well, I have that banquet for the Reitman Charity Association next week. I need to look my best. Frank told me I needed to sparkle." Vanessa made the statement without any emotion.

Piper shook her head again and wondered what that could possibly feel like, to constantly be challenged to maintain an appearance that satisfied somebody else. Piper wasn't fat, far from it. But she certainly would never tolerate being with someone who criticized her figure so other people might approve. It infuriated her that a marginally attractive, slightly pudgy man had the audacity to judge the appearance of someone as stunning as his wife. One who, let's face it, he would never have a chance with if he wasn't wealthy.

"I think you're beautiful the way you are and so should Frank." Piper offered the words because they were true and because she knew Vanessa needed a little booster. They heard the sound of car tires on the stone outside the front door of the carriage house.

"Have a bite of ice cream with me before you go?" she asked, knowing that Vanessa's quick exit was inevitable.

The way she came and went in Piper's world characterized every facet of their interactions. She came to Piper when she needed something. Emotional reassurance, sex, a sounding board, companionship, or an antidote for the loneliness of her life. Piper could be mad, but it wouldn't be genuine since it meant she could spend the balance of her night with her paints, and that was just fine with her.

She kissed Vanessa goodbye before opening the door and practicing her forlorn, disappointed look at the fact that Vanessa was leaving. Inside, she was already thinking of the painting calling her name.

CHAPTER NINE

B rook rolled out of bed early Thursday morning. The thought of the enormous job she had accepted had consumed the last few days. Shopping, planning and replanning the menu was making her crazy. She had to be sure she had enough food without overdoing it and carving out needless dollars from her small profit. She only had a day until the biggest job of her career, and she knew it could make or break her.

Meg snored away in her recliner, where she had been nonstop since yesterday. Brook quietly pulled a chopping board, bowls, and Tupperware from the overstuffed cabinets. The more filling, slicing, molding, and mixing she could get done, the easier Friday would be. She would make everything she could ahead of time and plan for assembly later tomorrow.

She finished mixing the spinach filling for the spanakopita, grating cheeses for her tiny quiches, and counting chocolate cups she would fill with raspberry-lemon mousse garnished with mint leaves. She made room in the fridge on the back porch, carefully labeling each item to make Friday's preparation seamless. She even numbered the dishes in the order she would prepare them, knowing which ones could be assembled early without wilting or becoming soggy. She had planned everything down to the number of seconds it would take to create each of the 1,400 items she would need for the party of a hundred people. She refused to calculate the amount of money she would actually make per hour after filling phyllo cradles, cutting fruit, stuffing mushrooms, assembling quiches, and chopping veggies, not to mention choreographing the time in the oven and creating her presentations. It was too depressing. Regardless, she could cement her footing in the social circle that people like the Warners moved in. She couldn't care less about their social standing, only that they kept throwing big parties and hiring caterers. It was her way up.

She moved through labeling each item she planned to serve, cutting garnish, separating tiny cuts of cheese, and setting aside the grape tomatoes that she would marinate in a balsamic glaze. Five hours later, Meg stirred from her chair and wandered into the kitchen, her eyes barely slits as she squinted against the bright kitchen lights.

"God. How am I supposed to sleep with all the racket you're making in here?"

"Good afternoon, Grouchy Greta." Brook wasn't going to let Meg's hangover spoil the joy that came of doing what she loved. "It's nearly one in the afternoon, you know."

"I went to bed late, I couldn't sleep." Excuses were the only thing Meg's tongue saw more than alcohol.

Brook stared at her, but she didn't reply. Meg had passed out by quarter after ten. She rarely woke in the night and Brook doubted she had on this night either, but it wasn't worth the argument. She certainly wouldn't start one.

"So is this all we're doing today? Making food I'm not allowed to eat?" Meg pulled the pot from the coffee maker and poured the remaining coffee into a large mug.

Brook wondered when the last time was they actually spent the day together doing something fun. They had planned numerous days over the last year, but either a hangover or the makings of one kept their plans from materializing. It had been months since either of them had bothered to try again.

"How about we go see that new James Milan thriller you wanted to see this afternoon? I should be at a good stopping place in time for a four o'clock show. What do you think?"

"Okay. That sounds fun. I haven't taken you to a movie in a while." Meg attempted a smile.

Brook was shocked by the glimpse of the woman who used to plan surprise dates and romantic evenings. She, of course, was long past being able to "take" her anywhere. She no longer drove and rarely used money for anything other than her habit. Brook caught her internal grumbling turning to resentment and she stopped herself.

"Sounds great. Why don't you look up the times so I can get in the shower right after you?" She meant to remind Meg that she needed to plan time for her own shower since she smelled like stale liquor and resignation.

"Okay. Just let me finish my coffee and I'll look it up." She shuffled out of the room and Brook heard her as she plopped back into her creaky recliner.

By three, Brook sealed the last Tupperware, labeled it, and shoved it into the corner of the now packed porch fridge. She checked the time and realized Meg had never told her when the movie started.

She wasn't surprised when she found Meg asleep in the chair. She gently shook her awake.

"What?"

"What time does the movie start?"

"Is it okay if we just stay home? I've got a headache for some reason."

Meg leaned up enough to reach for the coffee cup that Brook knew no longer contained coffee. She still felt the stab of disappointment despite having expected it. She couldn't respond. Instead she walked to the shower and stood under blistering spray until the hot water gave out. Dressing for an evening out of the house, she planned nothing but to be away from the now passed-out Meg.

She drove to the small independent theater and bought a ticket to the next showing of an indie film about a homicidal restaurateur. She chuckled at the comparisons she could draw as she accepted extra buttered popcorn and a large bottle of water.

Tucked into her seat, she took in the three couples poised to watch the show on what was a work night for the rest of the city. A man in a designer paisley shirt with contrasting fabric on the cuffs led his date by the hand and waited for him to choose a seat. Brook was jealous and envious, and she would admit to missing the closeness of someone who worried about where you were instead of when you'd be home to take care of them. She imagined Piper being that way, comforting and considerate. She smiled at the memory of Piper carefully arranging treats at the arts festival and wondered what she was doing at the moment. The theater lights went down, and she refused to look at her phone, vibrating incessantly in her pocket.

Brook lost herself in the unrealistic story, glad for the mental vacation where she wasn't thinking about crudité or crises. She felt a bit refreshed when she headed home, prepared to face whatever waited for her. She secretly hoped Meg had gone to the neighbors' again.

Resentment continued to grow, and she didn't want to end up hating Meg. She was, after all, still the woman she was once in love with. She pledged that this weekend would be *the* conversation. It was more than time.

A grip of anxiety squeezed her chest when she turned onto her street and saw every light in the house blazing. Distorted music bled from the open windows where she saw three figures crowded together with shot glasses lofted above their heads. She wondered if the other neighbors had grown weary of the constant party on their street.

"Unbelievable," Brook said out loud as she slid out of the van. She waited for a group to exit the crowded cottage, so she could enter. Chanting voices yelling, "drink, drink, drink" led her to Meg holding court in their den, making flaming fireball shots for an audience of ten, some of whom she recognized from the previous evening next door. Tommy was leading the chant and was the first one to hoist the shot glass of burning liquor. She imagined it was like parents returning from a night out and realizing their teenager had invited a fraternity to party in their living room. The sad part was that Meg was a law professor in her late forties and the fraternity was a bunch of twentysomething misguided losers from the neighborhood.

Meg passed another shot to a new girl in skintight spandex shorts showing more of her ass than they covered. Before the liquid could hit her lips, the glass slid from her fingers and shattered on the tile floor and her formerly white rug. Brook was stunned into silence as she watched the collection of irresponsible revelers trash their house. She began collecting stacks of discarded paper plates and cups that littered the tiny space, like trying to stanch a flood with a single sponge.

A tiny chocolate cup caught her eye. Tortilla strips sat broken on an end table, and what appeared to be spinach filling dripped from the mantel.

She stared in disbelief as she ran for the back door. "No. No. No. Please no." She stood, nearly vomiting at the sight of the fridge door standing open. What hadn't been removed from the shelves had been pawed through. The rest had been spread over the picnic table. Cheese squares and bowls of mushroom stuffing destined for phyllo bowls were nearly empty; spanakopita filling coated a mound of chips and looked as if it had been microwaved. Chocolate mousse had been spooned into plastic shot cups and topped with some sort of whipped cream from a can, evidenced by the frilly design wilting down the side of the cup.

Brook wanted to cry and then scream when sheer panic set in. She would have to cancel her job. This could end her career, her business. She didn't have another twelve hours or the food budget to remake what was lost. This couldn't be happening. Meg could be self-destructive, sure, but did she really care so little about her or their relationship that she would let this happen? The tears burned down her cheeks. They were tears of fury, frustration, and the final catalyst to the nagging decision she had previously been unsure she had wanted to actually make.

She stalked into the room where Meg was doing a snakebite shot from the chest of an equally inebriated guest. Brook stepped between her girlfriend and a cheap-looking blonde before the inevitable lemon suck and glared at Meg. She held up a dripping cup of chocolate mousse. When she spoke, she almost didn't recognize the growling tone cloaking her words.

"How could you? It's one thing to drink and party like you're some jerk who never made it out of high school, but to let them destroy all the food I spent days making? For a job that would have paid the rent? What the hell were you thinking? You have ruined *everything*."

Meg blinked, but the dulled edge of her stare told Brook that she barely registered what was happening.

"They needed something to eat. I told 'em you loved to cook, and they wanted to taste your food. I guess it got a little out of hand. You don't have to be a bitch about it, I'll get the rent from my mom. No big deal, and I'll get her to buy you some more food." She shrugged. The cheers and shouts continued behind her and Meg actually turned as if to see what she was missing.

Brook tried to assimilate the woman she had once loved with the scant shadow of the person in front of her who seemed intent on destroying both their lives with every tip of the bottle. She couldn't fathom climbing into bed one more night with this person she didn't recognize and was well on her way to despising. She had reached the place where she was finished. Completely and utterly done. The decision she had wrestled with for so long was made for her.

"That's it, Meg. This was the last straw. Drink yourself to death for all I care. I am *done*. I'll be back for my things this weekend. Rent's due in ten days. Guess you better call Mommy."

"Really, Brooklynn? Fifteen years and you're trying to leave over chocolate pudding? Don't be such a drama queen." If she was the least bit remorseful, she didn't sound it.

Taunts from the crowd and Meg calling her a party-pooper followed her until she heard someone tell Meg to "leave the girl alone." Brook found it fascinating that the one person who seemed to feel bad for her was not her girlfriend but a drunken stranger.

Brook grabbed her notebook and the file she had for the

reception and ran to the van. The tears flowed quickly, and she drove away. A glance back told her the party would continue unabated in a house she knew she would never sleep in again.

She pulled into a parking lot and cried for everything that burned down around her tonight. She picked up the phone and hoped she was making the right call.

❖

Piper reheated the last corner of the lasagna and set it next to the canvas she was sketching a new design on. She reached for a stick of blue chalk and sculpted the arch of a female figure's back as she reclined. She began to form the haphazard curls of hair around her shoulders as she chewed, more focused on the drawing than the taste of her food.

Her phone rang. "Rich Girl" by Hall and Oates sang through the speaker and she answered Vanessa's call immediately.

"Ready for dinner and birthday celebrations tomorrow?" Piper sounded enthusiastic and hoped she could continue the act satisfactorily.

"That's what I called about, sweetie." Vanessa sounded distracted.

"Uh-huh, you thought I forgot and took on clients tomorrow. Well, I surprised you after all." Piper put the phone on speaker so she could skim her finger down an errant line on the canvas to erase it and draw another in its place.

"I can't go." Vanessa dropped the words quickly, like she was absently checking off items from her list.

Piper stared at the phone. "What do you mean? Why not? Are you okay?"

"I'm fine, Pipe. Frank surprised me with a trip to Grand Cayman, and the charter leaves in two hours. Can we do it when I get back?"

"Well, yeah. Sure. I certainly can't compete with that." Piper wondered if it was okay to feel relieved. Relieved and a bit perturbed at the fact that Vanessa was furious and hurt just a few hours ago and the damage was somehow magically repaired with an extravagant trip. This was the modus operandi of the Devereaux. Make trouble, act with callous disregard, then throw money at the problem and watch it disappear.

"Piper. Don't be mad. I know you took the day off for me. I'll make it up to you, I promise."

"You don't have to make anything up to me, it was your birthday. No worries. Go have fun."

"Yeah. Okay, I better go. Talk to you in a few days."

Before she disconnected, Piper heard her tell the housekeeper to be sure to watch out for deliveries while they were away. Piper wondered why she felt irritated. Oh yeah, because once again, her schedule and her life were manipulated by a woman without common consideration for anyone else, despite expecting, even demanding, consideration from everyone around her. But then, what did she expect? She was Vanessa's distraction and would always come second. She was fine with it, generally speaking. Maybe, though, it was becoming less fine.

She returned to her canvas, slashing the chalk in a way that made the once soft, wavy hair on the woman resemble horns on some type of demon. She laughed at herself before using a damp towel to erase the entire image and begin again.

The clatter of car doors and luggage wheels on an uneven surface jerked her from the creative meditation she had fallen into. She had completed the outline and achieved the much softer figure of the woman she planned on coloring next. Piper considered that the woman of her creation looked, once again, nothing like Vanessa. A whole day crafting this new painting would inevitably be much more relaxing than the day she had planned for a birthday celebration.

Her phone rang again, and she considered ignoring it. She glanced at the screen and saw Brook's number on the display and snatched it from the floor.

"I'm really glad to hear from you." She felt herself smiling. "How have you been?"

"Well, I can honestly say this is one of the worst days in a long time, but I don't need to dump that all on you." Brook sighed a shaky breath into the phone. "I just wanted to hear a sane voice for a few minutes. Tell me what you're up to."

"Wait. No. Tell me what's going on. Broad shoulders, remember?" Piper chucked the nub of chalk into a plastic tray and knocked the dust from her fingers with the towel.

"I remember, but this is just too embarrassing to talk about." Brook spoke quickly. "How about I give you a call back another time."

"Luckily, I have a short memory and I am home alone, so you can be assured no one will hear it from me. This is the perfect time, so shoot."

After a bit more cajoling, Brook acquiesced. Piper listened to the whole story without saying a word. Brook cried several times, but the words kept spilling through the tears. Piper carried her plate to the sink and dropped her fork into the dishwasher.

"And so now I have to get up the nerve to call the Warners and tell them that I have to cancel. Careers are ended on much less, but the thought of it makes me want to throw up. Aren't you sorry I called?" Her laugh sounded like a half-sob. "Any suggestions on the excuse I can make that doesn't sound like 'stoner frat party broke out at my house and they all got the munchies'?"

"Actually, yes. Get over here as fast as you can and don't call anyone on your way, okay?"

"Piper, I appreciate it, but I think I'll just go to my mother's and hope she doesn't ask me why I'm there. Thanks for the offer, though."

"Brook. Seriously. Come here now. I have an idea. Please?" Her wheels were turning as she cleared the last item from the kitchen island.

"I'm a wreck. A total wreck."

"I'd really like to see you. How long till you can get here?" Piper was stripping off her painting clothes and searched for decent shorts and a shirt she wouldn't mind Brook seeing her in.

"Twenty minutes? Don't go out of your way for me, please." Brook had clearly reached the end of her arguments.

"See you then." Piper hung up and called the gate to clear Brook's entry to the property. For once, she thought, she would take advantage of the resources Frank and Vanessa let her share. She called Paul and told him she needed some information and a little favor.

❖

Brook crept slowly up the drive and stopped, unsure where to park or where Piper might be. She got her answer when Piper waved from the door of the little carriage house and guided her into the spot. The short drive over had been a concert of thoughts that bounced between needing to run and hide and needing to see the only person left in her world who didn't know every creak in the floor of her life and relationship. Someone who could be objective or distract her from the crash and burn of her current situation. It would have been too humiliating to call her parents.

She opened the door and slid out onto the cobblestone. "I'm still amazed at this house."

"Me too, sometimes." Piper pulled her into a strong hug and spoke in her ear. "I'm glad you made it."

Brook shivered at the tone and proximity. She couldn't decide if she was ashamed by what had happened or humiliated that Piper knew just how much of a mess she was.

"I'm sorry about today." Piper guided her through the front door and took her bag. "You didn't deserve that. No one does."

"Thanks. I still can't believe it. I could almost feel the business taking off with this job. I just never imagined I'd have to cancel on them. I'll never live this down. Once you make it through the gates, you don't get a do-over." She followed Piper into the cozy kitchen where Piper took her keys and chucked them into a basket near the smart speaker.

"You're not canceling." The delivery was final and succinct.

"Okay. Just not showing up is even worse. I have no choice. I have to be honest and decide if I'm going to work for some other caterer or do something else altogether. I clearly can't do this on my own." She watched Piper pour her a coffee and hand it to her. Her hand was strong and grazed hers as she took the mug.

"You haven't considered option three." She grinned at her as if she had solved the world's problems in the intervening minutes.

"And what is that, may I ask?" She sipped and then gulped the strong coffee. She regarded Piper through slit eyes when Piper unfolded an apron and draped it around her neck.

"Basically, I asked the Devereaux chef to lend me some stuff, like a bunch of utensils and bowls and pans and baking dishes. Some giant mixer thing, a food processor, a blender, stuff like that. The grocery delivery is on standby for a massive order and you and I are about to pull an all-nighter."

Brook shook her head vigorously. "Piper, there's absolutely no way. You're crazy." Brook started to pull the apron off when Piper steered her hands away from the knot she had just finished tying.

"I can't do this with all the ingredients in the world. There isn't time, Piper. Thank you, but there isn't time." She wished Piper's offer could fix this, but she knew it was impossible.

"Why not? Do you doubt my sous-chef skills? I might surprise you." She pushed a notepad at Brook and looped an apron string around her own neck. She tossed her head in Brook's direction. "Go on. Make your list."

Brook stared at Piper, who was grinning and looking expectantly at the pen and paper. Her unruly black waves framed her face and her intense eyes said she wasn't taking no for an answer.

"No way, Piper."

"We can do this. Go on." Piper pushed the pad closer to her.

Brook shook her head before she picked up the pen and tentatively began to write. Piper watched. The resulting list was two full columns, and she knew she had probably forgotten ten things. This was insane. She started scribbling small figures next to each item, mentally adding them up as she wrote.

"Piper, even if we could pull this off in a night, I don't have the money for what it's going to cost. I already spent over four hundred dollars on ingredients. I don't have anywhere near enough to do it again." She imagined what Meg would have said. She would have told her to call her parents and have them make everything okay. They'd had numerous arguments in this vein; after all, Meg was partially the mess she was because her wealthy parents had always bailed her out.

Piper cupped Brook's chin and gently tilted her face to look at her, as if she could tell her mind had wandered. The heat and her physical reaction to the touch stunned her for a second before she recovered and focused on Piper's words.

"Here's the beauty of living with too much money the way Vanessa and Frank do. They have accounts everywhere, and the market will bill me later. Trust me, that's not an issue. We'll make a great team, and it will be even better because you triumphed over the madness."

Brook stared at her and began to feel Piper's enthusiasm infect her. Just the excited grin on her face was enough to convince Brook it was worth a try. How did Piper manage to boil everything down into small, digestible bites?

"You really think we can make this happen?" She couldn't help but be skeptical.

"I am wearing an apron, I hate to fail, and I get to try new things with a pretty fantastic woman. All that makes me *know* we can."

"I can drop a couple of the complicated extras and just do more of fewer items." She glanced around the kitchen when Piper picked up her phone, the contact for Delmonica's Gourmet Market shining up from the screen.

"I think you might be insulting my abilities, but I will defer to your genius." Piper's smile was brilliant.

Brook studied her mouth, took in the olive tone of her skin, and landed again on the strong fingers hovering over the dial key.

"You're completely bonkers." Brook said the words with a smile she couldn't control and nodded just before Piper hit the dial key.

"Hi, Thomas, It's Piper Holthaus again. Can I hand the phone over to my chef for the big order I told you about?"

Brook took the proffered phone, her other hand clutching the list.

"I can't believe we're even going to try this." Brook stared at Piper before beginning to read what felt like an endless list into the phone.

She rattled off ingredient after ingredient to Thomas and didn't dare ask for a total. They were out of fresh rosemary and her preferred brand of tamari, but a few dried herbs replacing fresh and a different brand of condiment were the least of her worries.

She disconnected and forgot herself when she threw her arms around Piper's neck and squeezed.

"You are amazing, and I can't believe we're doing this." She released her and hoped she didn't look as flushed as she felt, which had little to do with their plan and a lot to do with the proximity to Piper. "I promise I'll pay you back for everything."

"Please stop it. We can worry about the bill later." Piper hadn't let her go, her strong arms still draped loosely around her waist.

"They said it would all arrive within the hour." Brook was still amazed by the astounding day she was having. Piper dropped her arms from around Brook when a loud knock broke into their bubble. She watched as Piper dashed for the hall.

"Reinforcements have arrived. Get ready to boss me around, okay?" Piper yelled from the hallway.

Brook jerked her attention toward Piper when the hollow clatter of metal hit the counter. A commercial grade stand mixer, huge metal bowls, baking sheets, a giant slicer and vast pots covered the surface. She ran a hand over the gleaming face of the massive Admiral mixer. She stared at Piper, who was hugging a tanned man in a white smock.

"I owe you big, Paul. You saved my ass here. If you can keep this quiet, you'll have it all back before the Devereaux return, okay?"

"Anything for you. You know that." He tapped a finger on her nose affectionately and turned to look at Brook.

Piper gestured in her direction and then waved toward Paul. "Brook Myers, meet Paolo Michele Stellini, the best chef Italy has ever produced."

"Ha! You flatter me so I make you pasta and don't tell Mrs.

Devereaux that you hide the salads she makes for you and eat my tortellini instead."

"Those are pretty good reasons, you know."

Paul looked at Brook seriously. "You've got a good woman in your corner." He held out his hand, which Brook shook immediately.

"Go dazzle them at this party. I'm rooting for you." His thick accent and deep voice combined into an almost melodic quality.

Brook was overwhelmed by the genuine warmth of the rugged man in the chef's coat. "I don't know how to thank you. This is all amazing."

"Piper says you're kind of a culinary artist." He raised his fingers to his lips as if tasting a wonderful flavor. "I'm sorry I missed your food the last time you were here. I'll be sure not to miss it twice." He raised his eyebrows and scanned the implements littering the counter as if imagining the creations he would make in her place. She refrained from begging him to do this all for her. If there'd been any way she could afford to pay his hourly fee, she'd have begged him to help.

"I hope I can live up to my press. You have made this all possible, and I don't know how to thank you."

"My pleasure." He turned for the hallway.

Within a few seconds he was gone, replaced by two teenage boys in Delmonica's shirts lifting bags of ingredients and boxes of produce and shuffling through the door.

Brook stared at Piper as she hefted the boxes into the kitchen, trying not to concentrate on the broad build of Piper's shoulders or her traps flexing under the smooth skin. She was well aware that Piper was currently saving her professional career, but Brook indulged herself in the momentary appraisal of her savior's physique. She couldn't move, assimilating the myriad of tasks, senses and feelings whirring in her mind.

The closing door shook her from the fantasy as she cut open bags of pastry flour and gourmet mushrooms.

"Chef Myers, Underling Holthaus reporting for duty. Tell me what we're making and what I can do given my limited expertise."

Piper smiled before stepping to the sink to wash her hands. She undid and retied her apron strings, which had gone slack from the labor of moving in the yards of groceries.

Brook didn't consider what Piper would think when she threw her arms around her again. The hug lasted only a few seconds, but Brook somehow knew tonight would change her life in so many ways. If she could overcome this disaster, she would know this was what she was meant to do, and leaving Meg once and for all was final. It had to be.

"You don't know me from Adam's housecat, and you're moving the world to save my ass. You can't know how grateful I am."

Piper stepped back from the embrace and grasped both her hands. The electrical charge was intense, and she wondered if Piper felt it too.

"I do know you. I've been in similar situations and I know what it feels like to be an island. Luckily, I have a free day tomorrow, so we're going to see what a team of two determined women can accomplish. I'm putting on some happy music and I'm all yours. Deal?"

"Deal. Let's do this." Brook was almost as sure as Piper seemed to be that they could move this culinary mountain. "Challenge accepted."

"That's what I like to hear." Piper barked orders for music at Alexa. Katrina and the Waves sailed through the speaker and Piper wiggled a silly dance move that elicited a laugh from Brook.

She nudged a knife out of its sheath and slid it, handle first, toward Piper, followed by a pile of mushrooms. "Start chopping, as finely as you can."

"Yes, Chef!"

CHAPTER TEN

By four a.m., twelve different bowls were filled with ingredients in various stages of completion. They had developed a system where Brook had assembled them and handed them to Piper, who had mastered the giant mixer. They chatted and laughed about surface things, teasing one another about tastes in music and sharing embarrassing school escapades. Piper had yawned more than once between some unorthodox chopping techniques and some near misses of more than a few fingers. A carving knife tumbled from her grip and bounced off the counter.

Brook screeched in warning and Piper stepped back just in time to see the point of the blade wedge into the wood floor.

"That's it, break time." Brook pulled Piper's arm, so she stepped away from the island as she retrieved the knife. "I had an instructor tell me once that the first accident or near accident should be the time when you take a break. So I'm calling breaktime."

"Fair enough. I could use a drink and an interim employee evaluation." Piper appraised Brook. The look of intense concentration and determination was sexy. Piper tried not to find her passion as striking as her cheekbones. Her determination was compelling, to say the least, and her haphazard bun completed the package, although she tried not to dwell on it.

"I think we're doing some pretty amazing stuff, yeah?" Piper hoped the work she was doing was actually helping Brook and their efforts would pay off in the end, because she never wanted to see that helpless look on Brook's face again.

"Are you kidding? If I had the money to hire an assistant, you would already have the job. You're awesome and I actually think your crazy plan just might work."

"Thank God." Piper exhaled, miming sweeping perspiration from her brow. "I had absolutely no idea that anything I proposed was actually doable, but I'm so glad you had faith."

"You mean, after all this, you doubted the plan?" Brook's look was incredulous.

"I mean, I've cooked for two dates and one birthday party where I made baked brie and crackers for six people. Even then, I'm fairly sure I bought the brie already 'en croute.'" Piper made air quotes as she spoke. "Beyond that, I don't think I've ever made more than a box cake and some stuffed mushrooms for anyone other than myself. If I'm honest, I'm pretty sure my friend Lana spotted me the stuffing."

"So, you're telling me that you convinced me that we could pull off fourteen hundred hors d'oeuvres for a party of a hundred people and you had no idea if you were even remotely capable?"

"Wait, *fourteen hundred?* Um. Well, I knew that *you* could because you are sort of fabulous, but I had no idea we had to do that many." She scanned the room trying to do a quick status count. She slipped a spoon into the mousse mixture and groaned at the flavor when it hit her tongue.

"You should know that I have the will and the power to be convincing, but outside of that, I'm relatively useless." She shrugged her shoulders, playfully gesturing with the mousse spoon.

"Stop eating the product. I should be mad at you for talking me into this." Brook snatched the spoon from Piper and chucked it into the sink.

"So are you?" Piper asked in a teasing tone.

"Absolutely not. You made me believe in myself again. That's worth a thousand secret leaps of faith and at least two get-out-of-jail-free cards. You've been amazing." Brook's face broke into a genuine smile.

"Whew. I was worried for a minute." Piper set another bowl under the mix arm and lowered the attachment into the bowl despite Brook's earlier call for a break. The actual numbers of things made her nervous.

When Piper added the last bowl to the collection, she found Brook watching her and tried to divert her burning attention. "In case you didn't know, you kind of light up when you get in the kitchen. You look like I feel when I'm painting. That's when I knew we could do this. Some self-centered idiots and a drunken party shouldn't be allowed to change that." She handed Brook a bottle of water and motioned toward the living room.

Brook followed Piper out of the kitchen and fell into an armless chair just beyond the bar. "That's the thing, isn't it? That moment changed everything, and not completely in a bad way."

Piper watched as Brook gestured with her hands and felt the words as clearly as she spoke them. "Expound, please." She decided she could watch Brook read the phone book, let alone give her the opportunity to peek into her heart and mind.

"I mean, if I'd canceled my contract and gone home, I would have found Meg where I left her, likely passed out in her chair. I might have continued to make excuses, to put off the inevitable. I've had a plan in my mind, but I kept figuring out reasons to put it off."

"I'm a firm believer in the universe and its plan."

"I used to be, and now I'm going to remind myself to listen to the universe again." Brook picked at the hem of the apron sporting the logo of some gourmet deli in the valley.

Piper saw Brook fade into the arms of the story she had grown resentful of and fought to bring her back to the present. "So tell me about what your plan is. I mean, if you want to. Sometimes it helps you keep your nerve." Piper wondered if Meg ever noticed the way Brook looked when she spoke about cooking and how happy she was when she was creating.

"If we were having this conversation fifteen years ago, I would have told you that I would spend my life with Meg. Open a business in some quaint shop and bask in all that a romance was supposed to be. I was in for the duration. I knew I would never leave. Never stray. Never give up."

"And now?" Piper sat on the rug and leaned against the wall near Brook's chair.

"I'd still never cheat. Even through all of this, no matter what, I would never cheat. That's a deal-breaker for me, you know?"

"Even if she did?" Piper wondered what Brook would think of her questionable relationship. She decided she never wanted to find out. Tarnishing Brook's opinion of her would be painful, and totally unacceptable.

"Even if. Take the high road walking before the easy road flying. That was my grandmother's favorite saying. She told me her husband cheated every day of their marriage, but she never left. Truth be told, I think she was secretly gay, and I longed for her to find a soulmate, but she never strayed."

"So even though Meg has caused you so much pain and checked out of the relationship, you'd never find someone else?"

"Not before it's completely over. I wouldn't consider it. I don't think I could be with someone who thought that was okay."

"People do a lot of things. You can't judge them for their past." Piper felt a twinge of guilt creep into her declaration. No, it wasn't the right way to do things, she knew. She briefly marveled at the unholy deals couples made with each other in the name of perpetuating the status quo in a marriage. She had helped Vanessa and Frank create the compromise she never saw coming.

"No. But I have watched it destroy lives. My family, Meg's, my grandmother. If you're in a relationship, know when it's over and stand up." She shook her head. "It's the advice I need to heed in my own life."

"Places like Shadow Glass Estates are quite the mecca of looking the other way. I think some people buy into the concept of happily ever after and then they just find out what they can settle for. Whatever works for them, right?"

"I just can't believe that people aren't miserable. Get out with your dignity before you sell it for a fancy car or status. Or when you figure out that coexisting isn't helping either one of you." She laughed and stared at her hands, perhaps contemplating her own statement.

Piper felt the twinge again. She wasn't trading on a relationship for a house or a car. She was accepting the assistance of a bored housewife with a cheating husband until she could manage on her own doing what she loved. It wasn't technically a relationship, and her husband *was* aware, so it wasn't at all what Brook was talking about. Her reasoning felt lame even as she tried to convince herself.

Brook stood and walked back to the kitchen and a baking sheet full of dark chocolate cups and began to fill pastry bags with raspberry lemon mousse, clamping the ends and wedging them into a box for transport. Clearly, she was done talking.

Brook was building a wall and Piper couldn't let her go beyond her reach. Somehow, ensuring Brook would stay in the present seemed crucial. "Does that mean you plan on being the Great Celibate Chef of the Millennium?"

"Are you asking if I'll go back to Meg because that would be the easy way?"

"Well, if you say you're committed to someone, regardless, for the long haul, I would be concerned for your safety, Brook. She doesn't seem stable enough to worry about putting you in harm's way."

"Don't worry. I can't go back, ever. We're done." Brook stepped back from the counter and closed her eyes for a second. "I can leave because the person I fell for doesn't exist anymore."

"I'm glad to hear it, but I truly am sorry for everything that's happened. Sometimes people are just too sick to cope."

"Sick is one thing. Blatant disrespect and callous disregard are something else entirely. I don't even know who she is. I would never do anything like that—even to my worst enemy." A flash of anger burned into Brook's tone. An audible deep breath allowed her next words to be calm and measured. "I just need to get through this job, you know? I saw a sign for an open house at a place downtown. If I can convince them to lease to a self-employed woman with irregular paychecks in the midst of a midlife crisis, I can start over."

Piper gripped Brook's arm and turned her so she could look

into her eyes now damp with traces of tears. "You'll get through this, all of it. I'm here if you need me."

"I know I will. It's just a lot right now. I couldn't have done this without you." Brook held her gaze. "Thank you." She turned away quickly when the warmth of it appeared to become too much.

They surveyed the kitchen surfaces, the oven, dining room table, living room, and end tables covered with trays and yet to be assembled bowls of food.

"I would like to think I was a factor, but I've watched you work and I'm pretty impressed."

Brook's stoic, stressed expression broke into a grin. "You're easily impressed, then."

Piper joined the smile and pulled Brook into a side hug. "Actually, I rarely am."

Brook handed Piper the bowl full of ingredients for her potato tarts and she made quick work of spooning it into a pastry bag. The heavy conversation was set aside, the music was loud, and they settled into the comfortable rhythm they'd been in before. But Piper kept going back to Brook's views on relationships, and it created a little knot of worry in her chest.

❖

"If I see one more shredded potato or sprig of parsley, I might never eat again." Piper lay on the living room floor barely able to bend her fingers. She rolled to her side to see Brook looking equally exhausted. The rising sun cast a streak of white light over her face.

"I already think I need to find a new line of work. I currently hate food and everything about parties." Brook chuckled. "But after all your hard work, I am going to make this happen."

"Good for you." Piper tossed a pillow from the couch toward Brook. "A few hours' sleep?"

"I wish. I have to go get my clothes and some serving platters I have at the house. I don't think the Warners would appreciate me serving their guests from cookie sheets."

Piper immediately felt concern. "Can I come with you? I'll stay in the car, but I would feel better if I could at least be there if you needed me."

"Thank you, but I'll be in and out. A quick shower and packing a bag shouldn't take me long. The serving platters are already boxed and waiting on my dolly. Meg's still passed out, I'm sure, if she's even gone to bed."

"How about you grab your things and just shower here? I'll have to worry about you less and you can take your time getting ready. You might even have time to sleep for a bit before we leave for the party."

"We? Aren't you sick of me yet?" Brook looked stunned by Piper's intention to see the party through to the end.

"No chance I'm letting you go without seeing our finished product. Besides, if you show up without me, you might take credit for all my genius." She was struck by the strange familiarity and protectiveness welling inside her.

The relief in Brook's expression was heartwarming and Piper felt a new, profound level of affection. She'd definitely have to get a handle on this.

"You really want to go with me?" She was drawing an invisible design in the carpet with her finger.

"I'll fill the phyllo like a champ. Mold a mousse, pack a potato, bake a brie, craft a…"

"Okay, I get it. You're a glutton for punishment."

"You just watch and prepare to be impressed." Piper stretched her arm across the carpet between them and waited to see if Brook would respond in kind. She could choose the high-five response or the hold-on intimate one. Piper didn't know which to expect.

"You couldn't impress me any more after today. I will owe you forever." She wrapped her fingers over Piper's and squeezed briefly before letting go.

Okay, there was a third response, but she would take it. Piper wanted the feeling of her touch back immediately.

"Nonsense. But I want you to hurry up and come back, okay?" Piper had an uneasy feeling. "I'm a little concerned about Meg's understanding of you being gone all night."

"It'll be okay. I'll be back in an hour and a half. Don't worry."

"It's too late for that." Piper hoisted herself to her feet and pulled Brook to hers. "Be careful, you're tired and stressed out."

"Thanks to you, I have a lot to be grateful for, which gives me energy." Brook tapped a kiss on Piper's cheek. "You're a lifesaver."

Piper watched Brook drive away until her van disappeared down the lane, the kiss still burning her skin.

❖

Brook felt her chest constrict as soon as she turned down the street. Such crippling anxiety had never been part of her life until Meg lost the footing on hers. Meg's father had been a practicing alcoholic until she was an adult, and Meg had more than resented the toll it had taken on her childhood. Brook wondered if Meg ever examined how history had begun to repeat itself. She knew well the signs of alcoholism, but she had obviously chosen to ignore them. She had officially lost everything, her job, her colleagues, her friends, and now her relationship. Brook couldn't imagine what was left for her.

She slowly eased open the back door into the kitchen, ignoring the plastic cups still littering the approach. She sighed with relief when she saw no lights on and heard the unmistakable sound of Meg snoring in the next room. She scanned the mess that beset the kitchen and the voided carcasses of liquor bottles scattered among beer cans, not to mention the remnants of her food growing stale on every surface. She carefully pushed the crates of serving platters from the porch to the van and loaded them in, lying the dolly on its side beside them. She slid coolers to the back and shut the doors as quietly as she could, still praying for a quick exit.

Stepping back through the door, her stomach dropped. Meg was leaning against the doorway to the den. She wore the same clothes from the day before and seemed to wobble slightly when she tried to stand independently. Brook considered that she might not have been asleep for more than a few hours, not nearly enough time to burn off the quantity of alcohol she had likely consumed.

"Where were you? I was worried." She slurred a reasonable facsimile of the words.

Brook worked to temper her reply. Fighting with Meg would do nothing but make things worse and accomplish nothing, but she couldn't ignore the absurdity of the statement.

"When did you realize I didn't come back last night, Meg? Just now?" She considered what might have happened if she had been in an accident or had needed someone to pick her up after the van broke down. Meg would likely have never even answered the phone, let alone been in any position to help. Brook was alone, whether Meg was in her life or not.

Meg avoided answering the question. "I don't know why you're so mad. They were just having fun. We could have gotten more food."

Brook was suddenly seething, despite her pledge seconds ago to avoid arguing. "You don't know why I'm mad, Meg? Really? The only chance we had to pay the rent this month was microwaved over tortilla chips for drunk and stoned idiots with the munchies and your answer is, we could have gotten more food?"

"Calm down and stop talking so loudly. You're overreacting and I have a headache."

"I am *stunned* that you care so little. But I'm so much sadder that we're at a point that it no longer surprises me. You know I spent days on this job, and you aren't even sorry. And by the way, you always have a headache, I can't imagine why." Snide and sarcastic, Brook thought to herself, so much for avoiding conflict.

"Fine. Okay. I'm sorry," Meg called after her when Brook pushed past, headed for the bedroom.

Brook was throwing clothes in a duffel bag hoping she could leave without too much more drama when Meg appeared again, this time leaning in the doorway of the bedroom.

"Did you hear me?" Meg looked as if she could be sick at any moment. She was holding her head and squeezing her eyes shut as if to stanch the pain.

"I heard you. It just doesn't matter anymore, Meg." She could barely get the words out. A combination of being up all night and having hours of work still to come was sitting heavily on her shoulders.

"What the hell does that mean?" Meg was now pinching the bridge of her nose.

"It means we've been doing this for too long. You're entitled to live your life exactly how you want to, it's just not okay for me anymore. I need to start the next chapter of my life and you need to decide what you're doing in two weeks when the lease is up. Maybe your parents will help you stay. I just know that I can't. I'm sorry." She blew out a breath and felt cautiously lighter. The words were plain and direct, not mired in some argument where they would pretend nothing had transpired the next day.

"So fifteen years together means nothing to you? You care so little about me you're willing to abandon me before I find a job? You're just going to leave me homeless?"

"Meg, when was the last time you even looked for a job? More importantly, when was the last time you went a day without drinking?" She waited a beat, knowing Meg couldn't or wouldn't answer. "Your mom would never let you be homeless, and you know it."

"I'm going through so much, and this is how you treat me. Unbelievable." She looked honestly perplexed that Brook was actually packing to leave.

"Yes, it is. All of this is unbelievable." Brook carried her bag to the door. Meg followed closely behind, her rant increasing in both cadence and volume.

"Look at me and tell me what is so horrible about me all of a sudden." She pointed at her chest as she spoke. "I gave you anything you wanted and at the first sign of trouble, you cut and run."

Brook saw the tremors in Meg's hands, formerly an occasional affliction she was never without now. Broken capillaries plagued her once smooth, even skin and her eyes were almost jaundiced.

Brook refused to play the game or dredge the arguments that had worn her down over the years. She could point out that she hadn't been able to provide so much as a bag of takeout in years, but what would be the point? "You're an alcoholic, Meg. Just like your dad. You need help, and if you can't see that," she looked around the messy house, "then…well…" She shrugged.

Meg stared at her, her jaw clenching, but didn't say anything.

"I have to go." Brook turned to the door. There was nothing else to say.

"New girlfriend so soon?" Her tone was taunting and angry now. "You find another chick who'll believe that you're perfect and devoted? You should give her my number so I can tell her about the real you."

"Megan!" Brook felt the stress finally consume her ability to speak calmly and reasonably. "I have a job in a few hours that your drinking and your so-called friends nearly ruined for me. I have been up all night replacing what you destroyed, and I am done enabling you. The woman I fell in love with ages ago doesn't live here anymore. You can ruin your life if you want to, but I refuse to watch. Insulting me won't change the shell of a person you've become."

"Go to hell, Brooklynn." Meg slapped an empty beer can from the counter and watched it land at Brook's feet.

"Thanks to you, I'm already there." Brook's body vibrated from anger and fear as she stepped onto the street and into the blank canvas of her future. She didn't even have the energy to slam the door, instead leaving it to rest lazily against the frame. Everything screamed for her to run. Her love for the real Meg told her to turn around, but self-preservation and the hope for a real future reminded her this was the only path left.

She threw her bag across the seat and shut herself in the van. She cried for wasted years and unexpected roadblocks where she would never have imagined them.

The future had to win this time, and even if she spent it alone, it was an improvement over watching a once-vibrant woman stubbornly self-destruct. Apathy was not an option.

CHAPTER ELEVEN

Piper finally heard the van rumble into the drive. Brook had been gone two hours and she had started to worry. "You okay?" She watched as she heaved a ragged duffel from the passenger seat and slammed the door.

"Yeah. I think the day is just finally catching up with me." Brook's expression said that a cooking marathon wasn't what put that look on her face, and there was more than exhaustion behind her red-rimmed eyes. Now wasn't the time to pull the details out of her.

"How about you shower and go crawl into the bed for a few hours? When do we have to leave?"

"We need to arrive by four thirty if I want to get all the assembly done without rushing."

"Fantastic, that gives you at least five hours to sleep."

Brook raised her finger to protest. Piper grabbed her hand and led her through the door to the bedroom. She dropped her bag on the ottoman at the foot of the bed and gently pushed her into the bathroom.

"Wow. This is fancy," Brook remarked as she took in the spa tub and double-headed shower.

"Too fancy for what I use it for. Five-minute showers over here. I've never even put water in that tub." She gestured at the copper Japanese soaking tub nestled into the corner of the slate-tiled bath.

"That is a true shame. I bet it would feel awesome." Brook danced her fingertips over the hammered surface.

"Maybe after the party, you can try it out." Piper reached into the shower to start the water, handing Brook a fluffy white towel and washcloth. "In the meantime, I suggest a nice hot shower and a good long nap. I put shorts and a T-shirt out in case you didn't remember to bring any."

"Thanks." Brook studied her. She opened her mouth as if she had something else to say but changed her mind and shut it again.

"You're very welcome. I'll wake us up at two thirty." Piper held up her phone to confirm she was indeed setting her alarm.

She turned to walk out, pulling the door closed behind her. Before the latch clicked, she heard Brook call her name.

She poked her head back through the door. "Yeah?"

"You're a little unexpected, Piper. I don't have words for what you've done for me."

"You don't need any. I think it's time you carve out some space for you. Sleep well."

"You too."

Piper closed the door again. She imagined what it would have been like to hold Brook as she slept, to chase her demons away. Piper would have told anyone before now that she didn't need or want a relationship. She wondered if that was because she hadn't met someone who made her want to be better. And conversely, whose life she wanted to make better. How infuriating it was to find that with someone so completely unavailable.

"Can you throw some more quiches in the oven? Those are going like crazy." Brook spoke quickly while she arranged crackers around a third wheel of brie. "These people act like they're starving."

"Maybe they love your food and can't get enough." Piper was thoroughly and inexplicably enjoying herself. If anyone had told her this was how she would spend a Friday night off, she'd have told them they didn't know her at all. But Brook's energy made her feel like a part of a very important team. Serving food to strangers aside, she couldn't wait to spend the night in the same place with her, despite her anticipated sleep on the couch. It had been so long since Piper had shared her space with anyone. The notion was unsettling.

"God, I hope so. They have no idea how much work went into canapés and crudités, do they?"

Piper liked that she and Brook had an inside story that only the two of them knew. "Nope, no clue. A few more hours and you can write this one into the history of how your business success began." Piper handed her another tray.

"Poke me if I fall asleep in the mousse, okay?" She shot Piper a now-familiar grin that Piper liked to believe was reserved for her.

"Deal." Piper stopped with loaded baking sheets in her hands and turned back to Brook. "You're staying the night, right? I have plenty of room and you need the quiet for a bit."

"If you're sure. I already feel like a giant imposition."

"Don't say that. You're anything but." Piper slid the trays into the oven as she spoke. She had realized in the last twenty-four hours that she wanted to be much more than Brook's friend, but she knew if that was all Brook wanted, she would live with that. "We're friends and I'll sleep better if I know you're safe, okay?" Piper meant it.

Brook stared at her; Piper could swear tears shined in the corners of her eyes.

"Thank you." The words sounded like she was fighting for each syllable. "I needed that."

Piper was just about to respond when Ellen Warner pushed into the kitchen.

"How's it coming in here? The quiches are gone, and that mousse is next, Brook. They love everything." Ellen clasped her hands together, surveying the next platters to head to the dining room.

"So happy they like them, Mrs. Warner." Brook lofted a plate of potato puffs after sprinkling them with paprika.

"Ellen, please. I have a feeling this might be a long relationship." She grinned knowingly. "You have no idea how easy you have made this for me. Parties like this are a pain if you have to manage everything. You're a gem."

"That she is. I hope you got to try everything before it was gone." Piper spoke from the corner of the room.

Ellen spun with surprise when she realized there was someone else in her kitchen. "Piper?" She made no move toward her. "Aren't you Piper Holthaus?"

"Yes, I am. Nice to see you again." Without the context or the name she had been given for this job, Piper would have never remembered Ellen Warner from the sea of people she met at the art reception.

She looked suspiciously at Piper. "Vanessa never mentioned that you worked in catering." The statement rang with clear judgment.

"Brook is a friend, and I love seeing her work these large parties. I just came along to help out today. Hope you don't mind?" Piper was finessing her confusion while inflating Brook and her business.

"Of course. Any friend of Vanessa's…" She raised her eyebrows and shot Piper a knowing glance.

Ohhhh, rumor mill, got it, Piper thought. *I'll be hearing about this again.*

"Well. Off I go." Ellen plucked a potato puff from the tray and spun back to her guests.

"Is this going to cause you any issues?" Brook shot Piper a concerned look.

"Heck no," Piper lied easily. "People like Ellen Warner have too much to do to wonder about Vanessa's houseguests." She wondered how long it would take for the news of Vanessa's pet project turned cater-waiter to reach Vanessa and her cronies. As long as the rumored story of who Piper was to Vanessa never reached Brook, she didn't care.

"If you say so." She sounded as dubious as Piper felt. Brook glanced back at her as she swept the next trays from the counter and headed for the dining room.

Piper made quick work of filling more mousse cups, rather proud of the fairly uniform ruffling she was achieving in the last two rows. She heard Brook's voice as she chatted with the guests about ingredients, ideas for wedding food, and several requests for her contact information. Piper listened and silently prayed for a groundswell of new business that could propel Brook to new professional horizons and out of dubious personal mires.

She wondered where Brook would go after tonight. As much as she would love to have her stay, it was completely impossible. She'd never had an overnight guest in the carriage house before, let alone a single, attractive female. Vanessa would lose her mind.

Of course, explaining to Brook the freedom with which Vanessa came and went at the carriage house would be impossible without disclosing the true nature of their relationship. And she sure as hell wasn't about to do that.

A loud vibration rumbled from the countertop near Brook's backpack. Piper checked that she was alone before she walked over to see Meg's name shine up from the screen. It ended in a few seconds later only to begin again in a few more. Piper turned it over and then pushed it into the open pocket of her bag. Brook didn't need the distraction or the chaos that would come of that call. Piper was making a decision that wasn't hers to make, and she tried to rationalize that it was good for Brook. In reality, Piper felt protective of Brook and she made her heart beat too fast.

The remaining hours sped by and Piper could barely remember her single trip to the bathroom. Brook looked a breath away from collapse when they finally reached the van.

"Can you believe there was nothing left?" Brook was weary but excited. "I mean, a few veggies and some crackers, but that's it. Those people can eat." Brook pushed her hand through her hair knowing it had sprung into a chorus of unruly sprigs in the last five hours. She was still buzzing with energy as she steered the van back to Piper's place.

"Those people *loved* your food. You did an awesome job." Piper slid off her shoes and stretched her toes. "I, however, would never make it as your full-time assistant. I'm too out of shape."

"You can't ever be in shape for standing for seven or eight hours, trust me. I'm feeling it too. I've been dreaming about your bathtub."

"Perfect. It's all yours." Piper yawned. "I might be passed out before you finish filling it up."

"Perfectly understandable. After all, you are a cater virgin."

"I've been called a lot of things. Rarely do they end in 'virgin.'" Piper wiggled her eyebrows, making Brook laugh.

Brook heard the buzzing in her bag. "Mind checking that for me?" Brook felt at once resigned and apprehensive. The old pit in her stomach raced back.

"You probably already know who it is." Piper fished for the phone.

"Of course. This is the time when she's partying the hardest and wants company." Brook heard the resentment in her own tone.

"Why don't you ignore it?"

"Because I have to face it sometime. I guess this way, I know she's safely in for the night and I don't have to worry."

Piper produced the phone, not handing it to the driver.

"You can look. I have nothing to hide." Brook slid her eyes to Piper as they stopped for a light.

Piper woke the phone and her home screen appeared. "You don't have a lock?"

Brook chuckled ruefully. "I took it off because I thought it would delay my calling for help when Meg fell or went into some alcohol-induced something or other." She stopped for another light and turned to Piper. "I just realized how every decision I've made in the past few years has somehow been about or related to Meg and her illness. It's amazing how that happens without you knowing it."

Piper squeezed her arm, and Brook briefly wished the distance between the van seats wasn't so wide. She caught herself. It was probably a good thing, since all she wanted at the moment was to have Piper put her arms around her. Rebounds were always bad news.

"So, what does she have to say?" Brook asked as she turned down the dark boulevard that would return them to the Shadow Glass gates.

Piper pulled up a string of messages. "Are you sure you want me to see these?"

Brook nodded. "I don't mind if you don't mind."

Piper scrolled up and began to read.

Where are you? I can't find my purple sweater.

At least you could answer me

?

??

Screw you

Very mature B. I can't believe you're doing this

Don't worry about me. I will be fine without u

Brook I mis u

I'm sorry

Ill stop if u come home

I promise

I can't believe u don't care anymore

Who is she?

I dont feel good

Baby cal me

I need u

Come here

I'm sick of this

Please

Please

Brook blew out a breath and she made the left into the gated drive and rolled down her window. Piper leaned forward so the guard could see her and waved.

"Have a good night, Ms. Holthaus."

"You too," she called, as the gate arm swung up.

"How are you?" Piper's question sounded cautious. The energy in the van had changed as if someone had opened a window during a snowstorm.

"I'm actually okay. I guess it's good to practice detaching myself. She doesn't remember that I had a job tonight, or more likely, she couldn't care less. It's all about her. That's the nature of the disease, isn't it? Self over everything and everyone else. Could you turn it off, please?"

Piper looked over. "Turn off the phone?"

"Yes. It's midnight. She's probably passing out, and I don't need the all-night texts if she isn't. I have to stop being codependent. Isn't that what it's called?"

"Yeah, that's what it's called." Piper held down the power key. "Good for you."

Brook looked at the clock on the dash. "I can't believe it's so late. I can't imagine doing anything but crashing." She slid into the parking slot for the third time in as many days. Her bones hurt she was so tired.

They both dropped out of the van, and Brook was happy that nothing needed to be taken inside. There was literally no food left. As a chef, she was beyond complimented, and as a woman who could barely feel her feet, she was beyond grateful.

"I might opt for a shower and save the tub for the morning." She was barely managing to speak above a whisper. She had zero energy suddenly. Somehow, the proximity to Piper energized her just enough to realize what was happening to her heart.

"I don't blame you. You want me to go first? I'll be quick and then the room is all yours."

"I can't take your bed again. Please throw me a blanket and a corner of a rug. I'll sleep like a baby." She felt the jolt of electricity when Piper draped her arm around her shoulders and guided her down the hall.

"Absolutely not. No arguments." Piper slapped on the can lights in the hall. "Do you need clothes to sleep in?"

"Actually, I found some in the tangle of belongings I brought. Go shower, I'm fine." Brook watched as Piper stripped off her button-down shirt, leaving only a thin white tank. The muscles in her tanned shoulders created a chiseled tableau for the straps to rest on. Piper smiled as she turned back to look at Brook.

Well, at least I know I'm not dead. Brook hadn't felt that twinge of attraction in a long time. Piper was stunning and strong and capable. She needed that in her life and was grateful for the friend Piper had become. Friend. That was all she could be. She wondered if Piper would still be available when she had managed to unravel her life. She couldn't believe she was technically single.

Brook mused about the last time she wanted to walk into a woman's arms or, better yet, be touched in way that made her hot, alive, and vulnerable.

She revisited the memory of Professor Meg Morris, who had always made her heart beat a little faster. For years, she marveled at the fact that her attraction for Meg had never dwindled. Being intimate with her was bliss and cemented the bond she had thought would last forever. She hadn't noticed when it stopped, when Brook had become her caretaker instead of her partner. When her lust for Meg had inexplicably become resentment.

She connected her phone to her charger cord and thought about turning it back on. Maybe she was being vindictive or stubborn. Maybe it was a challenge to see if she would be able to divorce herself from Meg and her incessant need to be cared for. She deserved the break and, damn it, she could do this.

She extracted sweats and a T-shirt from her bag and dragged her hair into a reconstructed messy bun. Piper reappeared in the room, rubbing a towel over her damp hair, the wild dark waves beginning to reclaim their bounce.

"So much better," Piper declared as she tossed the towel over the hook. "Water is hot, towels on the sink, and I put a new bar of lavender soap in the shower, though I don't think you'll need any help relaxing."

"I think I'll be lucky if I make it out of the shower still conscious." Brook pulled her gaze from Piper, determined to contain her attraction, which had no place in her life at the moment.

"Go enjoy. I'll be in the living room if you need me."

"Thank you. For everything, Piper." Brook didn't know how to adequately tell her how much she appreciated her and the lengths she had gone to in order to save the day and her business.

"My pleasure," Piper said as she turned for the hallway.

Brook turned on the water. Goose bumps scattered down her arms as she stepped under the spray, and she wondered how many of them Piper was responsible for. She let the water pound over her for a few minutes before she began the business of actually washing the day from her skin. She fantasized about Piper stepping in behind her, her toned figure melting against her body. She shook her head to chase the thoughts from her mind and concentrated on finishing the shower, which had gone on long enough to prune her fingertips.

She toweled off and stepped into her comfortable, albeit not sexy, ensemble. She placed her towel over Piper's on the hook and headed for the living room, which was bathed in the soft light from a small lamp next to the chaise lounge.

"Just came to say good night," Brook whispered in case Piper had drifted off already.

"How was the shower?" Piper pushed upright against a pillow and shifted to one side of the cushion.

"Better than any shower I can remember having in a long time." She chuckled at the fact that the statement was probably true. Her little rental bungalow had had atrocious water pressure, and the faucets produced water that was a slightly brown color from the old pipes.

Piper patted the space next to her. "Sit for a minute."

Brook didn't think much about the feeling the proximity to Piper might spur in her weary body until she sat. She took a deep breath and fought the inappropriate thoughts that again sailed into her brain.

"You okay?" Piper asked, squeezing Brook's hand gently.

"Yeah. Just super tired." She couldn't have moved her hand if she had wanted to, which she didn't. Piper's touch was as stimulating as it was stabilizing. "Please, let me sleep on the couch."

"Too late. I'm already here. Go get in bed and enjoy the quiet, okay? No alarms."

"I can't even set one, my phone's still off." She surrendered.

"You still okay with that?" Piper was looking at her carefully.

"I think I have to be, otherwise I'll spend my life in this circle." The dizziness of that circle had cost her so much.

"I'm glad."

"I'm sure I'll get an earful when I go to get the rest of my things, but that's for tomorrow." She didn't loosen her grip on Piper's hand.

"Let me know if you want me to go look at the rental with you tomorrow," Piper offered.

"I think I'll be okay, but thanks." Brook needed to start standing alone because she knew she would be for a long time. "Good night, Piper. You're a lifesaver."

Piper leaned toward her and Brook felt herself melt into the hug. She rested her head on Piper's shoulder and unexpectedly burst into tears. She cried for everything her week had been and that her life was becoming. She hadn't meant to. She had intended a grateful good-night hug before walking back to bed but she couldn't stop herself. She managed a tearful "I'm sorry" before dissolving into another bout of sobs.

Piper tightened her grip and stroked her palm over Brook's back. "Don't you dare be sorry. You've had one hell of a week, and I'm glad you're here."

"Me too." Brook sniffled, finally able to breathe without the stuttering brought on by hysterics. She straightened and took a shuddering breath.

Piper pushed a strand of hair out of her eyes before thumbing the tears from her cheeks.

"I'm fine. I'm super tired and it just hit me all at once. That's what you get for being nice to me. Waterworks." Brook pointed at her face and forced a laugh she didn't really feel.

"You deserve people to be nice to you. Don't forget that, okay?"

The look on Piper's face made Brook's heart clutch even more. Gorgeous, of course, but that only led to the mystery of the woman she was. The woman Brook could imagine in a hundred ways other than supportive, platonic friend, but now wasn't the time. "Yeah, okay." Her eyes locked into Piper's and she couldn't tear them away.

Piper leaned into her space and her mouth found Brook's. Warm, sexy, and intoxicating. She couldn't move. Her mind screamed for her to run away, but she felt the flush of desire and a warmth that had nothing to do with friendship. Eventually her mind triumphed over her weary body that craved more of this new person in her life. She was a friend, and that's all she could be. The mantra repeated in her mind as she relished the feel of Piper's skilled tongue explored her mouth.

Brook pulled back, covering her mouth with her fingers,

holding the kiss there or perhaps stopping her from letting it happen again. She stood and hugged her arms around herself, suddenly cold from the separation.

"Good night, Piper. Sweet dreams." She pulled her eyes from Piper, who looked jolted by her abrupt exit.

"Sleep well." Piper's voice was hoarse.

Brook leaned her head against the bedroom door she closed behind her. What the hell was she thinking? Five minutes out of a fifteen-year relationship and she was sobbing in the arms of someone else and kissing her? She wasn't technically cheating, but the effect was the same. No matter what, she owed Meg more than this. She wanted to exit the relationship with her dignity and leave Meg with what was left of hers.

She pulled the covers to her chin, and despite her speeding thoughts, racing pulse, and distinct wash of arousal, she succumbed to the exhaustion of the day.

CHAPTER TWELVE

Piper heard Brook moving around the bedroom. She had replayed the night before a thousand times. What she would give to kiss Brook properly and completely. To hold her before exploring what she knew could be between them. But Brook had made it quite clear that she wasn't in the same place, certainly not now. Piper was just as unavailable, albeit for different reasons.

She poured coffee and stacked the last of the bowls and trays onto the island ready to return them to Paul before the Devereauxs' return. Answering questions about the events of the past few days wasn't something Piper was prepared to do.

Her thoughts wandered to Vanessa and when she might be home. It was a strange place for her now. As much as she had thought she was content to continue living this way, an evening with Brook reminded her how being truly connected with someone felt. She realized that she needed an exit plan to come sooner rather than later. Not because of Brook's entry into her life—well, not *just* because of it. She wanted more. In what form, she couldn't begin to imagine, but she wanted more than stolen moments with someone else's wife. It wasn't about being in a relationship, it was about the freedom to make such choices without worrying about which part of her rented life would get yanked away in retaliation.

She wondered if Brook liked pancakes. She scanned her pantry for the ingredients when Brook, clutching her bag, began searching frantically around the kitchen.

"What's wrong?" Piper couldn't imagine what had transformed the exhausted chef from the last night into the frazzled woman before her.

"I have to go. Where are my keys?" She must have looked in their general direction ten times but never managed to focus.

Piper pointed to the counter where she had left them the night before. "Brook, what's going on?" She stepped toward her.

"They took Meg to the hospital last night. The neighbors called an ambulance and she's been at the hospital all alone since then. That's why she was calling and texting me and I just ignored her. I'm the most selfish person I know." Tears spilled down her face and she clutched the keys stiffly in her hand. Piper could see white patches where the metal edges pressed between her fingers.

Piper clasped her shoulders. "How is she now?"

"I don't know. Her mother just got there. She said that she was unresponsive in the ambulance. For all I know she could have died, and I wouldn't have known since I didn't even turn on my phone."

"You aren't responsible for this, Brook." Piper hated watching what the guilt of codependency did to someone in the mire of it.

"I could have been home with her. It was selfish to leave her alone. I'm all she has."

"That's a lie you're telling yourself so you don't have to blame her." Piper repeated the line her therapist used on her many years ago during her ex's crash to the rocky bottom of her addiction.

She barely focused on Piper when she pulled open the door. "I have to go to her. Goodbye, Piper."

Brook nearly ran to the van and Piper watched it vanish as Brook sped away. She tried to sort the myriad of feelings Brook had left in her wake. She was fearful that Brook would use this as an excuse to take Meg back. She felt the pang of memory. Kelly had been found outside their home with a .42 blood alcohol level. She should have died and nearly did. Piper had taken her back that time. Nothing had changed except Piper's hatred for their relationship and the prison Piper was in that stopped her from living. She hoped Brook could stop the same trajectory before it consumed her.

She wandered back inside, unsure where to start her day since, truth be told, she had imagined spending at least part of it with Brook.

She pulled two sticks of string cheese from the dairy drawer in the fridge and poured coffee into a tall black mug that sported a large driver above the words "weapons of grass destruction" in shiny gold lettering. A gift from a client who thought it was unique. She appreciated the gesture, but her collection of novelty golf merchandise was almost out of hand. It was a long way from the intimate pancake breakfast she had imagined consuming with Brook.

She strode to the sunroom as if some invisible force was pulling her. She fingered the coarse surface of a blank white canvas as she tilted it onto the new easel. She stared at the sharp white against the thickly lacquered frame. Without much thought she reached over and used her bare foot to nudge open her ancient rickety easel and dropped the fresh canvas onto the brackets of it instead.

More satisfied with the feel of it, she knelt on the cloth-covered floor and studied the mound of paints in a plastic basket. She pushed it over, causing the lot of them to spill onto the floor. The shades had to be perfect. She pawed through the contents selecting reds and oranges, yellows and golds. An energizing wave of inspiration washed over her as she squeezed out the earthy rainbow of pigment onto her pallet.

The first stroke of red and yellow produced alternating swaths of the primary colors and a murky orange band she highlighted in a cleaner, almost white hue. Piper focused on the arch and the texture. She layered and highlighted, retouched and replaced colors that refused to comply with the image in her mind.

By noon, Piper had cranked up her music and attempted to drown out the world that threatened her vision of what this piece should be, had to be. A haphazard array of discarded canvas in various stages of starts and stops littered the room around her, but she kept at it. Six attempts. Normally she would simply repaint them white and begin again, but somehow it had to be pristine.

Orange into the reds. No, gold first, maybe an unexpected hint of white? Nope. *Stop ruining this*, Piper scolded herself, painted, and scolded again before plunging her brushes and pallet knives into a fat Mason jar full of murky water. She began digging through a crate of her old paint supplies that were nowhere near the caliber she was using. Her first brushes. The ones she collected and scrounged when she was first finding her style and honing her talent. The shafts were coated in a mosaic of past projects long discarded or given away, their bristles a bit wild from use and lack thereof.

After hours of honing color and stroke, it was five thirty by the time she settled on, and was then possessed by, a painting that finally had potential.

A rush of brush strokes at the center created the last of the color and shapes that spoke to the vision of what she had intended. It was raw and deep and somehow commanding her to finish. She touched and retouched the canvas with the stubby nylon brush nearly frozen in her cramped hand.

She hadn't eaten. The second cup of coffee she managed on the return from her only bathroom break had gone cold in the mug.

It was worth it. It finally looked like the image in her mind. A perfectly imperfect projection. She stepped back to appraise the finished product only to realize that there was nothing finished about it. She stepped back to the painting, adjusting, adding, and appraising again and again.

Like an author who writes the last chapter of her life's work, the magic was spent. Laid out for whoever wished to consume it despite the intensely personal gift meant for just one set of eyes. She felt as if she could never create more of a masterpiece, as if she could accurately refer to *any* of her work as a masterpiece, but the emotion she had exhaled into this painting was everything she had.

She finally felt like an artist embracing her muse instead of a hack forcing some sad sophomoric attempt. Piper walked to check her phone, shaking herself from the high of working at her craft for so long. Nothing.

No text, no voice mail, no missed calls. Brook had to know something. She could call, but what if something awful was happening? What would she say? It was all too confusing and yet another reminder why the specter of a relationship felt cloaking and impossible. They weren't even dating, and Piper felt like any move she made would be the wrong one.

Her fingers hovered over the keys. Should she call? Would Brook welcome the concern or rebel at the intrusion? Fucking pathetic. She selected Brook's contact, and her thumb threatened to press the dial key and then the text key. Which one? Neither? Both? She hated herself at that moment. Then she selected to text.

I know you're busy, but I wanted to see how you were. And Meg of course.

To her surprise, Brook replied swiftly.

Okay. In a regular room. On fluids, mostly dehydration now. Scary to say the least.

You okay? She could ask that now that the omen of Meg's death or brain damage was apparently off the table.

Fine. Sorry I was a little crazed this morning.

You need anything?

Winning lottery ticket and a few hundred clients.

How about ten new clients and a little quiet time to start?

Definitely doable. I'll have the house to myself tonight.

Did you decide to stay?

Piper held her breath. Not for herself but for every unmet resolution she could remember from her own dubious dance in the past.

Just until Meg gets released. I did manage to slip away and go see that place. Small but also definitely doable.

You going take it?

Yup. They agreed to rent it to me. And guess what?

She loved that Brook felt like they were at least on their friend keel again.

What?

There is a small storefront right below it. A little cafe is closing, and their lease is up in four months!

Ever feel like some things are meant to be?

Piper was smiling at the news. At the new start for Brook and the possibilities she hoped for her own life one day. If Brook could make a fresh start and take a leap of faith, then surely Piper could too. She was hopeful this meant that Brook wouldn't take Meg back.

Actually, yeah.

So stoked for you. Glad I stowed away in your kitchen…you're pretty awesome, Brook.

Piper though how juvenile that probably sounded.

Thank you for everything. You're a great friend.

There's the word again. Friend. That was obviously all Brook wanted, and despite their kiss, their connection, it was all Piper was in a position to be, given the myriad of complications framing her life, not to mention Brook's. She would settle for friend. She had to. She would file the scorching kiss away for private fantasies.

Hope you can get some rest. Good night Brook.

Night

"Piper! I'm back!" The voice was loud and shrill in the wake of the simple silence and whisper of welcome fantasy.

"Back here," Piper spoke loud enough to be heard, but couldn't muster much more enthusiasm for the return to normal she hated to admit was her normal.

"Hi, gorgeous. Did you miss me?" Vanessa draped her arms around Piper's neck and pressed her body against the length of Piper's.

"Of course I did." Piper wasn't lying, not really. She did enjoy Vanessa, there was just a limit to what they could be and a limit to how much Piper wanted to continue to overlook the surface of it all. Despite a friend status blinking in neon with Brook, there was something about a future that made her crave a new normal. She craved a new way to live where she wasn't lying about who and what she was at every turn. The craving was colored more completely with Brook in it.

"I wish you had been on the trip with us." Vanessa punctuated the words with loud kisses along her cheeks.

"Something tells me that Frank wouldn't have felt the same, V." There was a limit to Frank's indulgence of their relationship.

"He was barely there." She flapped her hand dismissively.

"Apparently, my birthday trip was just a write-off meeting to contract some new client." She managed a nonchalant look, but her eyes burned with the disappointment of yet another surrender.

"That sucks. Did you at least do something you enjoyed?"

"Sure. The usual mani-pedi, facial, massage, sunbathing. Frank had a meeting with Kenneth, so I spent some time admiring the Berksoy Mansion on Seven Mile Beach."

Piper realized that she didn't know who any of these people or places were and didn't care to ask since none of the names in this or a hundred other episodes of the Devereaux saga ever changed the prevailing chronicle of aimless privilege.

"That sounds like fun. How was it?" Piper couldn't imagine it being fun, but Vanessa seemed impressed.

"The house is just huge. You would have thought it was over-the-top." She gave Piper a pitying look as if she was missing so much in life by not being impressed by excess.

"If you say so, then I probably would have."

"So…" Vanessa squeezed her shoulders up and wiggled excitedly like a small child about to get a present.

"So…" Piper couldn't imagine what was coming.

"I have a surprise for you." Vanessa reached for her phone and searched through her texts.

"It's your birthday, I'm supposed to be giving out the surprises." Receiving presents was always uncomfortable for Piper, and Vanessa had no sense of what too much looked like, so they made her even more awkward.

"I have the *best* surprise, though."

"Okay." Piper tried to match her enthusiasm.

"What do you want most in the world?" Her eyes were wide.

"World peace and a mortgage-free ranch where I can rescue animals and paint?" Piper mimed holding a microphone while sweeping imaginary tresses behind her shoulder in her best beauty pageant imitation.

"I'm serious, Piper." Vanessa's voice pitched as her eyes danced with impatience.

"Okay, sorry. I guess to be able to paint full-time." It was and had always been the essence of her dreams.

"And the more people who see your work, the closer that becomes." She rolled her hand in a "hurry up" gesture.

"Sure." Piper had absolutely no idea where this was going.

"So, one of Frank's associates is an art collector. They've moved in the same circles for ages with oil and gas jobs but his wife, who used to work for Gale and Harding, really loves art."

Piper thought Vanessa might have noticed a glazed look in her eyes since she sped up and abandoned the business detail.

"Apparently, they wanted to diversify and bought a local business." Vanessa looked expectantly at Piper.

"Great?" Piper was really trying not to be testy but this trip down business mogul lane wasn't helping her focus.

Vanessa sighed loudly for affect. "An art gallery, Piper. They bought an art gallery." Vanessa squealed and hopped in place while she waited for Piper's reaction.

"I assume you talked them into looking at a piece of mine?" It was exciting, but the only thing Piper could imagine was the strings that would come with it and the exorbitant commissions she would have to pay.

"I am thoroughly disappointed that you think so little of my abilities." Vanessa's mock pout was familiar.

"Okay. You convinced them to take and display some of my work." Piper smiled and hugged her. This truly was an amazing opportunity. "You're awesome, V."

"I should be insulted, but I just can't keep this going." Vanessa walked toward the sunroom and stood next to two finished canvases leaning against the wall. "These two pieces," she was clearly pausing for dramatic effect, "these two pieces will be joining," she stepped along the banks of artwork in various stages of completeness, "this piece, and this piece and twenty-one more of your paintings will be featured at the gallery's grand opening during art week, one month from today."

"Wait. What?" Piper was trying to imagine being shown at a

real gallery. Devereaux cocktail parties were one thing. They were sort of a captive audience. But real art buyers in a real gallery? *Holy shit.*

"Yes. You will be the resident artist in a high-end gallery downtown. Not only will you have a huge installation for the opening, you will be featured in the Abstract and Modern display *permanently.* They want to see all your work and will display as many as twenty-five at a time. Of course, they'll sell, so you'll have to keep up." She clasped her hands under her chin, waiting for Piper's reaction.

Piper scanned the room of completed projects. "We have a way to go before I run out." She chuckled and stared at Vanessa. "Is this for real?"

"You bet your very talented ass it is. As soon as Mr. and Mrs. Davinroy started talking about his new project, I couldn't believe it. Frank looked at me because he knew I was going to start talking about you. I thought he would be mad that I steered the business conversation away from tech, oil, and overseas shipments, but he said it would be good for him to diversify as well and…"

"Whoa, V. You're making me dizzy." Piper laughed and pulled Vanessa into her arms again. "So you're telling me that I'm going to be at a gallery. Like, all the time." She had always thought that, maybe, one day, it would happen for her, but she was still trying to process the possibilities.

"That's what I'm telling you. Frank and I invested in the gallery and we're sponsoring their grand opening. They expected a small soft opening, but I told them we needed to go big. This is it, Piper." Vanessa framed Piper's cheeks in her palms and kissed her triumphantly.

"Holy shit. Did I say that already? Holy shit. Holy shit." Piper spun Vanessa in a circle before lifting her off the floor and then did it again. "I can never repay you."

"You don't owe me. You're good, Piper. Better than good. People want to feel your work, own a piece of it. You deserve it. I'm happy you're happy." Vanessa smiled broadly as she watched the news affect Piper.

"You have no idea. I mean, I knew I wanted it to be about my art full-time, but I didn't know what that would look like and now it's here and real and awesome and…shit, when is this happening?" She raised her eyebrows expectantly and felt mild panic set in. "How much time do I get?"

"It's not a jail sentence. You have more than enough work to give them. If they want more, they'll ask. Peter Moffet is the curator. The Davinroys brought him in from Houser-Young in the city. His pedigree alone makes this a huge deal."

"I've been there a hundred times. It's one of my favorite galleries. They must be paying him a lot."

"Charles and Elizabeth said that they didn't want to get lost in the shuffle of new businesses. They want Paris Urban to be special and make a splash." Vanessa transformed when she talked about public relations and business. Piper wondered if following her passion would one day be more important than being Frank's overindulged wife.

"It's called Paris Urban? Are they French?"

"No, English actually. Elizabeth said the first gallery she ever went to was in Nice. She was talking to one of the curators and told them that she wanted to go to some art spaces in Paris. The woman sniffed at her and told her that Paris art was just too urban. I guess the experience stuck with her."

"That's kind of an awesome story for their brochure, huh? Will I get to meet them?"

"As soon as they get back from their business trip." Vanessa surveyed the canvases creating a wainscot effect around the room. "We won't be part of the day-to-day operations, but I think they're going to do great things. With Peter's experience and their eye for talent, it's only a matter of time."

Vanessa was firmly in business mode, and the moment of celebration was tempered by the demands of success and posturing.

"This is different." She turned to indicate Piper's new piece viced into the easel in the center of the room. "I'm not sure it fits the theme of your others. Let's start with them."

"Sure." Piper didn't tell her that the painting she was passing on wasn't for sale. It would be a gift one day. It wasn't for the public. It was personal.

Vanessa pressed her mouth firmly against Piper's. "We're going to blow up the art world, baby."

"I'll settle for a gentle rocking," Piper joked as she tried to assimilate what was happening. She couldn't wait to call Brook. She would, of course, wait for Brook's world to settle, but she was the only person she wanted to share the news with.

"You know…" Vanessa walked slowly backward down the hall toward the bedroom, her stiletto heels tapping a cadence on the floor. "We have about an hour before anyone will miss me. Maybe we could celebrate together? I've missed you."

"Celebrations can be fun." Piper followed her down the hall to her room when Vanessa's phone began to ring.

Piper caught the name Ellen Warner on the screen before Vanessa silenced it and chucked it onto the mattress, her dress followed, and Piper gave her what she was demanding despite the odd sensation that Brook wouldn't approve, not to mention it suddenly felt like a dirty trade-off—a chance at success, acknowledged with sex.

CHAPTER THIRTEEN

B rook stopped inside the small apartment with the last suitcase full of her clothes and all of the last-minute items that never have a place in a move. She found a candle, a hairclip, a pair of socks, and a half-open bottle of ketchup amongst the treasures that represented the dust bunnies of her former life.

In only a week she had packed everything, and Meg's mother had hired someone to clear Meg's things from the house. The echo throughout the small sagging cottage had been loud. Her copy of the house key next to Meg's on the kitchen counter had been the only blemish on the clear surface. She pictured the vacant remnant of the last chapter in her relationship. When Meg's mother found out that Brook was leaving her daughter, she was unapologetic when she asked Brook how it felt to "abandon her responsibilities." In truth, she wasn't sure.

Meg's text messages had continued, frequently at first, bobbing between desperate, pleading, loving, and angry. There wasn't much left to say, so the few conversations they had embarked on just made Brook sad. Her new home boasted a lone couch, a mattress, and her clothing. She mused about whether they felt like rewards in a hard-won victory or just salvage from the ashes of a fire.

She remembered Piper's words about losing your soul in the flames of a relationship. Since she felt hopeful and excited for the journey ahead, she hoped she had managed to escape in time. She visited the memories of Piper and their forty-eight-hour odyssey together and then chased the memory away. Their interactions since had been sparse and casual. Brook had told Piper that she was too busy to text the last time, even though she hadn't been. She hadn't dared embark on one more emotion, despite the fact that the ones Piper brought up were pleasant. She needed to stand on her own right now, not use someone else as a crutch.

Brook unpacked the kitchen boxes, although the bulk of her utensils would live in the tiny storefront space below her one day soon. The café was already out, months early. She couldn't wait to cook there, create there. The test would be a cocktail party next week and an anniversary party she owed to a lead from the wine festival. She could make it. She would make it. She knew that now.

She dropped the ketchup into the door compartment in the small fridge and took out the Chardonnay she had bought on the way there. On the way home. This was her home. She stared at the predominantly empty space, and peace suffused her. No more arguments, no more spilled whiskey or evenings full of dread.

She raised her glass as if to acknowledge the silence and the future. The wine tasted like this victory felt, sharp and strong. Her phone chirped from atop a box in the bedroom and she walked slowly to retrieve it, surveying every inch of her new space along the way.

How are you?

Brook's stomach jumped. How many times had she thought about Piper in the last few days, even hours? Wondered where she was or what she was doing? She had driven the feelings away but knowing Piper was obviously thinking of her made them hurry back.

Trying to figure out why I own 27 forks and 2 spoons. LOL
Don't invite me for soup and ice cream at the same time.

Brook laughed out loud and tapped in a quick reply. *Isn't pizza and ice cream traditional move-in food?*

What time shall I bring the pizza?

The message accompanied a selfie of Piper in a golf cart smiling from under the brim of a black ball cap. Her eyes glinted in the sun and Brook thought she was stunning. She stared at the screen and moderated the internal debate regarding the state of her new home, the message she would be sending Piper, her intense desire to see her again, and what Meg would think if she knew how much she already wanted to move on with someone new.

Brook knew it didn't matter what Meg thought, but the wounds were much too fresh for anything even hinting at a new relationship.

Maybe one day soon. When I get my bearings.

What were bearings anyway? It sounded good and gave her time to figure out the true nature of her feelings for Piper and what she wanted to do about them.

Sure. Have a good night. I hope we can spend some time together soon.

It sounded like Piper was sad. But then again, how did one sound sad over text?

"God, now I'm codependent over the woman who told me I was codependent. I'm an idiot." She realized she was talking out loud and decided to stop thinking for the moment. Instead, she snuck down to the kitchen that would soon be hers.

She surveyed the space, which was in desperate need of tidying. The old wood floor could use a good clean and a bit of staining. She wanted a couple of comfy chairs where clients could sit and review the photos of her work that she could load onto a wall screen. She daydreamed about being able to afford some artwork. Maybe Piper had something small she could start with. A large corner cried out for some color. Signs for a gift shop, an upscale restaurant, and some kind of gallery opening at the end of the block told her that she was lucky to have found the space when she did, as it was sure to be a hot commodity one day soon.

She couldn't help but imagine creating there. Adding shelves and displays for what she hoped might be a retail space where brides, event planners, and party throwers could come and taste her food, browse her menu, or sketch out a lavish celebration featuring Brook's cooking. She was getting ahead of herself but the dream, no longer distant and fuzzy, seemed as if it were within reach.

She would invite Piper to see it. She wanted her to share it. After all, she had helped save Brook's dream, hadn't she? Without the success from the Warners' party, she would never have the bookings or even the prospects of them. She could never repay Piper for helping make that happen. If she was honest with herself, repaying Piper wasn't the thought that was mostly on her mind. Kissing her thoroughly was. Feeling Piper's arms around her again was.

She imagined the space where they might both be creating a masterpiece one day, breaking only momentarily for a kiss or a quick meal, knowing that they could do anything together. Talk about kicking a fantasy down the path. She scolded herself for being quite ridiculous.

Her phone chirped again. Rose Snelling was confirming next week's cocktail reception. Something about confirming her next job and the paycheck to follow made the investment in her future that much sweeter.

❖

Piper abandoned the phone and marveled at the transformation Jack, the photographer, was making in her studio. Drapes and light canopies set the scene of an art studio where apparently no painting had ever occurred, given the blinding white fabric everywhere.

He chose the new easel, of course, claiming the other one would look too messy in the pictures he needed for the "package" shots. He staged painting after painting, requiring no assistance with the mechanics of it, and Piper wandered to the kitchen for a beer.

She checked her social media accounts and glanced for the hundredth time at Paris Urban's coming soon page. She checked her savings account balance and tried to calculate how much she needed for the next phase of her plan. She could live well for a year, decently for two, and hand to mouth for three. The closer her goals became, the less interested she was in postponing them any longer. She skimmed through rental ads, studio space listings, and some used car postings since she and her borrowed Bimmer would soon be parted.

"Piper. We need to do the artist portrait now. Can you come here?" Jack called over his shoulder as he tilted the umbrella in several different directions.

"The what?" Piper stared at him.

"Artist portrait. I just took all the catalog shots, but we need the mailer photos. You at work, a short bio, a head shot, you know, standard gallery stuff."

Oh, well, standard gallery stuff, of course. Piper smiled at the sarcastic inner dialogue she had with herself. She had dressed in black slacks and a black V-neck T-shirt, wanting to be presentable for the photographer, but had no intention of anything other than her paintings being photographed.

"Are you sure we can't skip that part? I'm not prepared for—"

"The marketing group gave me a list of shots I'm supposed to take." He held a wrinkled sheet of printer paper as proof. "I don't go back with these, I don't get paid, so let's get this show on the road, okay?"

"No room for negotiation huh, Jack?" Piper offered him a cheeky smile.

"Not in my world. Do as you're told, and no one gets hurt."

"Your world looks very similar to mine, my friend." Piper sat on a black stool he had placed in front of the empty easel. He riffled through her jars of brushes until he came up with a new black chisel tip and handed it to her. All at once she felt like a visitor in her own studio.

"Jack, I'm not telling you how to do your job or anything, but the stool hasn't got any paint on it. This brush has never been used and the easel looks like it just came out of an art store. I'm wearing dress clothes. No one will ever believe that I'm painting anything."

"It's not about what's there, it's about what they want to see. As an artist, you think you would know that. People aren't buying what you saw when you painted, they're buying what they felt when *they* saw it. They're buying the pretty, not the gritty. I don't have to tell you that." He gestured at the vaulted ceiling and sweeping views through the bay of windows.

"Yeah, I suppose so. Anyway, I don't live here, I'm just visiting." She marveled at how freeing that statement felt. She didn't have a home, but she would. Soon.

He tilted her head, angled her shoulders, turned her hips, and pinched her fingers just so around the brush. She thought she likely looked like a well-dressed contortionist instead of an artist. She tried to imagine the picture and then tried not to.

"Stay just like that, don't move." She froze in place and heard him rummaging behind her. He pulled the palette stand to her side and squeezed some dark umber, cadmium yellow, and crimson red onto the surface. Piper, shocked by the quantities, immediately began formulating a painting she could embark on to save the wasted pigment.

He stood between her and the easel, locking a canvas into the grips. "I really like this one. I think you really captured a mood here. What's it called?" He stepped aside and Piper saw Brook's painting.

"Wait. This one isn't for sale." She forgot her pose and twisted around to find him.

"Doesn't matter. It will translate well in print. The shading will work even in black and white. I have to think of those things. Why don't you let me be the artist right now, okay?"

She wanted to explain why this felt like a violation. Why this one was a secret shared with a special person. When she tried to formulate the story it sounded lame, so she just stared into it. She could feel Brook again, when she had told her the story. When they worked so hard side by side and she found in her what she always hoped to find in someone she could make her forever person. Brook, Piper realized at that moment, should be her forever person. She had many goals, but suddenly that was the most important. Unanticipated and important.

"…it called?"

"Sorry, what?" She jerked back from her daydream and heard Jack asking her something.

"What's that painting called?"

"*Brook's Peace*." Piper stared at it. It was the first painting she had named herself. The first steps on her new journey were unexpected but exhilarating. She knew the relatively few hours she had spent with Brook were the universe telling her to stop compromising her truth to be comfortable.

"Hey, Jack?"

"Yeah." He was distracted by his light, now sagging on the pole.

"If I told you that you could make triple what you make now, by doing something you didn't like, would you do it?"

"Nope." He shifted her this way and that, setting up the shot, careful to light the painting properly.

"Quick answer." She stared at the elk horns shining against the sunset rainbow in the painting and was proud of the detail she had managed.

"Nah, easy one." He planted her bare feet on the footrest under the seat and pressed her knees apart to frame the easel. "One feeds your bank account, the other feeds your soul."

"You know what, Jack? You're a pretty smart guy."

"I've got a fifteen-year-old boy who needs to hear that. I'm going to call and make you tell him that before I leave."

"You're on." Piper laughed.

"Sit still and look like you just painted something you're proud of." He bent to look in the camera.

"Easy one, Jack." Piper knew where she belonged now as she gazed into the landscape she had created, that Brook necessitated. She wanted to tell Brook about her day. She wanted to tell Brook everything. She wanted to ask her about her life and what she could do to make her happy. And show how much she loved her. That. That was clearer to her than any other decision she was making. She wanted to tell Brook how she felt, but she would need a plan, one that wouldn't drive her away. She stared at the painting, doing as Jack asked, her heart racing.

Piper's phone rang as the photographer threw a wave out his truck window and pulled away. She walked to the patio overlooking the green and answered. Vanessa's whispered voice was barely audible.

"Sorry I missed the shoot, Piper. Frank's deal nearly fell through and he brought the partners in for drinks. I just couldn't get away." Vanessa sound simultaneously irritated and empowered by the requirement that she be there to schmooze her husband's business dealings.

"It's totally fine. I managed all by myself. I wore a halter top and Daisy Dukes that said 'sexy' across the ass. Good, right?"

"Why do I bother?" She heard Vanessa laugh too loudly before she caught herself.

"It's a mystery." Piper was somewhat giddy and somehow freer than she had felt in ages. The smell of the fresh-cut grass and the chorus of crickets made her appreciate the gifts she had been given, but she knew it was her time to find a new way to move through her next chapter.

"I miss you."

"I miss you." It was true, in a way. She missed the Vanessa who used to remember having a solid foot in reality. The woman who longed to be whole and who still hoped for the love of her life. She had given up even talking about it, and Piper had watched her melt into the world of too much stuff and too little soul. Piper wondered how she would cope when Piper was gone. It was so close now. "Let's sneak off for some pizza and beer one night. Like we used to?" A little taste of her old self might mean getting Vanessa to feel alive again, to see what she was missing in life.

"Piper, you know the opening is coming up. I bought a fabulous Tom Ford that would show every ounce of pizza, so let's have a spinach salad and a little wine instead?"

"Sounds incredibly boring, V." Piper casually kicked the corner of the too-white drop cloth and saw the blotched and stained one underneath.

"You'll thank me when you see the McQueen pantsuit I bought you."

"V, I don't need new clothes. I'm a starving artist, remember?"

"This is your moment to shine, and as much as you hate the spotlight and the money and the show of it all, it's the reason that this is going to work for you, okay?"

To the extent that it was a necessary evil, Piper agreed. She pressed her palm against the railing and listened to the chorus of voices in the background. Could she do this on her own? Without Vanessa running interference, prepping and primping her every time? Doubt began to set in. Frank's booming baritone demanded Vanessa's presence.

"Got to go. Call you later?" The whisper accompanied the ubiquitous clip of her heels on the hardwood.

"Sure. Later."

She decided that continuing to analyze the transformation happening in her mind wasn't useful. Changing into paint clothes and using the fresh paint Jack had left on her palette would be much more productive. A heavy lesson schedule for the coming week would likely make this her last chance for some uninterrupted creative time like this.

By the time she was seated on her real stool, behind her worn easel, the sun was bleeding into the horizon, creating a fan of oranges and yellows across the bleached white walls. She manipulated a small chunk of charcoal into an arch that would represent the swell of Brook's full hip. It wasn't intentional to paint her again, it just happened. She had become Piper's muse, the predominant figure that escaped from her brush each time she attempted to create a figure. She used a thinner piece to outline her full mouth. Before Piper pushed back from the canvas, a scant twenty-five minutes later, Brook stood fully formed on a sixty-inch canvas. She had much farther to go, she knew, but she was proud of the easy progress and she needed to continue.

At midnight, Piper forced herself to walk away from the woman she had to compel back into her life. The painting of Brook was incomplete, and the decision Piper's heart was making wasn't far behind. Her goals hadn't changed, but the picture of her future now included another person. She saw Brook standing next to her.

CHAPTER FOURTEEN

A long day of lessons in the heat had made Piper weary and hungry. She contemplated what was likely in her fridge and still edible, determining that she would likely be much better off with takeout and a beer. As she slipped her wallet into her backpack, her phone rang.

"Hi, V." Piper threw a wave to Leo and felt the weight of her backpack hit against her spine.

"I need a favor." Vanessa's voice sounded rushed.

"Shoot."

"Frank got called out of town this afternoon and now he can't go to the reception tonight."

"Okay."

"Please go with me. I know it's late notice and, as a rule, you hate this kind of thing, but it will be short, and I don't want to go alone."

Piper scraped her front teeth over her bottom lip trying to figure out how she could produce a plausible excuse Vanessa would buy. She took too long.

"Please, Pipe. Cocktails, heavy hors d'oeuvres, and home by nine, I promise."

Piper was ashamed by the fact that the promise of good food someone else had to facilitate made the decision to go significantly easier.

"When does it start?"

"Seven. I'll pick you up at ten till."

"Okay, what's the dress code for this little shindig?"

"Dress pants and that great paisley shirt would be nice."

That was Vanessa-speak for "wear exactly that." "I'm on it. Usual suspects, I assume?" Piper couldn't decide if knowing people would make it worse or better.

"Probably some you will recognize. It's a thank-you reception all for the people who helped with the homeless charity ball last month."

"Only that crowd would figure out how to spend as much money congratulating themselves in a mansion as they raised for people without a house."

"Don't be a snot, Piper. I'll see you in an hour."

The phone flashed back to her home screen, indicating Vanessa had hung up. Piper slid the phone into the pocket of her shorts and ambled toward the guest house.

❖

Brook unloaded the last of the items from her van onto the metal cart before pulling it around back to make room for more guests. Her van smelled like onions, cheese, and chocolate, and she briefly mused about whether she did too. She had determined that great signature items were going to be her calling card and the thing that kept getting her invited to do more jobs. Onion tarts, potato puffs, and tiny mousse cups accompanied the standard fare of crudité and fruit-cheese pairings. Rose Snelling was standing in the entryway of her kitchen, appraising the trays Brook had already assembled.

"Everything look okay, Mrs. Snelling?"

"Yes. It looks fabulous and it smells even better. You know, I tried almost everything at Ellen's, and I can't wait to try it all again." She rubbed her palms together as she eyed the platters.

"So glad people are getting to know my food." Brook counted

on three or four jobs like this one to help her live. One or two extras would feed the savings account earmarked to take her business to the next level.

The sound of a doorbell summoned the hostess from the kitchen and Brook continued to feed pastries into the oven. Squealed greetings and celebratory toasts echoed from the front, but she had no desire to join in. She was finally doing what she loved on her terms, and this was enough. Simply, perfectly enough.

She filled mousse cups from a pastry bag and had a brief flash of Piper at two a.m. in her kitchen filling a myriad of the same cups that had been strewn around the counters. Brook refused to continue to reminisce about how much more fun the prep had been when they had done it together.

It was untenable and completely impractical but, damn, it had been fun. No, it had been sexy and like being part of a team again. She tried to steer her mind from the kiss, the intimacy, and the heat between them. It wasn't time, right? Brook had barely settled into the new place and was terrified every day that she could lose it all. Her remnant relationship with Meg consisted of varying degrees of hatred, desperation, and pleading. The messages she had received today just felt invasive. If there had been some degree of remorse or contrition, she might have felt bad; as it was, she just felt assaulted. She would save further analysis of the women she wished both in and out of her life for another time.

She loaded two silver trays and headed for the dining room.

❖

"Stop looking so grumpy, Piper. Nice food, great wine, and a chance to spend time together. I would think at least one of those would warrant a smile, no?"

"Not grumpy in the slightest. The food part sounds awesome, actually, I'm starving." She caught the exaggerated pout she expected when she didn't mention spending time with Vanessa as the element she was looking forward to first and foremost. "And of course, I like getting to hang out with you, don't be silly. I think it was just a long day in the sun. Thank you for inviting me, V." She didn't have to force the smile that placated her dinner companion.

"Better." She smirked and turned into the driveway of a smaller home, modest by Shadow Glass standards but beautiful nonetheless. Vanessa parked behind a couple emerging from a small Mercedes. Piper vaguely recognized the woman in a shawl grasping at her husband's elbow.

Vanessa waved as Piper met her at the driver's side and shut the door behind her.

"Ready?" Vanessa briefly glanced over the length of Piper's body and shot her a flirtatious smile.

"Sure. Find me food, woman." Piper smiled and briefly squeezed Vanessa's arm once she was relatively sure that no one was around to see them.

"Try not to knock anyone down on your way to the food table, okay?" Vanessa walked slowly over the uneven pavers, grabbing Piper's arm for balance. She released it just as quickly when another car approached from behind.

"I can't promise anything." Piper pulled at the front of her shirt and tucked in the back.

Vanessa had no time to respond before the door swung open and a petite woman sporting a round blond helmet for hair grabbed both of Vanessa's hands.

"Do come in. It's fabulous to see you." She swept her arm in a welcoming gesture.

"And you, Rose. Do you remember Piper?" Vanessa's smooth and practiced society voice floated off her tongue.

"Oh yes. The artist in residence at your house, correct?" If there was any allusion to their actual relationship, it wasn't overt.

"For another month, and then she will be the artist in residence at the Paris Urban Gallery on Fourth," Vanessa said proudly.

"Elizabeth's new gallery? Wow, Piper, congratulations. The opening is quite the buzz around the city." Rose Snelling framed Piper's shoulders with both hands and squeezed.

"Thank you very much. It's an incredible opportunity." Piper knew the game. It came too easily now. "I couldn't have done it without Vanessa."

"She is one of a kind, certainly." The platitude seemed genuine. "Will you have a drink? We have some fabulous food in the dining room. Please help yourself."

Vanessa guided Piper away from the door. "Nicely done, Piper. I'll get you a glass of wine I think you'll like."

Piper couldn't help but feel like a slightly defective pedigree dog deserving of a nice Snausage for her performance at the dog show finals.

"Sounds great. Can I get you some food?" She was hungry and already tired of the game that had started only moments ago.

"None for me, thanks. But I know you're about to eat your arm, so go." Vanessa flapped her hand, dismissing Piper to the dining room.

Piper wasted no time heading for the table. She had seen something that looked delicious pass her by on a guest's plate and picked up her own plate immediately. Before she had a good grasp on the silver tongs, she recognized the smell and the tiny signature swirl on the potato puff. Brook. She looked up to find the woman she had begun to believe was a part of a dream.

"I'd know your puffs anywhere." Unintended double-entendre aside, Piper thought the food was a close second to the woman who made it.

"I bet you say that to all the girls." A smile lit Brook's face.

"Ha. God, it's good to see you. Are you all settled?" Piper didn't ask what she wanted to. *Are you going back to Meg? Do you ever think about me? Do you ever think about that kiss? Can I hide out in your kitchen again?*

"Believe it or not, between all the jobs I've been booking, I haven't done much in the way of decorating. This is my fourth job this month for Shadow Glass clients. I can pay my rent next month already. I just can't believe it." Brook backed into the kitchen, never taking her eyes off Piper.

Piper followed. She could hear the ringing doorbell and happy voices at the actual party, but this was where she wanted to be.

"I'm happy for you." She *was* incredibly happy for Brook. She was also jealous that she was achieving her freedom to live her dream and regretted that she hadn't been a part of it. Not yet.

"Thanks. Part of me knows that I owe jobs like this to you, at least in part." She indicated the crowd of trays and half-cut fruit decorating every surface in the kitchen.

"Yeah, that was me. Taught you to cook, schmoozed people, won them over with my charms." Piper laughed and snatched a potato puff from a baking sheet just out of the oven.

"You saved my proverbial bacon is what you did, and you know it."

"I had more fun playing in the kitchen with you than I remember having ever." Piper forgot her appetite for a moment and could only recall forty-eight hours with someone who made her heart beat faster and who made her brain a little soft. "Probably shouldn't have said that out loud."

"It was pretty fun, despite the drama of it all." Brook looked like she meant it.

"So, can you tell me about your new place?" Piper wanted to know everything.

"I mean, I don't think *Vogue Home* is coming in for a photo shoot any time soon, but it's mine and it feels like home, you know?"

"Yeah, I get it. I can't wait for that too. And Meg?" There it was. The question was out there. Piper braced for the answer she thought she might not want to hear.

"You mean am I giving in to playing nursemaid? No." Brook busied herself with kitchen tasks, but she stopped to look at Piper when she spoke.

Piper managed a nod. She tried not to seem obviously grateful.

"She texts when she's sad or drunk, but even less now. She doesn't even know where I live, I don't think. Her parents won't speak to me because they consider what I did an abandonment of my responsibilities."

"Well, I don't know what says hot, sexy partnership more than that." Piper grinned at her overtly sarcastic comment.

Brook tried to stifle the laugh but couldn't. "Wow, I needed that. Thanks for the reality check."

"Any time. I guess I should go back to schmoozing, unless you need some well-trained assistant in here. I was an intern once you, know." Piper squeezed Brook's arm. The gesture wasn't planned, and she half expected Brook to pull away. Instead, she stepped forward and gave Piper a strong hug. It was over before Piper could respond, and Brook had already resumed sliding trays into the oven.

"I missed you more than I thought." Brook blushed and stepped to the prep counter.

"Can I call you?" Piper felt a warm flush skim up her neck. The short time away had allowed the memory of how Brook felt to fade, but that tiny bit of physical contact reminded her what Brook felt like and how she made Piper's whole body respond.

"Yeah. I'd like that. I feel like I'm ready to move on." Brook held Piper's gaze.

Move on? Hope for some future other than careful friendship danced in Piper's mind. "Me too. I have a kind of housewarming present for you, and I thought maybe I could drop it off one day." Piper wanted to place it in her hands and see her face when she recognized it. Piper briefly considered how she would transport the four-foot painting in the tiny, borrowed sports car, but she would think of something.

"Sure, I've been meaning to call you and ask you about—"

The door smacked against the wall.

"Piper. There you are." Vanessa looked pissed. Her tone was scolding.

Piper was irritated by the interruption and dug her nails into her palms rather than respond as she would have liked.

"I was telling Ellen Warner about the gallery, and just when I wanted you to talk about your recent paintings, I find you in the kitchen, of all places." Vanessa folded her arms and looked between Piper and Brook, first with annoyance and then curiosity.

Piper didn't move. She wanted to finish talking to Brook. She wanted to know what Brook was going to ask her. Screw Ellen Warner and her perpetual social yattering. She wanted to stay, but Vanessa was already pulling her away and out of the kitchen. Piper caught the strange look on Brook's face, which she was desperate to erase.

Piper tried to send her a silent message. Maybe she would text her an explanation when no one was looking. Maybe she could sneak off to the kitchen and find Brook once more. But then, what explanation was acceptable?

Vanessa gripped her arm tighter and spoke in a sharp whisper, "Maybe I should have been more specific when I asked you to come with me to this reception. I meant to be with me, not to hang out with the help."

Piper was barely able to contain her ire. She pulled her arm from Vanessa's grasp and policed the scowl she knew was present on her face. Ellen Warner descended on them both.

"Fabulous news about the gallery, Piper."

"Thank you so much. Big responsibility. But things are happening."

"You have always done well with your art." Vanessa smiled thinly.

"You have. And you'll able to sell your pieces without a party full of captive Devereaux cronies."

Piper stared and watched a flush creep up Vanessa's neck.

"Ellen, you should be happy you were included. Those guest lists are usually exclusive." Vanessa's voice had turned to ice. Apparently, the line between social friends and bitter competitors was constructed from a single wispy strand of rivalry.

"Well, I guess my money should be spent on something other than art by your pet project?" The smile on Ellen's face was impressive since the vitriolic words should have colored it.

What the hell just happened? That was enough for Piper.

"Excuse me." Fake friendship was uncomfortable enough. Strained, tight-lipped venom being spat at one another was just too much for her, especially when she was being used as the backdrop. She backed away and headed straight for the bartender. She felt sweat bead at her neck from the awkward exchange.

"Any recommendations?" She was hoping that she could disappear once again into the kitchen, assuming Ellen and Vanessa continue the battle of one-upmanship uninterrupted. She certainly hoped so.

The bartender handed her a martini glass with some violet-colored concoction. She should have specified a beer recommendation, but she was willing to try anything. She sipped the iridescent liquid and was pleasantly surprised by the taste of sour, vodka, and a tiny bit of sweet, which made it easy to finish in a few swallows. The bartender refilled her glass without request.

"Violet Vixen," the bartender replied when Piper nodded in appreciation. "Vodka, sour mix, blue curaçao, and a little magic by me."

"Good job. Depending on the rest of the evening, I might be back." She raised the glass in salute and walked toward the smattering of small groups assembled throughout the living room. She spotted Vanessa and Ellen in the same spot, fake smiles framing clenched teeth as they spoke. The look on Vanessa's face was something Piper couldn't decipher and wasn't sure she wanted to.

"No, thank you," she muttered aloud to herself, heading for a safer, quiet corner near the food table hoping to see Brook. Seeking her out in the kitchen was her first thought, but she imagined that Vanessa would be extra frosty when she had finished with Ellen and she didn't want to have to explain that to Brook. Piper was already formulating the text in her head about what had happened.

Brook pushed through the kitchen door with cucumber slices buried under rosettes of cream cheese and topped with carrot curlicues. Piper thought they looked cute, if food could look cute. She abandoned the thought when the hint of Brook's perfume found her, and she stepped into Brook's line of sight.

"Sorry about earlier. She's kind of relentless about this art thing." Piper's voice was barely above a whisper, hoping no one else could hear them.

"I can see that. She seemed…territorial." Brook looked confused, as if she were trying to appropriately classify the dynamic.

Piper wanted to steer her away from any supposition. She knew Brook's feeling about any sort of affair, and she wanted to be far removed from it before Brook ever found out the true nature of her relationship with Vanessa. And if she could stop it from ever happening, she would prefer it. She hated the deception and half-truths, but she didn't want this to go south before it even had a chance become something special. Brook had changed every flavor in her formerly bland existence.

In her life. Piper realized, at that moment, nothing was more important than Brook Myers in her life.

❖

Brook glanced over at Piper and then over the room to assess the crowd, the swelling numbers of them and their potential appetites. She had a recurring nightmare about standing over an empty table and angry guests demanding more food she couldn't provide. Ridiculous, since she always overprepared, but the fear was always present.

She watched Piper as she sipped from a large martini glass and secretly wished for one of whatever that was. Brook followed the lines of her torso, suggesting its toned, athletic form beneath the fabric. She caught herself staring and quickly focused on Piper's face, hoping hers wasn't as flushed as it felt.

Some people exuded cool confidence. Piper wore it like skin. The combination of that and her effortless charm made Brook's vision tunnel, and her sweaty palms confirmed Piper still made her unfocused and unable to concentrate.

She counted cucumber towers, even though she had counted them in the kitchen. It forced her brain to be in caterer mode rather than smitten girl mode. Instead, she lost count three times when she caught Piper watching her.

"I don't know where my head is this evening. I've been trying to count one tray of these things for the past two minutes." She hated to admit being scattered, but Piper made her need to reveal everything without qualification.

"I've been a little distracted myself. I think you and I have had a lot to talk about."

"True. It has felt like a whirlwind." Brook considered the understatement.

"Like I said, a lot to talk about."

"What have you been doing lately?" Brook wondered if their mutual attraction was still as strong. It was all she thought about lately.

"I'm working on moving into my own studio and concentrating on the art as much as I can." Piper's eyes danced with excitement, but she kept her voice to a whisper.

"That's fantastic. What about teaching at the club?" Brook pictured her solid form in golf shorts and then mentally slapped herself for going there again.

"I don't know if I'll be working there after I move out." Piper looked as if there were more to the story but didn't elaborate. She seemed to be momentarily satisfied when she spotted Vanessa and Ellen Warner locked in conversation.

Piper stood closer to Brook as she rearranged mousse cups and swept crumbs from the table. Brook smelled her cologne and recalled the kiss for the millionth time. She wanted another one.

Piper started to speak just before a wine glass hit a nearby tray with a thud.

"Piper, take me home." Vanessa Devereaux looked furious and sounded even more so despite her obvious attempt to hide it.

"Give me a minute, I was just talking to—"

"I need to go now, please." Vanessa was leaving no room for negotiation.

Piper looked at once embarrassed and frustrated.

"We can talk later. You better go." Brook wondered why she was suddenly a bit jealous and a little put off by the woman Piper had characterized as her landlord and benefactor. The grip of Vanessa's fingers on Piper's arm was definitely more than a simple gesture to move Piper to the door more quickly.

Brook stared after them. Piper glanced back to Brook and mouthed, "I'll call you."

Brook was studying the duo as they marched toward the door. Vanessa waited for Piper to open the door for her before striding through it. She lost sight of them when Ellen Warner approached with an indecipherable expression on her face.

"So you and Piper are pretty close, huh?" Ellen swirled white wine in her glass before sipping it.

"Well, we're friends. I haven't seen her in a bit, actually. Why do you ask?" Warning bells were going off in her head and she couldn't decide why.

"I was just telling Vanessa how Piper came to help you at my party, and she seemed shocked." Ellen sipped again, her eyes shimmering over the rim of her glass as she watched the words settle over Brook.

Brook took a step back and tried to analyze whatever was going on. Piper must be in trouble for something. But she didn't work for Vanessa, she worked for the club, right?

"I think it was her day off." It was lame and sounded more so when the words landed. Brook felt oddly protective when she thought Piper might be in trouble for helping her.

"Honey, you must know how territorial Vanessa can be over her special friends." Ellen punctuated the words with air quotes and didn't try to hide a smile when Brook looked confused.

"I'm not sure what you're saying, Mrs. Warner?" Alarms were ringing in her head.

"Oh, honey. Surely you knew." She paused and looked unreasonably delighted as she delivered her salacious gossip.

Brook stared at her, attempting to formulate a question. Ellen Warner rendered it unnecessary.

"Vanessa Devereaux doesn't spend all that time and money on Piper because she makes good paintings. It's a well-known fact around the club. You should know that if you do any other events in SGE. It might not be a good idea to bring her."

Brook felt a punch in the stomach. She was trying to manage the cacophony of emotions that were barraging her.

"I'm sorry. I don't understand." Brook hoped she didn't. She didn't want to understand. She didn't want to know anything negative about Piper, who had snuck her way into her heart. She hadn't imagined a future where she couldn't weave Piper Holthaus into it one day.

"I'm sure you know that it's a pretty common thing in this place for husbands and wives to have an understanding. I mean, not Dan and I, of course, but having some sort of arrangement with a married partner isn't uncommon here." She paused as if to wait for Brook's reaction. When she didn't get one, she kept going. "Brook, Piper is no dummy. She takes full advantage of the situation and then some."

How could this be even remotely true? Piper let her go on and on about her feelings about infidelity and neglected to mention any of it while they were together for endless hours? She couldn't picture it. Vanessa and Piper, under her husband's nose? Or perhaps the three of them? She shook away the thought. Yuck.

"I wouldn't worry, Mrs. Warner. I can manage my work on my own. That was just a friend helping out. Nothing more." Brook scrubbed her palms down her thighs and forced a smile. "Back to work." She was grateful that the door to the kitchen was barely three steps behind her. The burn of Ellen's stare lingered as she rushed through it.

She was trying to figure out what she was feeling. Anger? Betrayal? Manipulation? They had poured their hearts out to one another, which included a discussion on fidelity and how important Brook thought it was.

She guessed Piper had been speaking from experience when she talked about the compromises within Shadow Glass Estates. Compromise was one thing, but treating a marriage as a casual convenience was something else entirely. Brook had stopped at the words "special friends" and felt the sweeping emotion that cleared out any longing for Piper and made betrayal the prevailing emotion. She would remind herself of that when she thought back to the warm place she had put Piper in.

Piper didn't owe her anything, not technically. But Brook had bared her soul to her. Maybe she was just angry with herself for believing that Piper was the perfect antidote to her disappointing life at the moment. Thinking she felt like a friend, was so attracted to her, had kissed her. The same person who suddenly felt like a stranger and one more letdown in a string of them. Was she wrong for thinking that Piper should have been honest with her? She had told her that she had a friends-with-benefits thing, but wasn't revealing the other party in that scenario pretty relevant information? Especially when it was Vanessa? Perhaps she was making Piper responsible when she wasn't. Maybe she just wanted to be disappointed.

Ellen was the sort of woman who would have delighted in passing on such gossip disguised as a casual conversation. Brook imagined that knowing such a secret was the highlight of Ellen's evening.

Her duties were thankfully winding down and she began to condense the leftovers. She texted her mother.

Up for a visit? I need a little reality check from my mom.

Brook needed a reset, and she hadn't had time to visit with her family. It always made her thoughts clearer. Her mother was her voice of reason, and she was feeling like she couldn't make sense of much lately, just when she felt hopeful that her life was ticking all the boxes.

Her phone delivered the excited text from her mom telling her to hurry at the same time Piper's request to call her and explain popped up.

She simply replied that it was probably best that they didn't communicate for a while. It was too much. Just when she had believed that Piper was enough, it seemed glaringly obvious that she wasn't. She wondered if anyone would be. Perhaps she was being ridiculous or just angry at herself for allowing the thoughts of Piper to feel like a light at the end of a long, dark tunnel. An escape to her mother's would be a welcome respite from her warring thoughts.

❖

"Would you like to try to make me understand what you were doing with that girl? What is your relationship, exactly? How did you end up at Ellen Warner's party? And without telling me? How could you let me be humiliated? I'm not even sure what to say to you right now."

"Really? Because you've been going on without taking a breath for the last five minutes." Piper attempted a chuckle that sounded resentful instead of amused, something she realized she would pay for dearly.

"Unbelievable. You are unbelievable, Piper. Are you sleeping with the cook?" Vanessa's condescending tone was intolerable.

"She's a chef, Vanessa. She catered for you at your last party, remember?"

"Why would I? I was out selling your art. Apparently, you were selling something else entirely. When was this? When I was away for my birthday?"

"You mean how was I free from my gilded cage long enough to talk to people whose address is somewhere other than Shadow Glass Estates? Yes, you were in the Caymans and a friend needed my help." Despite the darkness of the moment, Piper felt elated that her investment in the drama of Vanessa and the elite set was going to end soon.

"Maybe a better question is how long were you making a fool of me? Ellen couldn't wait to throw it in my face that you had been working for her."

"Vanessa, how is my helping someone out after you canceled plans at the last minute making a fool of you? Or better yet, where is the fine print on my lease that says I can't have *friends*?"

"I have an image to uphold, and your traipsing around the country club as one of Ellen's employees is humiliating."

"Seriously? Are you so elitist now that you can't even abide people who don't marry for money or trade on it to get what they want? This place has ruined you, V."

Vanessa whipped the car into the cobblestone court and jerked to a stop outside the carriage house. "Get out."

Piper looked back at Vanessa before shutting the door. "Think hard about why you're mad at me. Try to figure out when my being a normal human being started to go against your plans and your image. I deserve a life too." Piper slammed the car door before Vanessa had a chance to respond.

Piper walked inside and felt, very clearly, that her presence in this place had to be over. She was a guest who had overstayed her welcome. She looked at her phone. No notifications. Vanessa wouldn't call, not even to yell. She was too furious.

Brook was likely trying to figure out what was going on and Piper couldn't bring herself to lie, so perhaps silence was preferable. She dialed her number anyway, despite the text that told her not to. She wanted to tell her how she felt, what had happened, what her plans were, or just good night. Brook didn't answer, so it didn't matter anyway.

She wanted to paint but she couldn't be creative when she felt defeated. She opted for a hot shower and bed, where she likely wouldn't sleep. The text from Brook declining communication from her was more than she could process. She knew her fear of moving on had likely cost her a future with Brook.

❖

Piper eventually dragged herself from bed and into an early shower when chasing sleep had just become annoying. She mentally inventoried her lesson schedule, which thankfully didn't require her presence at the club until ten. She would mainline caffeine until then and hope that work would take her mind off whatever was, or in this case wasn't, happening in her life at the moment.

She absently sorted through her canvases trying to stack together the pieces that felt more commercial, more saleable. She grouped them by size, and then color. She still tried to wrap her head around the idea that she would soon be in an actual gallery. In just a few weeks, she would be standing at a grand opening doing all the things she hated. Chatting up potential buyers and telling stories about what inspired her. At least those people would be there because they liked art, not just because they were trying to impress the Devereaux. She knew if she wanted to support herself as an artist this was the best way to start.

She heard the door open followed immediately by the tap of heels on the hard floors. Vanessa whooshed into the room and studied the stacks Piper was making. She mentally prepared for the next round of the fight she knew wasn't over.

"I don't really see *Uncommon Beauty* being right for this show. Add it to the no pile for a little while until we see what sells."

Business Vanessa scared Piper a little bit. Hence the reason she was racking her brain to figure out what piece she was referring to or further, what pile, she considered the no pile.

"Um, okay. Which ones do you like the best, then?" Flattering Vanessa was the only way to stay away from their earlier conversation, a necessary feat given the current circumstances.

Vanessa marched to the stack just beyond Piper and removed a forty by forty abstract, a busier piece featuring orange highlights and turquoise strokes, one of her earlier attempts and one of her favorites. She dropped the canvas in front of the window and began collecting others from Piper's to-go pile. Piper watched her work being stacked in a discard area. It felt uncomfortable, but she reminded herself the price would be worth the outcome.

"There. We need to put your best pieces out there." Her voice was cold and aloof.

"Sure." Piper was desperately trying to sort out Vanessa's mood and anticipate what might come next.

Vanessa finally turned and skimmed her fingers along Piper's neck, fisting a chunk of hair in her hand. It was something she had done often when they were in bed, but never standing in this very unsexy place together.

"Your performance will reflect on me, you know." The sentiment was controlling and contained a hint of warning Piper couldn't name. Vanessa pressed her mouth to Piper's, less of a kiss than a demand, and Piper pulled back to look into her eyes.

"Did something happen?" Piper's skin chilled with the cold shift from Vanessa, who usually purred into her submissively. Piper didn't like this version of her.

"Like what?" Vanessa released Piper's hair and moved to smooth her own despite no strand being out of place.

"I don't know, you're acting different right now." Piper should have let it go, but a pissed-off Vanessa didn't soften with time, she simmered and then boiled into something with razor-sharp edges capable of serious damage.

"Do you like what we have, Piper? Our arrangement?" Vanessa returned to rearranging canvases along the wall.

"Of course." She knew this wasn't the time to wax philosophical about Vanessa's concessions or her own. Or to admit to her plans of starting over.

Vanessa released the painting she was studying and let it fall back against the stack. She stalked to the couch and crossed her legs instead of discarding her shoes and inviting Piper to join her, as routine.

"Can you imagine how embarrassing it was to hear that I must be losing my touch with you since you were off with some cook?"

"Wait a minute. I was helping out a friend, who was the caterer, by the way. And since when do you worry about what Ellen Warner thinks?"

"Piper, you're either an artist or some hired help. Your art is linked to the Devereaux, and what people think is sometimes more important than reality, you should know that by now." She was rebranding the narrative from the night before, but the message was the same.

Piper bit back a myriad of retorts about Vanessa's reality and her ridiculous notion that she was some authority on society dos and don'ts since she was as common as the rest just a few years ago. The fact that Piper could see her way out of this unholy deal if the gallery took off the way she had hoped made her measure her response. A battle would get her nowhere.

"So, I can't have friends?"

"Of course you can. Just don't make me look foolish by making poor selections. Please tell me you didn't sleep with her."

Piper nearly replied that it was none of her business but thought the better of it. She bit at her bottom lip instead. "No, I didn't." It was honest, but it felt like she was betraying Brook. "I told you, I was helping out a friend."

Vanessa seemed to visibly relax. "I told Ellen there was some other explanation."

Piper blinked and shook her head. "You actually talked about who I may or may not be sleeping with in the middle of some cocktail party?"

"What does it matter? The important thing is that you aren't."

"*That's* the important thing?" Piper was trying to decide what was making her angrier, being property that needed to behave or having others praise her for behaving.

"Forget I said anything, Piper."

Piper couldn't help but notice that she was only willing to forget about it when her control on their relationship seemed to remain intact.

"Sit with me?" Vanessa patted the couch cushion as she tossed her shoes to the floor.

Piper wanted to scream that she had lost all respect for Vanessa, but her self-preservation wanted to get through to the opening. Once that was over, she'd be gone.

Piper fell against the back of the couch, not particularly close to Vanessa and even less so emotionally.

Vanessa didn't seem to care as she rose to straddle Piper's thighs and pulled Piper's hands to her hips.

"I missed you, Piper."

Unbelievable. She was no longer compelled by the old physical attraction to Vanessa, and she had the ability to walk away, to stop it. She guided Vanessa off her lap.

"Duty calls, V. I'm due at the club." She could lie easily because she felt nothing for this life now.

"Call in sick." Vanessa was direct.

"I can't." Piper was equally so.

"You can't or you won't?"

Piper declined to address the question. "There is a lot to do, and I need to go."

"The gallery's coming to pick up your artwork today or tomorrow. We should talk about it."

Piper marveled at the shift in the directive that Vanessa used for control.

"I still have to work." Her voice was flat.

"I guess I'm in charge of selections. You'll have to trust me to pick everything out." Vanessa's tone was taunting.

"Of course. Who else would be?" *Certainly not me. This is your show.*

Piper headed to the bedroom and noticed she still had ninety minutes before her first client. Maybe she could have an hour on the driving range with her thoughts and her plans. What a mess.

She wanted to call Brook and try again to fix what had inevitably broken because she'd failed to be honest in the first place. She wanted a lot of things; she just didn't know how to get them without pissing off the world.

❖

Brook padded into the plush living room that felt like the home she always remembered. Morning light was seeping through the curtains that had hung in the windows as long as she could recall. The white couch cushions were slightly dull and misshapen from years of wear, and inherited antique carpets made it look and feel the way her parents' home always had. She absently toed the fringe on the hundred-year-old rug before wedging herself into the corner of the sofa. She picked up a magazine and dropped it back to the coffee table without even opening the cover.

She reviewed the twists of her life in just a few months. She caught herself counting off the milestones on her fingers. New business, moving, bad relationship, no relationship, nearly losing a business, near death of an intimate partner, messy breakup, moving again, falling for someone too soon only to discover she wasn't who she thought she was. She had just wanted to feel a new peace in her life where emotional obstacles weren't hiding at every turn.

How had she ended up sleeping in her childhood home waiting for her mom to talk some sense into her? How had she fallen for a woman who made her dream come true by living off some married couple's money in exchange for…well, she didn't want to finish that thought. It was too gross and too slimy.

"…coffee?" Her mother's voice broke through the thoughts spinning in her mind.

"You have no idea how much I need that." Brook took the antique Blue Nordic china teacup and saucer her mother held. Her mother's cherished Meakin China tea set had been in her family for years and had remained without so much as a chip despite regular use.

"So, you want to tell me what's happening?"

Sandra Myerson always looked as glowing and polished at six a.m. as she did at six p.m. Brook always thought that good genes and an unwavering commitment to seeing the bright side of every situation contributed to her mom's flawless appearance.

"I just needed a Mom visit." It was true but significantly understated.

"Lies. You don't need those unless something's weighing on you. Is it Megan?" She turned and sipped from her cup before placing it on the saucer in her hand. She set it on the table and waited.

"Luckily, no. I mean, it's been hard, adjusting to everything, I guess, but other than a few texts when I'm pretty sure she's drinking, it's been quiet."

"Okay then. Is it work? Are you stressed about work? Your father and I would be more than happy to help you with the business. We remember what it felt like to start a business. Your father talks you up to everyone. You should know how proud he is of you."

Brook felt the swell of warmth as she thought about her father, undoubtedly already at work at the warehouse by now.

"Thank you. I'll be sure to let you know if I'm drowning, but I've got a lot of jobs coming up. I'm pretty lucky. Please thank Dad for the free publicity." She leaned over and kissed her mother's cheek. She knew that she had been just as ready with a quick promotion for her only child's business as her father.

"Too proud to let your parents chip in as a little investment?"

"Of course not. It's the eventual hostile takeover I worry about, Mom. You know that." She smiled happily, grateful for the cocoon of comfort her mother always offered.

"I can see that, given how ruthless we are." She took another sip of coffee. "So what's making you look like the weight of the world is on you, then?"

Brook contemplated avoiding the subject of Piper Holthaus. After all, it didn't matter. What could they have in common now? Their core values were too different. But, that was a big part of what was on her mind. "I met someone." She held up her hand when a delighted expression formed on her mother's face. "Wait. It's not like that."

Her mother let her expression return to neutral and nodded for her to continue.

"She talked me off a ledge when someone insulted my food."

"Go on." Her mom gestured for her to continue.

Brook hadn't told anyone but Piper what had happened. Ashamed and defeated, she'd been afraid of what her parents would think about it all. But she hated keeping things from them.

"You remember my first big job at Shadow Glass Estates—the art reception?"

"The one at the Devereauxs'?"

Brook knew that the job was, in part, due to her father's association with some of Frank Devereaux's clients.

"Yeah. It was for an artist named Piper Holthaus. She's pretty close to Vanessa Devereaux." She hoped she had kept the distaste out of her voice. She pictured a furious Vanessa dragging Piper out of the kitchen the night before. "Anyway, I pitched a couple of smaller things after that, and then Ellen Warner hired me for a huge party. I'm pretty sure I was in over my head, like, fourteen hundred pieces over my head."

"Obviously, you managed as you always do." Always an unwavering support, her mother nodded encouragingly.

"So, I planned ahead, prepared everything I could beforehand, and I was really thinking I could do it, you know? It took every dime I had, but I could feel it coming together."

"That's my girl. You've never been afraid of hard work and sacrifice." She took Brook's hand and squeezed.

"Yeah, well, you have no idea how much work went into this thing, more than I even thought," she said wryly. "So, I drove up and found out that Meg had thrown a party. Not a nice, invitation kind of party. A drunken free-for-all." She took a breath and fought the same feelings of fury despite retelling the story these many weeks later.

"I take it she was drinking a lot."

"Understatement of a lifetime. She was hammered. Of course, that didn't surprise me. That was the norm, as you know, for the last couple of years."

"I'm so sad that she let that disease get the better of her. She was such a smart person."

"She's still smart, she just lost sight of who she was, I guess." She wondered why her first instinct was to manage Meg's reputation, even now.

"Sorry. Go on." She reached out to squeeze Brook's hand again.

"I pull up and see the party and I'm irritated, but that's nothing new. I walk in and before I've been there a minute, I find that all the prep work I had done for days had ended up as chip dip or under whipped cream from a can." Fury rose up once again, filling her to overflowing.

Her mother clapped her hand over her mouth in shock. "How could she let that happen?"

"She said it was no big deal, that we'd just get more food. I guess she was so into her own stuff that she didn't care, or maybe she wanted to punish me, consciously or unconsciously. I don't know." She thought it may have been a little of both. "Anyway, I kind of lost it. I broke up with her right there."

"Of course you did. It was a long time coming, sweetheart." Her mother was watching her carefully.

"So, I called a friend. I mean, I guess she was a friend. I had only met Piper a couple of times, but I just needed to vent to someone who didn't know all the people involved, you know?"

"Impartial third party."

"Exactly. So I called her, crying like a big baby and freaking out."

"You could have called me, you know."

"I wasn't keeping it from you, I just didn't want you to know how much of a spectacular disaster my life was."

"We knew you weren't happy, Brook. You hadn't come over with Meg in almost a year. It doesn't take a genius to figure out things had changed between you two."

"I know, but saying it out loud to your family makes it much more real."

Her mother waited for Brook to continue.

"So I tell Piper what happened. She tells me to drive over to her house right then. She lives in the Devereauxs' guest house." Brook pictured Piper standing in the driveway, looking gorgeous and ready to welcome her, be her savior. She could recall the butterflies anytime she was near Piper. She forced the memories away.

"Long story short, she called in a hundred favors, set up the kitchen and stayed up with me all night, recreating what I had lost. After all that, she went with me to the party and worked for free."

"Sounds like a pretty amazing person, this Piper." Her mom poured more coffee from a silver carafe on the table, topping up Brook's when she held out her cup.

"Yeah. I thought so. She's gorgeous, funny, and driven. I kind of let things go too far, though."

"Did you sleep with her?"

"Mom!" As old as Brook was, she and her mother rarely discussed sex, certainly not as it pertained to her own intimate life, and she was perfectly comfortable that way.

"What? It's a reasonable and relevant question." She sipped, obviously still waiting for an answer.

"No. We just kissed." Brook hadn't even intended on revealing that much but it was relevant, she supposed.

"Okay. Go on." She regarded Brook over the rim of her cup.

"Anyway, I hadn't planned on anything like that but the

adrenaline, the all-nighter, the realization that my fifteen-year relationship was over, all of it…I realized I was attracted to her. But it was too soon."

"Who says that anything is too soon if you get a chance to be happy?"

Brook loved her mother's no-nonsense declarations. She could have been honest about her feelings, but she hadn't really come to terms with them herself. And everything had changed now that she knew Piper was involved with Vanessa Devereaux.

"We talked about my feelings, about fidelity and Grandma's relationship and how I would never be with a cheater."

"Being the moral police is a very taxing job, Brook." Her mother's brow creased just slightly, and Brook recalled their many discussions about the fact that Brook could be hard on people.

Brook jumped to her own defense. "I wasn't judging, Mom. I just don't want to have a relationship that isn't built on trust."

"So, what did she do that's so terrible?" She cupped Brook's chin and held her eyes until she answered.

"I found out that she might be having an affair with a married woman." There, she said it.

"What do you mean you 'found out' or 'might be'? Where did you get your information?"

"Last night, someone told me that she was sort of in an open dirty-little-secret part of a married couple."

"So a third party, who apparently enjoys gossiping, passed on a rumor that your single friend might be part of an open marriage? Wow, is there room for her at the next public hanging in the town square?"

"What do you know about open marriages?" Brook considered her parents about as pure and naïve as they came, so such worldly revelations felt shocking.

"About as much as you know about Piper's circumstances. But I know that consenting adults have the right to set the rules in their lives without other people judging them."

"You and dad would never do something like that." It went

without saying, but she liked the distance it created from the uncomfortable scrutiny.

"No, but not because it's a capital offense, because it isn't right for us. It took Steven two months to ask me out on a date. Add a third person and we would all die of anticipation."

"Okay, I guess." Brook laughed at the notion.

"What did Piper say when you asked her about it?"

"I haven't talked to her. I told her I wasn't ready to have a conversation." Brook shrugged.

"Wow, Brooky. You know better than that. If you truly thought that there might be a future for you two, then I suggest you leave some of that judgment at the door."

Brooky. Well, she must be completely wrong to get *Brooky*. That was reserved for heinous crimes and epically serious missteps.

"I wouldn't even know what to say, Mom. I'm not doing this again. I'm not trusting someone with my heart when we find no common ground on the important things in life."

"I think you know better, and being so black and white isn't going to make life any better." She stood. "How about breakfast?"

Apparently, they would just agree to disagree from here on. Brook needed to think some more. A healthy breakfast instead of a rushed granola bar might help that along. At least she hoped it would.

"I'd like that. Thanks."

Her mom spared no time whisking her cup from the table and heading into the kitchen. Brook padded after her, planning to assist where she was needed. Her love of creating in the kitchen came from her mother and grandmother, and times like these made her feel like an eager chef-in-training again.

Her father lumbered through the door seconds after the egg timer went off.

"Sounds like I'm just in time." His smooth tenor and sturdy hugs always made Brook feel safe and steady, like she could manage anything.

"Mom said you were still here, so I better get my butt home for breakfast." He smiled as he walked to her mom for a squeeze. "To what do we owe the pleasure?"

"Just needed a little grounding, I guess." Her dad wouldn't pry, she knew.

"I know I have limits in the advice department, but I'm always here if you need me." He chucked the mail on the table at his seat and picked up the pile of silverware to begin laying the table.

"We both are." Her mom linked her arm through his.

"See? This is why I come here. So I can remember what relationships are supposed to look like." Brook kissed her father's cheek.

"Don't let her fool you, she thinks I'm a giant pain." Her dad offered a peck on her mother's cheek before he brought a stack of plates from the cupboard.

"A pain that I hitched my wagon to forty years ago. And I have no intention on breaking in another one." Her mother handed Brook a bowl of fruit.

They sat and chatted, around bites of scrambled eggs and toast. Her father talked about their latest clients, Brook's new apartment, the clogged gutters, and plans for Thanksgiving.

Her dad sifted through the giant stack of magazines, advertisements for primary election candidates, and bills, which he still insisted on paying one by one, albeit online finally. He slid a large shiny postcard her way.

"That's the new gallery in your neighborhood. Elizabeth Davinroy and her husband have been moving quite a few pieces through the warehouse lately. The opening is coming up if you want to go with us."

Brook drew her finger across the hues of a painting she recognized. She stared at the solo image framed in a white border. She knew who had painted it before she flipped the card over. Piper, the outline of her broad shoulders clearly visible in the black shirt, was perched in front of her easel and a painting that made her stare.

"...the woman you were talking about? This is *the* Piper?" She heard her mother's voice too late to catch the beginning.

"Yeah. This is her." She felt the flush of attraction surge when she saw Piper. She couldn't believe that she'd come this far, that she didn't know what was going on in her life. To be fair, she hadn't exactly made herself available.

"Why do you look like you've seen a ghost, Brooklynn?" Her father sounded concerned.

"No. Nothing like that. It's just that this piece she's working on in this picture looks incredibly familiar."

"She's very talented. Her work has a lot of soul." Her father had been around the art and collectibles world his whole life.

Brook could feel her mother's eyes on her. "It does, doesn't it." She couldn't stop staring at the faded antlers breaching the dusky skyline.

"Perhaps you should call and congratulate her. Or you could just come with us."

"No. I'm not sure that would be such a great idea."

"Up to you." Her mother shrugged and speared a melon wedge, her eyes never leaving Brook.

CHAPTER FIFTEEN

Piper pulled her golf shirt away from her neck and pictured the cold shower she planned to have as soon as her student's last three balls found a home in the grass of the driving range.

Luckily, between the gallery opening just a week away and Frank's heavy entertainment schedule with his clients, Piper had barely seen Vanessa. She had felt her art flourish and a few extra golf clients had padded her bank account just enough that she had searched for a live-work studio near the gallery. She didn't care much about the live part—a bed, a small kitchen, and a functional bathroom was all she needed, but the work part was essential. The place on Second and Market had good lighting and the space for her new pieces. She had signed the lease on the spot. Once the opening and all its fanfare was behind her, she would move out of the carriage house and into her new place. It was time. The thought of the conversation with Vanessa made her nauseous. It wouldn't be easy.

"Great job, Tina. Your game with the ladies' club tomorrow should be great." She could see a look of satisfaction blossom over her student's face.

"I'll settle for any improvement I can get." She slid her club back into the bag and lifted it over her shoulder.

"Good luck. See you next time." Piper picked up the few scattered range balls from the turf around the tee. Tina leaned in for a glancing hug and was walking toward the parking lot when Piper's cell vibrated in her pocket.

"Guess where I am?" Vanessa's hushed tone meant she was close to people who shouldn't know who she was calling.

Piper didn't want to play the game just then. "I don't know, Paris?"

"Funny. I'm on my way back in a limo that Frank's client sent for him complete with champagne and the biggest charcuterie tray you've ever seen. Frank couldn't get away from a call, so he told me to grab some friends and go have fun."

"Wow. Hope you have a great time." Piper chucked a few towels in the bin and grabbed her backpack. She threw a wave to Leo, who was poring over month-end paperwork in the office, and started the walk home.

"No, silly, I want you to come with me. I'm a few blocks away."

"V, I can't." She could, she just really didn't want to. "I just got off work, I need a shower, and I have to paint."

"No, you don't. I'll wait for you to shower so you can come have fun with me."

It was the last thing Piper considered fun. No, she didn't *have* to paint, but she wanted to. She wanted to go home, shower, and most of all she planned to call Brook and see if she could mend things. She didn't want to make small talk with Vanessa or have to pretend any longer.

"V, can I take a raincheck, please? I'm really tired."

"Or do you just want to go visit your new shiny toy?" A bitter cattiness leaked through the phone.

"What?" Piper gripped the phone tighter. "What are you talking about?"

"She isn't welcome at my house, you know."

Piper felt her blood pressure rise as Vanessa was now blatantly dictating her free time, the people she could have in her life, and who could visit her where she lived.

"First of all she is not a toy, that is rude and incredibly demeaning which is, of course, how you meant it."

"Piper, I give you everything and this is how you repay me." Vanessa was no longer whispering.

That was it. Her whole life was a negotiation, a compromise of what she was willing to do for the easy existence she no longer wanted, certainly not at the price she was being asked to pay.

"Wow. And there it is. I should behave as you demand so that I'm not punished?"

"Piper, I will not be humiliated because you find some low-rent distraction to play with."

Piper was beyond livid now. She was insulting Brook, and it felt like a gut punch. "Brook is a talented chef and makes a living feeding snotty, self-important socialites. You have many talents but chose to give them up for a staff and a limo that drives to nowhere. Don't take that out on me." Well, she'd done it now. She knew there was no going back. She had never wanted it to end in a fight but, after all, it didn't surprise her.

"My talents got me living on an estate, traveling the world, on the charity circuit and the arts council. And don't forget, I'm a major investor in an art gallery showing your tacky canvases."

"Wow, a few days ago I was a genius, now I make tacky canvases?" She knew Vanessa was just angry, but the subject of her art was the tender place that bruised easily.

"Why don't you take a few minutes to calm down and think about what you are doing, Piper. This isn't you. You're smarter than this. I'll see you in a few minutes. Be ready."

"I said no. Goodbye."

She tapped the phone to her forehead and resisted the urge to throw it into a sculptured hedge. So many internal arguments were warring in her head. She needed to fix this; she'd come too far. No, she needed to walk away with what was left of her dignity, no matter the cost. She knew it would end one day, but she didn't plan it to be at the point that everything seemed to be reaching its pinnacle.

She rounded the gate and had just stepped onto the cobblestone drive when she heard the vehicle approach. She didn't have to turn around to know it was the limousine containing a furious Vanessa.

She continued to the carriage house without looking back and snagged a beer from the fridge. She knew the fight was just about to begin.

Before she had swallowed her first sip, the front door slammed and the clack of angry heels echoed down the hallway.

"I can't believe you want to throw away everything we have built together over some distraction you won't be able to pick out of a lineup in a few months. Don't you understand what our partnership could mean for your future?"

"Gee, V. Why don't you make it sound sexier? Make sure I trade my personal life choices for your husband's money? I've been doing that long enough. You said you wanted me to be successful, but I guess you meant on your terms. Let me ask you something. Did you ever see me leaving this place, or did you just assume I would be at your beck and call forever?"

"I've done everything to make all this happen for you. I have asked so little in return."

"You asked me to sell my soul, and I just realized how much it's costing me."

"Oh, poor Piper. Forced to live in the lap of luxury and take torturous limo rides and drink four-hundred-dollar champagne."

"That's just it. Where's the Vanessa who knew how over-the-top all of this was? You used to tell me that you would never become the person who existed just to go to the next gala or buy the next extravagant accessory, and that's exactly what you've become. Don't be angry at me because I don't want that for my life."

"Judgment? You'll see what it feels like when you have to start figuring out how to pay the electric bill on your salary, if you even find a job." Vanessa was just as enraged as Piper now and clearly wanted her to know that she held all the cards. Her influence, or at least her husband's, was a weapon Vanessa wouldn't hesitate to wield.

Piper felt the fear of scraping by without an income. She wondered how fast this particular house of cards would fall around her despite her years of planning. Yes, she had savings, but years of believing there wouldn't be enough money while she was growing up consistently fed an irrational panic.

"You have a choice. I'll check with you tomorrow to see if you've made the right one." Vanessa spun on her heels and marched out the door. Vanessa didn't want anything per se, she just didn't like the thought of not being in control. Of Piper no longer being her play toy. She expected Piper to continue their arrangement without Piper's pesky need to have her own life.

Piper scanned the room for the things she would take with her. The question was, of course, when would she go. Did she go before the gallery opening and risk having it pulled from under her? Or did she stand up, take control, and damn the consequences?

She took a long pull from her beer and grabbed her phone. It was time to take the next step.

❖

Within a couple of hours, Piper had selected a dubious, drab green Range Rover almost a decade old that sported a gray patch of Bondo where a rust repair had been made. It was in relatively perfect condition and, more importantly, wasn't expensive. She could have used her savings to buy a newer car, but this felt like the ideal compromise. A side benefit would be the look on Vanessa's face when she saw the pedestrian selection she had made. The best part was that most of her things, as well as Brook's painting, would fit nicely inside it.

Okay, living, that was the next step. She assessed her belongings and found that she owned very little. Her art supplies filled up the Rover, and she decided that they were a must for the first run. She'd come back with more boxes to pack up the rest. There wasn't much more than a tiny stove and junior-sized refrigerator in the new place, but the light from the picture window was fantastic. She could afford the rent for years on her savings, and the thought of finally being in control of her own destiny made it feel like moving into a mansion instead of escaping one.

She pulled through the gate as if she was absconding with the estate's loot. She blew out a loud breath when she cleared the guard shack, having not encountered a soul. Particularly Vanessa.

She slipped her key into the half glass door and heard the creak echo through the sparse apartment she hadn't planned on moving to this soon. Her heart was beating as if she was doing something wrong. The secret would be out soon enough, and she had no doubt Vanessa would lose her mind. In the meantime, arranging paint supplies on the built-in shelves flanking the Murphy bed was deliciously satisfying.

She placed her old splotchy easel in front of the window and watched a smattering of traffic spill by. Her view wasn't silent, nor did it frame the sweeping length of the ninth hole, but it was more inspiring than she had expected. She reclined on the hard floor and stretched her legs out in front of her. She fingered the grain of the ancient wood floor under her hands and took in the faint musty smell that would soon be replaced by acrylic and sealer.

A car horn jolted her from the solitude, and she stood to head back to her car. She would make one more trip tonight.

A misty rain coated her windshield and she attempted to find the proper wiper control in her new vehicle. She signaled left, then right, started the cruise control at twenty miles an hour, and turned on her brights. She was laughing to herself when she finally found the wiper switch and jumped when her phone rang from the console. She tapped her speakerphone. It was Vanessa. No time like the present.

"Where are you?" she demanded.

"On the way back, why?"

"The Bimmer's in the drive. Who are you with? You better not be with her."

Piper just hung up. As much as she dreaded it, this had to be it.

Piper parked the Rover in front and entered the foyer, shocked that she was alone for the moment. She wheeled the suitcase full of her clothes to the hatchback and slid it in. Her third trip with the boxes of toiletries and books would fill the remaining cargo space.

She pulled the tailgate shut and wandered back inside. The rain was steady now, and Piper imagined painting with a view of the wet streets from her new home.

"Who the hell owns that piece of crap in my driveway?" Vanessa called from the open door.

Piper exhaled and pulled a beer from the fridge, scanning briefly for the food supplies she would take for the new place. "Well, that's my piece of crap. What do you think?" Piper swallowed another large gulp and peered out the window to assess her new purchase.

"It's gross, Piper. You aren't parking that thing in here. The next thing I know there'll be oil stains all over the drive."

"Nope. I won't be parking it here."

Questions seemed to drop like blocks over Vanessa's face. "What's going on, Piper? You owe me an explanation."

"It seems I owe you a lot lately, Vanessa. I bought a vehicle." She shrugged.

"Why?" Her tone softened.

"Because it was time." Piper was matter-of-fact and stood as far from Vanessa as she could without being obvious that the distance was calculated.

"For what?"

"For me to be independent."

"Because we had a fight?" Vanessa looked incredulous.

"No, because we keep fighting about things that remind me who I want to be."

"A successful artist, thanks to me." Vanessa managed smug easiest of all now.

"Exactly. Thank you for your help, but it's time to do this for myself. I can't keep being the show dog you parade around, doing what you want, when you say, in return for treats. I won't."

The light of realization hit Vanessa. She marched into the living room and saw the empty spaces where Piper's paints once were.

"You're abandoning me? Us? Because we had a fight?"

"I'm doing no such thing. You and I both know this isn't healthy anymore. Hell, it probably never was. I was hoping you'd be happy for me." Piper knew that was unrealistic.

"Frank warned me about this. People take you for granted when they know you have money. He said I should watch out for opportunists like you. I will never forgive you for this."

"Vanessa, stop. This isn't you. You are more than some woman with a rich husband and social calendar. At least, you used to be. Can you really not understand that I don't want to trade my possible success for a non-relationship and a place to stay? Really?"

Vanessa's lips peeled from her teeth. It wasn't a smile. "You will regret this, Piper. Listen to me carefully. Your whole world is about to change. You should decide what's important to you before it all goes away."

Piper thought she saw a tear glistening in the corner of Vanessa's eye, but she couldn't relent. "The things that are important to me, you can't take away. I've made my decision." Piper clutched the beer until she felt the joints in her fingers go stiff.

"Is this because I forbid you to see your little friend?" She wound her arms across her chest.

"No, but the fact that you think you could isn't helping."

"Have your things out by Friday, there's nothing left to say. Oh, and leave the silver, you don't own anything in here."

"That was a cheap shot. Besides, there isn't any silver, I already checked." It was snarky, but this conversation was going nowhere productive.

"Make sure you get all those paintings out of here as well. There'll be no gallery for them to go to, so be sure they're out."

And there it was. The compromise. Live your own truth and have the one good thing ripped away. "Why does it have to be all or nothing, Vanessa? I just need my space, it's not about you." It was a bit of a backpedal, but she'd really wanted to see her work on the walls of a gallery.

"It's very much about me. I can only imagine the rumors when you leave."

"That's what you're worried about? What some bored housewives think? You used to pray they didn't know."

"I have better things to do than stand here arguing with an ingrate. Good luck with all your new space. Oh, and go to hell."

She slammed the door so hard the wall clock in the hall tilted on its hanger.

If there were tears, Piper would never know. She wondered what Vanessa would tell people, not because she could manage the narrative, but she wanted to be ready for it. She slid another beer from the fridge and went to inventory her remaining belongings and her dignity. She stopped to appraise *Brook's Peace*, which leaned against the wall. She would take it last and one day watch Brook's face when she gave it to her. That is, if she could salvage any potential relationship.

None of this was what she planned, but none of it was unexpected. She stroked her fingers over the gallery invitation; it was slipping away as fast as it had come. If anything, it was a reminder that for things to work, she couldn't let anyone else call the shots. She had to do it on her own.

She skimmed her thumb over the list of numbers on her phone. She searched for Brook's contact and pressed it. The call went to her voice mail immediately, and she wondered if her phone was off or if Brook had simply dismissed her call.

Before she could analyze too much, she grabbed a cooler and loaded it with the meager contents of her fridge and aimed the Rover toward her new, albeit dubious fresh beginning on Market Street. She passed the club office and thought about calling Leo. She wondered if he would fire her immediately or simply tell her to leave quietly on her own after Vanessa called him. She would miss working for him. Good bosses were hard to find.

She reminded herself that she had a healthy savings, and she could find another job to tide her over. She'd been independent before Vanessa, and she could be again.

Rain pounded the windshield now, and very few cars were with her on the late-afternoon drive. For the first time Piper felt not just alone. She was lonely. Her own decisions and compromises had contributed to where she was now, and it was an unfamiliar feeling she hated.

❖

"Who was that, Brook?"

Brook looked up from the screen after dismissing Piper's call.

"No one," Brook lied.

"I don't believe that." Her mother looked up from her book.

"I just can't talk to her right now." Brook nervously spun the phone in her hand.

"Because you have feelings for her, and they scare you." It wasn't a question.

Brook stared at her mother and ignored the twinge of emotion in her gut. "I'm here to visit with you." It would have sounded completely plausible to anyone except her mother, who wouldn't let her avoid owning her truth.

"No, you're here to avoid being hurt by your feelings for her and having to decide if she's worth the risk after Megan. You and Meg have been over for such a long time, I just want you to be happy."

There was the twinge again, except now it was more of a punch to her gut. "I think I need to concentrate on building a business and not on some woman who trades her integrity for a place to live."

"Ouch." Her mom stood from the table and cleared her calendar from the surface. Brook knew the look. The expression on her mother's face was disappointment, and Brook was always gutted by it.

"I really don't think that integrity is an unreasonable standard." She was intent on defending herself however precarious her position might be.

"Your assumptions about her life are uninformed. Sounds like she helped you without expecting anything in return because you needed it. Don't you think avoiding her calls without letting her explain is unfair?"

"Why are you so intent on me having some sort of relationship with someone you've never met?" She knew she had been hiding out, and she needed to get herself together. As always, the visit home had given her the little boost she needed. Her next steps were unclear, but she felt like she was strong enough to make a plan.

"I saw the way you looked when you told me about her, the way you looked when you saw the gallery invitation. I just want you to be happy, and there is something about her that brings the light back to your eyes."

"I know you think she would make me happy, but I can't get past the betrayal."

"That's a little harsh and you know it. How did she betray you? By not revealing her maybe complicated relationship status to someone she'd known for a few days? Come with us Friday, at least show your support for someone who helped you out when you needed it."

"Fine. If I say yes can we talk about something else?"

"Of course." A glimmer of a satisfied smile lit her mother's face.

Brook took her empty mug from the table and dropped it in the dishwasher. She chatted about upcoming jobs, possible bookings, and new recipes, anything but Piper Holthaus. Her thoughts, however, never left her.

"Where did you go?" Her mother was staring at her.

"What? Nowhere. I was just thinking how I want to get home and try out some new recipes for a job next week, that's all." She knew the lie was as transparent as the previous one had been.

"Uh-huh."

The sideways look told Brook her mother believed none of it. She gathered her belongings from the foyer and tapped a kiss on her cheek.

"Thanks for being there, as always. I love you."

"Love you. And get out of your own way." The tone was stern, but there was a smile in her eyes that was always there for her.

The drive home in the clattery van gave her an excuse not to call Piper. It was too loud. Anyway, she would see her Friday.

❖

Piper steered the Rover back to the carriage house and had to slam on her brakes to miss the large truck pulling away from her front door. She watched it roll away before she could register what they had been doing there. She rushed inside to see that the "go" pile Vanessa had assembled of her canvases was now missing.

She tried to figure out what was happening. Vanessa had decided to sponsor her show anyway? Nope. Piper couldn't imagine an altruistic bone left in Vanessa's body.

She'd been robbed? Highly unlikely since her laptop still sat on the sofa next to cash tips from her golf students.

Big mistake? Probably that. Now she had the humiliating task of calling the gallery to ask what to do next. She would tackle that task in a bit.

She scanned the few remaining boxes and the stacks of art that remained before carrying them out. She had managed to finish loading the rest of her art before the next run-in with Vanessa or the next rainstorm. They seemed similar in their threat of destruction.

An hour had passed before she shut the final items into the car. Her phone rang.

"Piper Holthaus? This is Elizabeth Davinroy from Paris Urban."

"Yes, Mrs. Davinroy." Piper didn't know what she should use for a greeting in a situation where she hadn't ever met the woman in charge of hiring and presumably firing her before they had even met.

"First of all, I wanted to say how sorry we are to hear that the Devereaux pulled their sponsorship for Friday."

So there it was. *Pulled their sponsorship.* What on earth could she say now? "I assume that means none of my work will be in the gallery, then?" Rip off the Band-aid.

"Well, you can imagine that several paying artists were waiting for wall space to open, and Vanessa suggested I reach out to them."

"Of course she did. I assume that the truck that picked up my work shouldn't have?"

"That's why I was calling. Embarrassingly, I forgot to take the pickup off the schedule, and I could have died when they unloaded all your pieces into the warehouse. We would be happy to facilitate bringing them back to you at your convenience."

"Sure. Great. I'm in the process of moving, could we do it next week? I'll be just around the corner from the gallery." Piper hoped the tremble in her voice wasn't detectable.

"Of course. This was our error." She sounded as if she genuinely regretted the circumstances.

"Thanks, I'll contact you next week." Piper was nearly in tears.

"Thank you. And Piper? For what it's worth, you're very talented."

"Thanks." She managed to hang up before the tears fell.

You're talented, but you don't have the clout of Vanessa Devereaux pushing your agenda. If she ever doubted that money talked, it was confirmed now.

She remained locked to the floor as if her feet were cemented there. How many hits could come in one week? Brook refused to speak to her, Vanessa was punishing her for having a spine, and now her dream of showing in a real gallery had been dashed before the first canvas was hung, let alone sold.

She felt as if she was wading through mud. Every step was an effort and there was no clear path. Her phone vibrated in her pocket, but she ignored it. She couldn't talk to anyone.

Piper couldn't help but wonder how every shred of time she had spent with Vanessa over the past few years could be wiped away once she ceased to obey or concede her every desire. She wasn't angry yet, just thoroughly disappointed that she hadn't done this sooner. Her heart thrummed heavily in her chest as she closed the tailgate on the remaining paintings that made up the last of her presence in the carriage house. Normally, she would have had a final appraisal of the view through the beautiful window, of the studio that had given her peace and solace, but now it felt like a structure for which she held no attachment.

She sat behind the wheel and scanned the giant house she had seen every day and thought how sad and dark it looked. An artificial façade that hid so much dysfunction, more than she ever could have imagined when she first arrived.

She accelerated too quickly over the cobblestone toward the exit and pushed out a sigh of relief. It was a messy disaster, all of it. She had lost almost everything she knew in the span of a few days, but she was determined to rebuild a life where she stopped trading her self-respect for convenience.

She passed the gallery and noticed a quick-fix banner with the words "featured artists" covering the spot where her name had been. She felt the heat in her cheeks. It was disappointing, sure, but worse, she imagined what people would think. 'Oh look, that's the artist that got fired. I wonder what she's doing now? It's so sad, isn't it?" She had been so close.

The rain had stopped, and Piper made quick work of jogging inside with stacks of canvas she couldn't wait to arrange on the walls. *Her* walls. Her phone rang again, and this time she reached for it.

Brook.

Her heart leapt as she hit the button.

❖

Brook heard the phone ringing and wondered if she should hang up and just send a text. After all, she had been very clear about Piper not contacting her. Would she even answer?

"I'm really glad you called. I wanted to explain. The last time I saw you was pretty uncomf—" Piper's words sounded rushed as if she was afraid that she had limited time until Brook hung up.

"How are you?" Brook cut her off.

"Honestly? I've had better days, but I'll survive. I've just moved the last of my things into a little studio on Market."

"You moved out of the guest house?" Brook was trying to decide what she should ask first. She needed too much information.

"I told you that was the plan." Piper's tone was defensive.

"On Market? That's near me." Brook tried to navigate the conversation back to friendly waters.

"Yes. That wasn't intentional. I just had to jump on it before anyone else could."

"I mean, I figured with the gallery opening you would be concentrating on that. In fact, that's why I was calling. My parents do business with the Davinroys and they asked me to go to the gallery on Friday, insisted actually. I wanted to see if you thought that would be all right, with Vanessa, I mean. I don't want to make trouble for you."

Piper didn't respond for a few seconds.

"Hello?"

"I'm here. No, it would be fine. Except I won't be there."

"What do you mean? I passed the gallery just yesterday morning and saw your name."

"Like I said, things have changed. My sponsorship fell through, so they decided to go with other artists willing to pay the freight."

Brook spoke before the notion had reached her brain. "Can I come over?" Then she panicked and rushed to cover. "I'm sure you're busy. I just wondered if we could talk and I could see your new place? I won't stay long." Her voice shook like a child's.

There was the pause again. Overstepped. Asked too much after dismissing her so definitively before. *Why would I be welcome in her home?* "Maybe another time." Brook was prepared to end the conversation. The silences were excruciating.

"No. Now is fine. I was just thinking that I don't even have one spoon, let alone two, and you'll have to drink a beer out of the bottle because I don't own so much as a plate or a glass yet."

"Are you sure?" Brook waffled between the mental happy dance and apprehension about what would likely be an uncomfortable conversation.

"Keep in mind, this is literally my first day here, so it looks more early storage unit than art studio so far. And I'm not sure it will ever look like a home."

Brook breathed through the smile tugging at her cheeks. "You scared me for a minute."

"Sorry, I haven't been processing very quickly today. What time works for you?"

"Is now too soon?" Brook was determined not to let this opportunity pass her by.

"It's 202 Market. Park behind the green Range Rover."

"Can't wait to hear about what's been happening. See you soon. Oh, and Piper?"

"Yeah?"

"Sorry I kind of pushed you away. I can explain." Brook was determined to fix this.

"I understand."

"No. I'll explain if you let me."

"See you soon." Piper hung up. Her voice was missing its normal cool air and trademark bright tone. Brook knew she had contributed.

She changed out of her sweats and into a pair of tight jeans. She appraised her reflection before trying to refashion a haphazard bun into an intentionally messy one. She found a thin cotton sweater that she thought didn't hug too many of her bulgy places and realized she was rarely in anything other than work clothes or sweats. She was thankful her jeans still fit.

Brook pulled behind a drab green Range Rover and leaned forward to take in a tiny storefront conversion. Light glowed from behind the glass-topped door and she squinted to make out the black metal address numbers above it. She smoothed her sweater and tugged her jeans down where they had ridden up at the ankle. She carefully avoided puddles in her best black boots and tried to quell her nerves as she raised her fist to knock.

In seconds she was staring up at Piper in a paint-spotted Henley and black jeans. She could smell her cologne and forced herself to focus on moving her feet over the threshold instead of putting her arms around her.

Piper stepped back for her to enter, and Brook's shoulder brushed against her chest. She riffled through her brain for something cool and pithy to say but ended up just staring at Piper anyway.

"Nice to see you."

Brook noticed Piper's blotchy face and slightly bloodshot eyes. There was a story here and she hoped she wasn't the cause.

"Thanks for letting me come over. You, um, need to catch me up, I think." Brook placed her hand over Piper's forearm and saw her look away abruptly.

"Beer?"

"Yes, please. Oh, and I have a present for you."

Brook dug into her jacket pocket, producing a fork and a spoon from her kitchen, and to her relief, Piper laughed.

"Are you sure you can spare the spoon? I seem to remember you only having two."

"Well, I might have to ask you to bring it with you if you ever come to my place."

"Fair enough. We're a great pair, aren't we?"

"Twin souls on the train to freedom, it sounds like." Brook couldn't decipher the energy, but she had never seen Piper anything other than confident and carefree.

"Indeed." Piper squeezed her shoulder as if she was cautious about touching Brook. Brook leaned into the gesture for just a second.

"So. Time for the grand tour?" Brook peered down the hallway.

"Oh yes. I hope you can make it all the way through without needing to sit down." Piper seemed to force a smile.

"Try me."

Piper steered her down the short hall, stopping at a tiny bathroom boasting a narrow stall shower and a toothbrush on the tiny wall-mounted sink. "Just in case you need to go."

"Nice." Brook thought it could use a coat of paint.

"Hardly. But sufficient and clean."

Two steps later Brook stood at the archway to a good-sized room boasting soaring ceilings. Stacks of art she recognized from the guest house leaned against the walls near Piper's easel and a stool. The only other item was a large wall cabinet near a kitchen area not more than six feet wide.

Piper spun Brook in a circle. "And you're done. Tired yet?"

"The light in here is great, Piper." Brook walked to the bay of windows.

"It's the reason I rented it. Well, that and it's ridiculously cheap given the fact that it's miniscule. I'll get furniture one day."

"You going to hang some of your work?" Her eyes fell to an abstract she recognized from the carriage house.

"I thought about it. I do own a hammer and some nails."

"Want some help?" Brook hoped the offer of some joint project would help Piper relax.

"Maybe. Let me get you that beer. And we can sit."

Brook could only describe Piper as stiff. Rigid. Something she had never experienced.

Brook tried to scan the room without being obvious, hoping to find a place to sit other than Piper's art stool.

"Place to sit coming up." Piper snapped a side latch on the cabinet, and Brook watched a bed and small nightstand descend from it.

"That is pretty fantastic." Brook was impressed.

"Please excuse my asking you to go to bed with me in the first five minutes of you being here, but this is the best I have at the moment."

"No offense taken." Brook accepted her beer and perched at the end of the surprisingly comfortable mattress.

"Should I go first?" Piper sounded a bit stronger now.

"Sure." It was Brook's turn to be nervous.

"I should have told you before, about Vanessa. I'm assuming you know, right?"

"Yeah, Ellen Warner couldn't wait to tell me."

"Figures. The funny thing is, Vanessa always thought no one but Frank knew."

"So her husband knew?"

"Oh yeah. They have an arrangement. We just kind of... happened. We got along really well when she first started taking lessons with me. She told me about her open marriage, and she liked my art and wanted to promote it. At the time it felt like a cool alternative to the starving artist thing, you know? It worked for everyone involved, until it didn't. I'm not a cheater. I happen to know you hate that."

"My mom called me the moral police." Brook offered a sheepish grin and shrugged.

"You told your mom about me?" Piper smirked and regained a bit of her cheeky bravado.

"Yeah." Brook could feel her face burn now.

"I hope you were able to come up with at least one nice thing to say about me."

"Of course I did. She already likes your work."

"I'm sure she'll be less of a fan when you have to tell her about my colossal fall from grace."

"Want to tell me what happened?" Brook pushed back and made herself more comfortable on the mattress.

"Let's just say that the Devereaux generosity extends to the end of their driveway or the end of Vanessa's patience, whichever comes first." Piper raised her beer and clinked the neck against Brook's.

"Did she make you move out?"

Piper shook her head, looking thoughtful. "No, the situation just came to a head, and I refused to do what she wanted. We fought, and she pulled her sponsorship."

"So that's it? No more gallery?"

"Not unless I can pay for the wall space before they take a fifty percent cut of any sales."

"Holy crap. Fifty?"

"Some more established galleries take sixty. That's why prices on art seems crazy. The artist gets less than half."

"I'm so sorry, Piper. I know this was your dream."

"I'll just have to see if I can make some connections on my own. The gallery is bringing all my work back here next week."

"What about the club? Are you still giving lessons?"

"So far. I've been a little afraid to call Leo, but I'm supposed to work tomorrow, so I guess I'll find out what other damage Vanessa's done."

"I don't get it. You were her girlfriend, or whatever."

"I think I was more of a rent-a-companion. The art was just a project she thought would keep me on the hook."

"Were you committed to her?" Brook didn't know how much she should ask, but the door was open now.

"Of course not. That honor goes to Frank. I was simply her friend with benefits. And, admittedly, I got the benefit of a place to stay and a nice car to drive, as well as introductions to people with money to buy art." She winced at the description and seemed to search Brook's face for some verdict of guilt.

"I'm sorry, I just don't get it. It seems crazy to me, but I shouldn't judge. It still feels like cheating."

"It wasn't. It just wasn't particularly fit for public consumption. You would be surprised how many husbands have similar arrangements, Frank included, but that's not really my story to tell."

"I'm never going to be able to look at these people again without wondering." Brook laughed at the absurdity of all the posh society players having secret lives with people outside of their marriages.

"Careful. That might be a stain you can't erase from your mind. Anyway, it's a place I won't go again, I can assure you."

"I wanted to apologize for jumping to conclusions. I was surprised and, if I'm honest, a little bit jealous."

Piper looked like she couldn't believe what she was hearing. "Jealous? You were jealous of me?" She did a small playful wiggle.

"Don't make a big deal out of it." Brook laughed, her cheeks burning at the scrutiny.

"I'm not. I'm just flattered that Brook I've-got-it-all-together Myers cares that much. I kissed you once and I thought you were going to run screaming from the room."

"I was in a much different place then."

"Where are you now?" Piper's expectant look was hopeful.

"A little less freaked out and a little more open to…stuff." Brook wished for some element of smooth, but it was not coming easily.

"Jealous *and* eloquent." Piper nudged her shoulder playfully.

"I think you're teasing me." The tingling in her face intensified.

"I think you're pretty beautiful when you blush."

"Well, I imagine that's worse now. Thank you very much." Brook rubbed at her cheeks and tried to take in Piper calling her beautiful.

"Tell me what's been keeping you busy. Have you heard from Meg?"

"Almost never now, which is progress, I think. I'm still getting used to letting go of wondering if she's okay, but I'm moving on.

I'm actually booked into the new year already, so business is great, I'm relieved to say. Other than the little chat with Ellen Warner and my mom, I talk to food more than people."

"Are you happy now that it's behind you?"

"Yeah, I am. Business happy, living happy, the rest will come in time. I'm miles from where I was. What about you?" Brook placed her hand over Piper's, causing Piper to flinch. Brook moved it away and instantly missed the feeling.

"Sorry."

"Don't be." Piper opened her hand and waited.

Brook slid her hand into Piper's and she closed around it.

"You said you wanted to ask me something at the party before we were rudely interrupted," Piper said, looking at their entwined hands.

"You mean before the warden came to drag you back to your cell?" She hoped Piper took it as a joke. She didn't want to sound bitter.

"Yeah. What was it?"

"It seems silly after everything, but I wanted to know if you would like to come over for dinner."

"Like a date? With the cutest chef in town?"

"According to my mother, a judgmental chef who needs to apologize for the way she acted." Brook plucked at a loose thread on the comforter.

"Hardly, it wasn't exactly news you expected. How did you finesse the Ellen conversation?"

"I'm not sure I did. I babbled about you being a friend and she warned me that you were Vanessa's *special friend*." She shook her head at the recall.

"You know V would die if she knew how public her secret was. I'm sorry Ellen hit you over the head with it."

"Hey, I'm a grownup, I could have acted less like a naïve teenager. I hope you can forgive me for telling you not to contact me."

"If there are potato swirls and mini quiches in my future, I'll forgive anything."

"Opportunist." Brook was happy for the release of tension.

"You're not wrong. And yes, I would love to have dinner with you. I guess I should confess something." Piper turned slightly to face her.

"Uh-oh." Brook swallowed against the swarm of butterflies trying to escape her stomach.

"That night, when I kissed you...I haven't stopped thinking about it."

"As long as we're confessing things, if Meg hadn't caused drama that night, I would have likely spent the morning eating scrambled eggs in bed with you." Brook slapped her hand over her mouth, instantly regretting the confession.

Piper stared but didn't speak. She stood up and pulled Brook to her feet. She kissed her, and Brook thought her lips tasted like beer and bliss. She accepted Piper's arms around her neck and pressed against her body.

Piper broke the kiss and held Brook's face against her cheek. "I guess you know how much I wanted to make you those eggs."

"I do now." Brook was still catching her breath.

"If I owned sheets and a cup for morning coffee, let alone an egg, I wouldn't let you leave right now."

"And I wouldn't have wanted to. How about I make you that dinner Friday night and we can explore missed opportunities." Brook felt the swell of confidence that came with the confirmation that her future was likely standing in front of her.

"Sounds like a plan." Piper's arms were still firmly around her.

"I'm so sorry I doubted you."

"I'm so sorry I didn't kiss you again before now. I'm sorry I evaded the truth."

"You didn't owe me anything." Brook realized it was true, and she wondered how much time she had wasted casting people aside because they weren't who she thought they should be.

"See you Friday? Let me know what to bring?"

Brook walked slowly to the door, still holding Piper's hand. She had plans now, and they involved more than starting new adventures with an amazing person.

The searing goodbye kiss felt more like a beginning she couldn't wait to explore.

Brook nearly danced to the van, stopping to wave at Piper leaning casually in the doorway. Before she got in the car, she turned and ran back to collect another intense kiss. She remembered a similar feeling fifteen years ago when she met Meg, but this was different. Piper looked like a promise and tasted like a forever she couldn't wait to get to.

When she finally managed to pull away from the curb, she dialed her parents' house hoping she could manage not to sound as giddy as she felt.

"Mom. I have some things to tell you, and I need some advice. I'm on my way."

CHAPTER SIXTEEN

Piper hadn't been able to sleep despite the early morning lessons she was on tap to deliver. She couldn't stop thinking about Brook. She shifted and organized her collection of belongings, making a list of needs, starting with sheets, coffee cups, and eggs. She had replayed kissing Brook a thousand times, stopping only to text with her at least a dozen times before finally calling her to say good night. Dinner was two days away.

As she scanned the parking lot of the club, she saw only Leo's car. It was early and Piper had hoped to get the impending humiliation over with. She had no idea what to expect when she swung open the door to Leo's office.

"Morning, Piper." Leo faced a pile of invoices and member billing statements on his desk.

No scowl or obvious disdain, so far so good. "I figured you would want to talk to me, so I came in early." Piper stood rigidly in the doorway, still clutching her backpack.

"Why did you think that?" He glanced up briefly and returned to his paperwork.

"So, you aren't going to fire me right now?" Here it is. Throw it out there.

Leo's stern expression cracked into a smile. "Oh, you mean because a certain lady of the estate called me to inform me of your royally pissing her off?" His tone was as casual as his expression. He pushed his paperwork away and reclined in his chair.

"She said that?" She dropped her voice and rechecked the room to be sure they were alone.

"Not in so many words. She simply let me know that you had been asked to leave her property and she thought I could do better with another pro at the club."

"I left on my own." She hated having to defend herself, but at least she knew what she was up against. The hurt of it all took her by surprise.

"Don't care if you didn't. You're good at your job and *most* of the members like you. Half of them call me names behind my back, so we need someone who can curry favor around here." He stood and chucked his pen on the desk.

"I was pretty sure I would be unemployed after today." She mimed wiping her brow and dropped her backpack on the counter.

"No such luck. You should have more faith in people, Pipe. Especially me."

"Yeah. My faith's been tested over the last few days." She could breathe again. The relief was amazing.

"You're forgiven." Leo scratched out an appointment card and held it out to Piper. "Cameron called out and I'm going to need you to cover first thing tomorrow. I know you're off for the art thing, so I just gave you the early one."

Piper slipped the card from his fingers.

"Well, turns out the art thing was a condition of my living arrangement, so I'm pretty free tomorrow." There, all out on the table now.

Leo shook his head in disgust. "I really am sorry, Piper. That's some unfair shit."

"Who knows, maybe I'll give up art and work for you full-time." She wouldn't give in that easily, but it was good to know she wasn't going to be unemployed.

"Uh-huh. Get out of my office and go earn what I pay you too much to do. Tina's already here." He offered a casual hug before playfully pushing her toward the parking lot.

"Yessir." She practically danced out the door and waved at Tina. Little victories. Big opportunities and some unfair shit. In the grand scheme of things, she wasn't going to complain. She had her own job, her own place, and her art. Not to mention something that could be special with Brook. She was finally on the right track.

By the time her last appointment canceled, Piper had seen and critiqued all the golf swings she cared to. She texted Brook under the guise of confirming tomorrow's dinner plans and asked again what she could bring.

Just you. Dinner will be ready at six.

Perfect. Shall I bring my spoon?

Nope, I stole some from the Chinese buffet last time I was there, so we should be good.

Am I having dinner with a felon?

Actually they're plastic so I think I'll get by with a misdemeanor.

That was close. See you then. Xo

Xo

The exchange made her smile, and it felt good to feel so free again. Piper pointed the car toward Target to clear her list. Two comfortable chairs, a rug, dishes, and cookware had driven her purchase total to well over six hundred dollars, but the news that she still had a job made that feel okay. The balance of her evening was spent placing art on the walls and doing a mediocre job of decorating the tiny space. It was all hers, and that's what mattered.

She heard from Brook, who sent her kiss emojis and pictures of food she was prepping.

Piper had forgotten how it felt to want to see someone instead of having someone demand her time. She had more than one fantasy involving cooking with Brook, creating memories with Brook, and waking up with a very naked Brook, but she could wait for it all. She wouldn't rush this.

She looked forward to getting her work back from the gallery so she could finally give Brook her gift. Piper still felt the sting of losing the gallery spot, but she would have traded it in a minute for a future with Brook. She was fairly perplexed by that realization since a few days ago, it felt like the end of her future.

CHAPTER SEVENTEEN

Piper ignored her phone as she worked product through her hair. She still had two hours before dinner, but at the rate her stomach was flopping around, she would need the time for the Tums to kick in.

The phone chirped, indicating a voice mail, and she pressed the button to play it.

"*Piper, this is Elizabeth Davinroy. Could you please arrive at the gallery no later than five thirty? There are things we need to discuss.*"

Piper stared at the phone and checked the number on the missed call, reconciling it with the time stamp on the voice mail. Same time.

She called the number and got a recording for the Paris Urban Art Gallery. Surely they weren't trying to load out her paintings just before the opening. If so, that smelled like a vindictive Vanessa Devereaux stirring the pot.

Now she needed to let Brook know that she would be late.

"Hi." Brook answered on the first ring.

"Any chance we can postpone an hour or so? The gallery called, and I guess they want my paintings out before the opening. I'll be dressed and ready to come over afterward, though. I hope that's okay."

"Perfectly. I'm running a bit behind myself. One of my clients needed some last-minute items for a party, so seven thirty would work best for me."

"Great. Thank you. I've got a gift for you." Piper hoped the look on Brook's face would surpass the one Piper had imagined so many times.

"Your company is enough." Brook sounded busy.

"This is special." Piper let herself fall for the possibility that Brook would one day be hers. "I'm really looking forward to spending the evening with you."

"I can't wait. See you later." Brook's voice was raspy as she disconnected.

Piper checked the clock and pulled a French blue Armani dress shirt from the clothes rack, a contribution from her former life that seemed appropriate to help secure her future one. She paired it with slim black slacks and mused that Vanessa would have approved. Adding socks with tiny multicolored easels all over them would have sent her into a spin, and that made Piper laugh out loud.

Just after five fifteen, Piper verified that the Rover's cargo area was clear, and she made the three-block drive to the gallery. She could see a myriad of activity, no doubt gearing up for what should have been her night. The sinking feeling in her stomach still appeared when she thought about being nary a footnote in the celebration.

She pulled behind the building and hoped to avoid any uncomfortable run-ins with people either pitying or gloating. The small dock door stood open, and she saw two men separating a sculpture from its packing.

"Excuse me, I'm here to pick up some paintings?" She scanned the area for any of her items.

"Sorry, ma'am, no pickups until tomorrow between ten and two. All the sold items will be available then."

"No, I didn't buy anything, I got a call to come and get some pieces. I was an artist. Am the artist. An Artist." Geez, what the hell was she in a situation like this? *Hi, I'm the novice hack who made some tacky canvases the gallery wants far away from here before people see them?* Yeah, maybe a little softer than that.

"Sorry, ma'am. I don't know anything about a pickup like that. Nothing back here. Maybe ask Elizabeth or Sandra? They're inside." He pointed toward a nondescript wooden door that read "GALLERY."

Great, she thought. There was no way she was getting out of here unscathed. She turned the knob and peeked through the resulting crack. Nothing. Voices in the distance, but maybe this Sandra person was nearby. More voices, but she couldn't make out the words. She was pretty sure she was sweating everywhere. She saw a well-dressed woman in a tight green suit carrying a plate of food and gesturing to some canvas she couldn't see. It was probably better that way. She would compare her work to theirs. Then she'd critique their use of color and wonder if she should ever pick up another brush. God, could this be over already?

"May I help you?"

The voice from behind her made her jump, and she hoped she looked less guilty than she felt.

"Yes, I'm Piper Holthaus. Elizabeth asked me to come by at five thirty."

The woman was beautifully put together and looked the tiniest bit familiar. One of the Deveraux crowd, perhaps. She smiled broadly and grasped Piper's hand in a firm shake.

"Piper, it is such a pleasure to finally meet you. My daughter is a huge fan, and now that I've had a chance to see your work, you can count me as one too."

"Wow, um,...I..." *Well, this is going swimmingly.* Surely, staccato one-syllable words should help her blend in with the educated art set. Piper mentally shook herself and tried to get a grip on her nerves.

"Thank you. I'm looking for Elizabeth." All she could think of was ending the humiliation rather than explaining why she had been fired.

"Pardon my manners. I'm Sandra Meyerson. My husband and I are sponsoring your exhibit here tonight."

Piper turned around as if there was someone behind her to clear up the mess swirling in her brain. A tiny blond woman with sprigs of hair escaping from her ponytail appeared, fanning herself with the gallery brochure.

"I'm sorry. What? I'm afraid I won't be showing here tonight." She considered how many times she was going to have to explain the same thing before she could get out of there.

"Elizabeth! So glad you're here. This is Piper." Sandra placed a comforting hand on her shoulder.

"Oh, thank goodness. I thought you were going to leave us on our own for introductions." Elizabeth Davinroy's impeccable English accent sounded a bit weary.

"Mrs. Davinroy. I got your message about picking up my canvases. I'm sorry if I misunderstood about your delivering next week."

Elizabeth smiled at Sandra as if she had an amusing secret with her. "Oh, call me Elizabeth. And you *are* a bit behind, aren't you, love?"

"Walk this way, Piper."

Sandra led her the rest of the way down the hall to a grand space with walls displaying artwork, pedestals holding sculptures, and shelves offering gifts. There were at least fifty people milling around the softly lit rooms appraising exhibits, chatting, and sipping champagne from tall flutes. Piper briefly scanned the crowd and prayed Vanessa wasn't among the guests. She could picture the smug grin she would shoot at her.

"Quite a crowd this early. Congratulations." She was proud of herself for not sounding bitter.

"When our daughter explained what had happened to your sponsorship, we couldn't have been happier to step in. Like I said, I'm already a fan of your work." Sandra walked at quite a clip and Piper hustled to keep up.

"Wait. You're showing some of my work? You sponsored me?" Sandra's words were finally penetrating the fog. She expected someone to reveal a big practical joke any moment.

"Well, not all of it, of course, we saved some pieces for later. And two pieces sold in the first hour during the buyers' tour." Elizabeth spoke in a hushed tone.

"Two of *my* pieces?" Someone bought her artwork without Vanessa strong-arming them into it?

"Don't look so stunned, dear." Elizabeth patted her arm in a motherly fashion that calmed her slightly. "People are really interested in your work."

"I'm afraid I *am* stunned. I'm really confused." Piper attempted a smile and began to let the light of hope seep in. *I'm in a gallery after all. Wait till I tell Brook.*

Elizabeth gestured to where Sandra was standing, clearly taking in Piper's still bewildered look.

"We have two minutes. I'll give you the quick version and then you're on." Elizabeth straightened a large watercolor as they walked.

"On what? How?" Sweat was sliding down her back and she straightened in hopes it wouldn't stain her shirt.

"The Myersons took over the sponsorship of your exhibit. Of course, Sandra had a pretty big push from her daughter."

"I guess I owe her a huge thank you. Is she here?" She wondered where she might have seen any of her pieces. She had managed a pedestrian attempt at a website but couldn't fathom anyone digging through the internet deep enough to find it.

"Of course. But right now you need to put on this name badge and go talk to all the people about your paintings." Elizabeth was patting a gold printed name onto her shirt.

"I think I'm going to pass out. I have to make a call. I'm not prepared. I don't even know what paintings are on display. I need a drink." The room was a blur and a woosh of air moved Piper's hair into her eyes when the door opened to more visitors. Thankfully, the chilly air served to snap her out of her confusion.

"No time for anxiety, Piper. We just opened the main doors. Look happy." Sandra Myerson took over, walking her into the swelling crowd.

"The front two displays belong to you." She swept two glasses of champagne from a passing tray and handed Piper one before giving her a reassuring nod.

Sandra held on tightly to Piper's forearm when she began to address the crowd; perhaps it looked like she was going to run. She'd considered it.

"Thank you all so much for joining us. We are so proud of Elizabeth's vision, and Steven and I feel so lucky to be a part of bringing you such talented artists like Myriam Garrett, Tucker Bannon, Ruth Daniels, and the artist whose work you see behind me, Piper Holthaus. I'd like to introduce Piper first."

Oh God. Please don't let me pass out in front of all these people. She rubbed her sweating palm along the thigh of her pants before changing champagne hands and repeating the move.

She felt Sandra squeeze and gently nudge her toward the center of the room. She barely registered a few familiar pieces as she stepped in front of a seven-foot wall of her work.

People were staring. Waiting for her to talk, right? Yes. *I'm standing here sweating and people are wondering what's wrong with me.*

"Um. Wow. Is it hot in here?" She wiped her forehead and shoved her free hand in her pocket. "You see, people like me paint because they are horrible public speakers." She received a chuckle from the crowd and took the opportunity for a much-needed deep breath.

"This was all impossible until these two people came into my life, like *really* recently." Another chuckle spurred her on, making her slightly less anxious. "I paint because I love it. If you like it a little, I'd be honored. Like I said, I'm so bad at this, but I am so grateful to be here. Thank you for coming to see what makes me get out of bed in the morning. Enjoy your evening. I hope to get to speak with some of you later."

She was pretty sure the room went black for a moment. She stepped back when Tucker Bannon walked in front of her and began talking about his sculpture. *He'd* clearly done this before. She turned to find another drink and nearly walked into a center wall holding a single canvas. It was *Brook's Peace.* Oh God. There was a Sold tag hanging from the corner.

No, this was not happening. She had to find Elizabeth to undo this. The only painting that shouldn't have been sold, hung as a glaring reminder that she couldn't count the ways this week had been a tornado of things that she should have done differently.

Fifty paintings, numerous colors, sizes and even shapes, why this one? Sandra appeared next to her.

"It's truly lovely. When she saw it on the invitation her face lit up, and I knew I wanted to buy it for her. She said it looked familiar. What did you call it?" Sandra fingered the Sold tag that whipped in the breeze every time the door opened.

"*Brook's Peace.* It was a gift for someone. I don't know how to say this without sounding incredibly ungrateful, but it wasn't for sale. It was for her. For Brook." She would beg if she had to.

"You painted it for me?"

She felt the words, her voice. Piper turned to see a damp-eyed Brook standing behind her. "Oh my God, you're here."

Brook wore a narrow black skirt and a deep V-neck sweater in pale green. Piper had never seen her dressed up. She was just as beautiful as every other second she'd seen her in the past.

"Of course it was for you. You actually painted the picture for me, I just put it on canvas. But Sandra says that she bought it for her daughter." She tried to communicate how blindsided she was by all of this. "I'm so sorry."

"Why?" Brook smiled at Sandra.

"Because I wanted to bring it to you as a housewarming gift. It wasn't supposed to be part of the show. Of course, I didn't know there even *was* a show." She imagined trying to paint another one, but she knew it wouldn't be the same.

Sandra looked amused. "You two have a lot to talk about. We can catch up later." Sandra patted Piper on the shoulder before walking away.

"Oh my God. I have so much to tell you," Piper whispered. "I came to pick up my paintings, or I thought I did. Then Sandra Myerson came up and told me her daughter is a fan and that she and her husband sponsored the show and now my work is hanging here and I'm part of the show...God, what if I'd showed up in jeans? I would have, if you hadn't invited me for dinner."

Brook began laughing. Piper stared as tears welled at the corners of her eyes and she daintily dabbed at them so she didn't smear her makeup.

"What the hell is so funny? I probably looked ridiculous up there." Piper was amused, but she still had no idea what was happening.

"Actually, you looked pretty sexy up there." Brook laced her fingers through Piper's and squeezed.

"You're laughing too hard for me to believe anything you're saying right now." Piper felt herself join in with Brook.

"We have a lot to learn about each other, you know." Brook pulled her closer. "For instance, my full name is Brooklynn Myerson. I shortened it so no one would make the connection or give me a job because of some association with my parents." Brook raised an eyebrow as if waiting for the light to come on.

Piper stared at her. She wrenched around to see Sandra in deep conversation with Elizabeth a few yards away. She looked at the painting and turned back at the sound of Brook's laughter once again.

"Can you break this down for me? I suddenly feel like I've just come out of a deep sleep." She was confused, and Brook took her other hand. The soft laugh lines around Brook's eyes relaxed.

"My mom and dad own Myerson Imports. I called her when I found out what Vanessa did to you and asked them if they would consider having MI sponsor the show. The next thing I know, they agreed to buy Vanessa and Frank out and they've invested in the gallery. I told her how much I would love your painting for my new place, and they surprised me with it just before you came."

"So you knew I was going to be late for dinner? And you made up the part about food for a client to distract me?"

"Of course I knew. I wanted to see you last night, but I was sure I would blow the surprise. And my dad asked Elizabeth to let me bring some samples for the guests. So it was kind of true."

Piper stared at her, the full information stirring into a euphoric cocktail in her head.

"Why would you do all that for me?" Piper stood closer and pulled Brook against her.

"Because you deserve to succeed. The same reason you did it for me."

"And because you fell stupidly in love with me over potato puffs and mini quiches at four in the morning like I did?"

"Precisely." Brook slid her palm along Piper's cheek and kissed her.

Piper knew it was far from art gallery decorum, but Brook made her forget everything. She was the perfect person she had never expected or thought she wanted. She silently vowed that she would spend every day painting an uncompromisingly beautiful life with her.

Epilogue

Piper snatched a piece of cheese from the tray and Brook responded with a swat of her kitchen towel.

"Aren't you supposed to be painting or something?" She moved the platter farther away.

"Nope. I'm hanging at the café with you since Sophie is out today. You're sexy when you work."

Brook noted Piper's relaxed response instead of the panicked look she used to have every day. She no longer labored under the guilty pressure to paint in order to survive. The gallery opening and subsequent business had been a resounding success for the Davinroys, as well as for Piper. The catering business and now the busy café had allowed them both to build up enough savings to plunk a nice down payment on the three-story brick walk-up in what was now being called the "art district."

"You're just saying that so I'll make you the grilled cheese special." Brook dragged a tray full of small side salads across the stainless-steel counter and dropped a radish garnish in the center of each.

"Probably true. But since we moved out of the building, I don't get to be here as much."

"I think the townhouse has a lot more perks, and your clothes don't smell like sauteed onions anymore."

"Definitely a perk."

She thought they both missed the us-against-the-world feel of the tiny space every once in a while. Piper's apartment, just a short walk from their new place, was strictly an art studio now. Golf lessons had dwindled to about five a week, but it was a good outlet for Piper. Once the café had taken off, they had converted Brook's old place to storage and staging space for the catering side of things. Brook imagined owning the building one day, but reminded herself not to do too much too fast.

"I dropped the Rover at Bill's Garage for an oil change. Hopefully that's all it needs." Piper pulled a crate of glasses from the dishwasher. "Can we go by and pick it up later?"

Brook shook her head. Their same playful argument was about to start.

"Or you could sell the damned thing and buy gold bricks instead. We have the new car and van." She placed some slices of the cheese and a few grapes on a plate she passed to Piper.

"I can't sell the freedom wagon, sweetheart. It was my first step to capturing your heart." She munched on a grape.

"I can assure you, that leaky heap had nothing to do with it. You just like it because it made Vanessa nuts."

"Ahh, fond memories." The series of door chimes alerted them that the Painted Lady Café was going to be busy as usual on Friday.

"I'll get the drink orders if you wouldn't mind bringing some to-go cartons from upstairs for me. We're low down here." Brook grabbed an order pad and rushed over to give Piper a kiss on her way out the swinging doors.

"On it."

Brook scanned the room of ten tables, three now occupied with duos perusing the menu. The nervous excitement of seeing customers come in just to eat *her* food in *her* restaurant was a dream she couldn't believe had come true in less than two years.

She stopped to collect drink orders from the two tables near the front. She summarized the soup and grilled sandwich feature for each before walking to the corner table, where she could see the customer's stiletto shoe bouncing impatiently into the aisle.

"Welcome to the Painted Lady, can I bring you a drink or do you already know…" She stopped mid-sentence when she recognized Vanessa Devereaux. She was intently scanning the menu and hadn't looked up. "What you want," Brook finished.

Vanessa's companion, a polished woman in a crisp dark suit with short blond hair, spoke first.

"Water with lemon for her, and can you do an Arnold Palmer for me?" She smiled and made eye contact with Brook.

"Lemonade and iced tea, right?" Brook wrote it down even though she rarely forgot an order.

"Yes. Thanks. And could we each have the Farmers Garden salad. She'll have the dressing on the side, please." She gestured to Vanessa, who still seemed to be digesting the menu.

"Be right back." She walked quickly toward the kitchen feeling like she might burst before she got back to Piper. She rushed through the doors.

"You will never believe who is sitting at table four," she said quietly.

"Who?" Piper started for the doors so she could see for herself and Brook grabbed her arm.

"No, don't look. She'll see you."

"Who will?" Piper chuckled at Brook's conspiratorial whisper.

"Vanessa Devereaux." Her eyes were wide as she pointed in the direction of the dining room.

"Stop it. Really? I have to see this."

"Okay. You can peek, but be cool." Brook pushed one of the doors open so Piper could see.

"I think one of us needs to work on our definition of cool, babe."

Brook rolled her eyes. "This *is* cool. Do you think she knew this was my place when she came in?"

Piper smiled and peered into the dining room. She immediately saw Vanessa chatting with another woman at the window table.

"Doubtful. I can't even believe she's eating at a place that serves any combination of bread *and* cheese. I'll bet you ten bucks she orders water with lemon and a salad with a side of balsamic vinegar." Piper pictured many a miserable meal where Vanessa never permitted herself even the tiniest bit of enjoyment, only deprivation and discipline.

"You got it. Exactly." Brook laced her fingers into Piper's. "Are you going to go say something to her?"

Piper shook her head. "I haven't talked to her since I left. I doubt we would have much to say to each other."

"I'm not sure what she's going to say to me, either. I better get all the drinks going." She walked toward the beverage station and began to assemble a tray full of glasses. She drained the last of the iced tea into a tall glass tumbler.

"I'll go bring down some more tea," Piper said.

"Coward."

"I prefer avoidant, with a side of self-preservation."

"Chicken."

"That's fair." Piper flashed her a wide smile before heading out the side door.

She walked past the restroom and stopped to pick up a leaf someone must have tracked in. Brook was meticulous about the restaurant's appearance, and Piper had adopted a similar eye for that detail.

"Piper?"

Her voice had a tone of surprise. She turned around to see Vanessa coming out of the restroom. Dressed in her signature couture pants and blouse with coordinating heels, Piper thought she looked pretty good, albeit a bit shocked at running into Piper.

"Hi, V. How are you?" It was unoriginal, to say the least, but the hundreds of questions swirling in her head probably weren't a good icebreaker.

"Really good. You having lunch here?" She looked like there were a hundred other things she would have preferred to ask as well.

It was a reasonable assumption, Piper supposed.

"Actually, Brook owns this place. I'm helping out today."

"Brook?" She asked and answered her own question when she made the connection. "Sorry, I'd forgotten her name. So, I guess it worked out for you two?"

Piper was reasonably sure that the grapevine of art, money, and politics had already provided Vanessa with that information, but she played along.

"It did. I'm happy. What's going on in your world? How is everything?" She had stayed away from the Shadow Glass rumor mill, but she had heard that there had been a recent change in the Devereaux marriage.

"It's all final now." She held up her hand and wiggled her ringless finger in demonstration. "I moved out to the beach house for a while, but I was spending so much time at Marie's, it made sense for us to get a place together."

"Marie? As in your broker Marie?"

Vanessa laughed and seemed to relax a bit further.

"Yes. Marie Layman. She and I are together. Officially for about six months."

Piper's mouth hung open in exaggerated surprise before she pushed up her chin in a comic move to close it.

"I'll be damned. Good for you. I must say you look happy. How did Frank take it?"

"You know, better than I thought. It's a lot of work pretending to be happy. He's dating a bunch of women half his age and he never has to lie about where he is or what he's doing. I think he's glad to be free. We still talk a couple times a month, just to check in."

"I'm proud of you, V. I hope you don't mind my saying that." Piper was shocked that she'd had the guts to leave the security of the relationship she'd clung to so tightly.

"I told myself I would tell you this if I ever saw you. So here it goes." She took a deep breath before she spoke. "You were right. I'd forgotten who I used to be before my marriage and how much I'd been compromising for what I thought was an easy life. It wasn't worth it after all. And I'm sorry I made it so hard on you before you left." She smoothed her hand over her perfectly creased pants and stood a little straighter.

"That's nice to hear. I hope you know that I appreciate everything we had, while it lasted." Piper was now grateful they had run into one another. She didn't realize how much she'd needed that little bit of closure.

"Thank you. I wasn't the easiest person sometimes."

"None of us are." Piper wanted to steer clear of any uncomfortable recounting of their last few weeks together. "So, what're you doing with your time now?"

"I kept doing the social circuit thing for a while, but I started to feel pretty useless. Marie finally told me that if I got one more facial, she wouldn't recognize me. I remembered how much I loved the charity work I did before, so we decided to start a nonprofit for homeless families. I run the marketing and fundraising part of it and Marie does the money and all the regulatory bits I hate."

"I can testify that you are a force to be reckoned with in the fundraising department. They don't stand a chance." Piper found a glimpse of the Vanessa that Piper had always known was there.

"I'd love to have you meet Marie before we leave. I think you'd like her." Vanessa looked over and waved at Marie, who glanced up from her phone and smiled.

"We'll come over in a bit?" Piper wouldn't go without Brook.

"Sure. Thanks." She started to walk toward her table before turning back. "I mean it, Piper. Thank you. I always wanted you to have a great life. I'm happy for you."

"Thanks, V." Piper took a deep breath and headed up to get the iced tea. Sometimes, things just worked out.

❖

"Well?" Brook decanted her homemade balsamic vinaigrette into small ramekins and lifted colorful salads onto a tray.

"What?" Piper played dumb.

Brook issued a light slap on her arm before reaching for bowls of soup she placed on another tray. "I saw you two talking in the back hall. You better tell me everything, I'm dying in here. How'd it go? What did she say?"

"Oh that. Yeah. Well, she left Frank for her broker. Her and Marie are living together, and they started a charity for the homeless." She reached over to lower the gas under the soup when an escaping bubble of liquid caused a hiss on the burner.

"She looks fantastic." Brook rolled silverware into cloth napkins boasting the café logo Piper had designed.

"A couple mil and a beach house will do that for you," Piper joked.

"Not to mention a relationship with a cute little money mogul who looks like Sharon Stone." Brook wiggled her eyebrows.

"Um, do I have something to worry about?" Piper grabbed Brook around the waist and dipped her playfully.

"Oh yes. I'm over my dark, brooding artist phase." Brook laughed as she struggled out of Piper's hold and jogged away. "Watch out. You should know I love a blonde in a suit."

"You aren't getting away that easily. Besides, your mom said she'd pay for our wedding one day, so you're stuck with me."

Brook shrugged. "True. I guess I'll stick it out with you after all."

"You know, I never thought she'd go through with it—leaving Frank for a woman, but she looks happy."

"I don't how she did it as long as she did."

"She wants us to come meet Marie. That is, if you can control yourself."

"I'll do my best." Brook assembled the last tray, spearing a toothpick through slices of pickle and tomato and plunging it into a sandwich. "I'll drop the rest of the food and we can go over together. This is super weird."

"Completely. So, I guess dinner with Meg is next?" Piper balanced a tray in each hand.

"Hardly. The apology letter was plenty for me."

She had read Piper the lengthy missive Meg had sent after rehab. Piper admired Meg for embarking on what turned into a two-month stay followed by a brief relapse. She had recently begun seeing a woman named Tina and was doing some teaching at the community college. She was happy, and she and Brook had mended some fences.

❖

The café was finally empty. Brook slumped against the counter and rubbed her temples. "I need a foot rub and a long sleep." She snapped the lid over the fruit salad, and Piper slid it into the cooler.

"I can handle both when we get home. Ready when you are."

"I think chatting up Vanessa and Marie was extra work." Brook flicked on the Closed sign. "Don't we still have to get the Rover?"

"No. Bill called and said he needs to order a part. I guess it might be time to sell, like you said." Piper handed Brook her backpack.

"Up to you, sweetheart. I was only teasing." Brook took Piper's hand, pulled her toward the front doors, and watched her lock up.

The early evening was fairly quiet, but people weren't used to the windy, rainy weather they had been having the past two days. Brook tilted her head back and relished the fresh air and mist on her cheeks.

"I needed this." Brook appraised the construction progress of the new gift shop opening next door to the café as they walked.

"You aren't too cold?" Piper pulled the sleeves of her shirt down and rubbed her arms.

"No, it feels great." Brook felt the spray increase to a steadier sprinkle.

The three-block stroll to their new home had become their daily wind-down session, to talk about anything other than the daily special, catering, or gallery business.

"I'm happy Vanessa and Marie came in today. I know it was awkward at first."

"I'm glad they did too. I really liked the guilt money she left as a tip." Brook had tucked it into the animal rescue collection box after they left.

"I guess she felt bad about how she treated you when she first met you."

"Then a hundred bucks for mistreated dogs seems perfectly fitting." Brook bent to pet the neighborhood Siamese cat that always followed them for a few yards before he lost interest and headed back to his family's house.

"I like the parallel." Piper squeezed Brook's hand. "Are you happy?"

"Of course. What makes you ask that?" Brook stopped to look at her.

"Just checking in. You're the best thing that's ever happened to me, FYI." Piper wrapped Brook in a hug.

"Why are you so perfect?" Brook had found it. The peace she had longed for. She took the key Piper held out for her, and she unlocked the front door to their home.

"I'll settle for perfect for you."

About the Author

Cass Sellars (http://www.casssellarsauthor.com) is a certified fraud examiner and criminal justice professional. She has led white-collar criminal, corporate and financial fraud, and theft investigations. Formerly an editor of a small magazine, a creative journalist, and a public speaker, she's always been a writer at heart.

She loves writing about powerful women and their adventures and searches for justice.

Sellars grew up in the Midwest and in Great Britain but spent much of her adult life on the East Coast. She dabbles in interior design, event planning, travel, and all things wine. And she works at being a vital part of the lesbian and creative communities.

Books Available From Bold Strokes Books

Can't Leave Love by Kimberly Cooper Griffin. Sophia and Pru have no intention of falling in love, but sometimes love happens when and where you least expect it. (978-1-636790041-1)

Free Fall at Angel Creek by Julie Tizard. Detective Dee Rawlings and aircraft accident investigator Dr. River Dawson use conflicting methods to find answers when a plane goes missing, while overcoming surprising threats and discovering an unlikely chance at love. (978-1-63555-884-5)

Love's Compromise by Cass Sellars. For Piper Holthaus and Brook Myers, will professional dreams and past baggage stop two hearts from realizing they are meant for each other? (978-1-63555-942-2)

Not All a Dream by Sophia Kell Hagin. Hester has lost the woman she loved, and the world has descended into relentless dark and cold. But giving up will have to wait when she stumbles upon people who help her survive. (978-1-63679-067-1)

Protecting the Lady by Amanda Radley. If Eve Webb had known she'd be protecting royalty, she'd never have taken the job as bodyguard, but as the threat to Lady Katherine's life draws closer, she'll do whatever it takes to save her, and may just lose her heart in the process. (978-1-63679-003-9)

The Secrets of Willowra by Kadyan. A family saga of three women, their homestead called Willowra in the Australian outback, and the secrets that link them all. (978-1-63679-064-0)

Trial by Fire by Carsen Taite. When prosecutor Lennox Roy and public defender Wren Bishop become fierce adversaries in a headline-grabbing arson case, their attraction ignites a passion that leads them both to question their assumptions about the law, the truth, and each other. (978-1-63555-860-9)

Turbulent Waves by Ali Vali. Kai Merlin and Vivien Palmer plan their future together as hostile forces make their own plans to destroy what they have, as well as all those they love. (978-1-63679-011-4)

Unbreakable by Cari Hunter. When Dr. Grace Kendal is forced at gunpoint to help an injured woman, she is dragged into a nightmare where nothing is quite as it seems, and their lives aren't the only ones on the line. (978-1-63555-961-3)

Veterinary Surgeon by Nancy Wheelton. When dangerous drugs are stolen from the veterinary clinic, Mitch investigates and Kay becomes a suspect. As pride and professions clash, love seems impossible. (978-1-63679-043-5)

All That Remains by Sheri Lewis Wohl. Johnnie and Shantel might have to risk their lives—and their love—to stop a werewolf intent on killing. (978-1-63555-949-1)

Beginner's Bet by Fiona Riley. Phenom luxury Realtor Ellison Gamble has everything, except a family to share it with, so when a mix-up brings youthful Katie Crawford into her life, she bets the house on love. (978-1-63555-733-6)

Dangerous Without You by Lexus Grey. Throughout their senior year in high school, Aspen, Remington, Denna, and Raleigh face challenges in life and romance that they never expect. (978-1-63555-947-7)

Desiring More by Raven Sky. In this collection of steamy stories, a rich variety of lovers find themselves desiring more: more from a lover, more from themselves, and more from life. (978-1-63679-037-4)

Jordan's Kiss by Nanisi Barrett D'Arnuck. After losing everything in a fire, Jordan Phelps joins a small lounge band and meets pianist Morgan Sparks, who lights another blaze—this time in Jordan's heart. (978-1-63555-980-4)

Late City Summer by Jeanette Bears. Forced together for her wedding, Emily Stanton and Kate Alessi navigate their lingering passion for one another against the backdrop of New York City and World War II, and a summer romance they left behind. (978-1-63555-968-2)

Love in the Limelight by Ashley Moore. Marion Hargreaves, the finest actress of her generation, and Jessica Carmichael, the world's biggest pop star, rediscover each other twenty years after an ill-fated affair. (978-1-63679-051-0)

Love and Lotus Blossoms by Anne Shade. On her path to self-acceptance and true passion, Janesse will risk everything—and possibly everyone—she loves. (978-1-63555-985-9)

Suspecting Her by Mary P. Burns. Complications ensue when Erin O'Connor falls for top real estate saleswoman Catherine Williams while investigating racism in the real estate industry; the fallout could end their chance at happiness. (978-1-63555-960-6)

Two Winters by Lauren Emily Whalen. A modern YA retelling of Shakespeare's *The Winter's Tale* about birth, death, Catholic school, improv comedy, and the healing nature of time. (978-1-63679-019-0)

Calumet by Ali Vali. Jaxon Lavigne and Iris Long had a forbidden small-town romance that didn't last, and the consequences of that love will be uncovered fifteen years later at their high school reunion. (978-1-63555-900-2)

Her Countess to Cherish by Jane Walsh. London Society's material girl realizes there is more to life than diamonds when she falls in love with a non-binary bluestocking. (978-1-63555-902-6)

Hot Days, Heated Nights by Renee Roman. When Cole and Lee meet, instant attraction quickly flares into uncontrollable passion, but their connection might be short-lived as Lee's identity is tied to her life in the city. (978-1-63555-888-3)

Never Be the Same by MA Binfield. Casey meets Olivia, and sparks fly in this opposites attract romance that proves love can be found in the unlikeliest places. (978-1-63555-938-5)

Quiet Village by Eden Darry. Something not quite human is stalking Collie and her niece, and she'll be forced to work with undercover reporter Emily Lassiter if they want to get out of Hyam alive. (978-1-63555-898-2)

Shaken or Stirred by Georgia Beers. Bar owner Julia Martini and home health aide Savannah McNally attempt to weather the storms brought on by a mysterious blogger trashing the bar, family feuds they knew nothing about, and way too much advice from way too many relatives. (978-1-63555-928-6)